You Can't Kill a Dead Man

A Vanessa Sterling Suspense Novel

You Can't Kill a Dead Man

A Vanessa Sterling Suspense Novel

Fran Blacketer

SUNSTONE
PRESS

SANTA FE

Sunstone books may be purchased for educational, business, or sales promotional use.
For information please write: Special Markets Department, Sunstone Press,
P.O. Box 2321, Santa Fe, New Mexico 87504-2321.

Book and Cover design ✦ Vicki Ahl
Cover art by James Blacketer
Body typeface ✦ Perpetua
Printed on acid free paper

Library of Congress Cataloging-in-Publication Data
Blacketer, Fran, 1944-
You can't kill a dead man : a vanessa sterling suspense novel / by Fran Blacketer.
    p. cm.
ISBN 978-0-86534-834-9 (softcover : alk. paper)
1. Women lawyers--Fiction. 2. Family secrets--Fiction. 3. Chicago (Ill.)--Fiction.
I. Title.
PS3602.L325294Y68 2012
813'.6--dc23

                        2011040978

WWW.SUNSTONEPRESS.COM
SUNSTONE PRESS / POST OFFICE BOX 2321 / SANTA FE, NM 87504-2321 /USA
(505) 988-4418 / ORDERS ONLY (800) 243-5644 / FAX (505) 988-1025

To my husband Jim

1

Oregon Coast
2004

Vanessa Sterling gripped the steering wheel, her cold hands as numb as her mind. The winter storm came out of the south slamming into the Oregon Coast; sleet pelted the windshield as the Jeep's headlights cut through the nearly impenetrable fog covering the roadway. She careened along Highway 101, the main artery along the coast, while the fierce storm made this otherwise breathtaking scenic mountain route a dangerous snarl of twists and turns.

Less than an hour ago a nurse from the hospital in Florence had called. Vanessa knew her old friend Kate Remington was there and had put off seeing her until it was almost too late. Now, guilt pushed her along the pitch-black highway. Try as she might to keep her mind on the road, the past kept intruding.

Back when Vanessa was thirteen and Kate only ten, they took a blood oath that their friendship would endure for all times.

Vanessa blinked back tears as she let up on the gas to steer into the next curve. An ominous mood crept over her.

The lights from the hospital pierced the fog. Vanessa pulled at her parka as she made a dash for the entrance. A night nurse directed her down the hallway to Kate's room.

She slowly pushed open the door. A fluorescent light flickered above the bed illuminating her friend's pale, gaunt face. Kate's once curly blond tresses were lost to chemotherapy and her once shapely frame withered. Breathing tubes, saline drips, and wires from the heart monitors ran from her frail body to humming machines. Vanessa choked back the medicinal stench.

Slumped in a chair on the opposite side of the bed was a tall, lean young man, his drawn face in shadow.

Vanessa's mind reeled as recognition sunk in. After all those years, not knowing if he was dead or alive, there sat her son. She flashed from disbelief to anger and back again. It was all too much. Feeling light headed, she staggered, grabbing the back of a metal chair, causing it to scrape along the floor. Startled, her son straightened, blinking back his slumber.

"Michael?" Vanessa whispered, as she desperately tried to make sense of the scene before her. "Is that you?"

Kate awakened and squeezed Michael's hand as she struggled to raise her head. He quickly stood and propped a pillow behind her head.

"Vanessa." Kate gasped for breath, but managed a faint smile. "My dear friend. Thank god you've come. I had to see you. To explain…"

"Explain what? What's going on?" Vanessa asked, with an edge to her voice, her mind spinning out of control. Michael here with Kate, it didn't make sense.

"Michael, please…tell your mother. You owe her that much."

"Yes, tell me, Michael!" Vanessa wanted to scream, to shake Michael and tell him how for ten long years she'd mourned for him. She struggled to control her emotions, fearing if she unleashed them he'd leave again. She couldn't bear that.

"There's so much…" Kate's voice became shallow and weak. A dry raspy cough took her breath. She grew still, her face ashen.

Panic overtook Michael. "Kate! Don't leave me! Please."

Just then the heart monitor screeched. Michael clung to Kate's hand and stared at the machine. Medical staff rushed in. Vanessa and Michael were ushered into the hallway. Color drained from his face. He started to speak, but his shoulders' trembled. He hung his head, staring at the floor. A few minutes later a doctor emerged and confirmed what they feared: Kate Remington was dead at the age of 48.

Vanessa leaned against the wall, her mind flashed back ten years. Then struggling through a nasty divorce, Kate had left Chicago without word. She'd abandoned Vanessa just when she needed her most. Feeling desolate and lost, the final blow had landed when Michael, at 18, disappeared. This pushed Vanessa over the edge. After an extensive search conducted by several private investigators, Michael could not be found.

Devastated by her losses, Vanessa moved to the Oregon coast, a place she remembered from a vacation years before as isolated and remote. There she had carved out a new life for herself free of corporate greed and a punishing marriage. Her new life was void of friends and family. She convinced herself that the all-consuming loneliness that overwhelmed her late at night would someday end.

Michael stood, shoulders slumped and weary. She struggled for the right words, but gave up, too tired and bewildered to make sense of it all.

Finally she simply asked if he'd like a cup of coffee.

After getting directions from an over-worked intern, they took the elevator down to the lower level where they shuffled along to the cafeteria through a dimly-lit, antiseptic-smelling hallway, past idle gurneys and wheelchairs.

Other than two nurses in green scrubs, who talked in hushed tones, as they ate their late supper, the place was deserted. Mother and son filled their cups at the stainless steel urn, before settling at a small table along the back wall. Sinking her tall, slender frame into the chair, Vanessa released a long slow sigh. Her unruly auburn mane was pulled back into a ponytail, her scarf hung lopsided around her neck and her energy at its lowest ebb. She massaged her throbbing temples hoping to stave off a migraine. The clock read three-ten.

Michael fidgeted in his chair while Vanessa peered at him over the rim of her cup. He still had a strong-set jaw. His once blond hair, a little darker now, fell into his sad blue eyes. *Where do I begin?*

As an attorney, she had no problem arguing a case, but managing to stand up for herself was another story. Raised by nannies in a cold, indifferent family, she had been shuffled off to boarding school at age five, where loneliness had plagued her. Her parents, too occupied with career or social engagements, rarely visited. Kate became her friend and savior. Each summer Vanessa went with Kate to her family's summer house on the shores of Lake Michigan, where the stately, but loving grand-dame of the Remington family, Kate's grandmother, who had long since died, made Vanessa feel wanted and cherished.

Now Kate was gone. And Michael, for some inexplicable reason, sat across from her.

Vanessa set her cup down, her anger getting the best of her. "Do you have any idea what you've put me through? For god's sake, Michael, where have you been? Say something!"

"I…" He hunched over his cup for warmth. "Kate's gone, that's all I can think about right now."

"Did you leave back then to be with Kate? Have you been with her all this time?" Vanessa found it hard to swallow.

"I didn't run off with her, if that's what you mean. We both just happened to end up in San Francisco."

San Francisco! How many times had I been there in the last ten years? A dozen? Had I passed him on the street? Sat near him on the cable car?

Michael methodically stirred his coffee. "When she found me I was barely alive. She saved my life."

"Saved your life!" Vanessa realized she was still wearing her coat. Suddenly hot, she shrugged it off her shoulders.

Michael pushed his chair back. "Yes, Mother! She saved my life. At the time I was hooked on heroin."

"Heroin!" she cried, tears welling in the corner of her eyes. "Is that what Kate was talking about when she said to tell me the truth?"

He ripped the top off a sugar packet, flicked his finger against it, releasing the granules into his cup. "Look, I can't deal with this now!" His eyes avoided hers. He rose to refill his cup. When he returned, he sat uneasily. "You've got to understand! I've made some terrible mistakes."

"Oh, Michael, I've made so many mistakes, too." Her tears released. She grabbed a napkin and blew her nose.

"I've got no place to go," he said. "I just got into town on a Greyhound, the only way to get to this god-forsaken place. I haven't slept in days. Would it be possible to stay with you for a few days?"

Vanessa caught a sob climbing up her throat. *Maybe he doesn't hate me after all. I'll give him time. I need to know what caused the pain in his eyes and the lines on such a young face.*

2

Newport, Oregon

Several days later, Vanessa balanced the latte on the corner of her gray metal desk and surveyed the cramped quarters located on the third floor of the Lincoln County court house. She set her briefcase on the floor before she nudged her office door closed with her elbow. Boxes of current files lined the perimeter of the walls, with more piled on metal chairs that surrounded her small conference table. She sighed, recalling the past few days since Michael's return. She couldn't go there right now; the court didn't slow down for her personal problems. With three pending trials and new cases coming in every day, she had to focus. As the sole public defender for the county, her clients had been arrested for manufacturing, dealing or using methamphetamine. Most did all three. At first smug and defiant, they soon came to realize Vanessa was their only hope.

Funny, the one person she really wanted to help didn't want it. Michael had been sullen since Kate's death. He'd known her his whole life so Vanessa understood his grief. But she still wondered about Kate's last words.

Then this morning, before leaving for work, Michael surprised her by saying, "I would like to stay. I know you're ready to burst with questions, but you can't be asking me anything. Not right now." He looked away, his face hardened. "I'm just starting to deal with things myself. I've got a few dollars, so I'm thinking about getting a place nearby, maybe find a job."

Her heart lifted. He wanted to stay.

"Focus!" she chastised herself, she needed to keep her mind on track. Now that she knew Michael would be around for a while, she had to get back to business.

She pulled a Stone Mountain box from the teetering stack to review a particularly appalling case needing her full attention. Different from most she handled, it involved a sixteen-year-old boy named Billy Welsh, charged with sexually molesting a ten-year-old girl. An ugly case by anyone's standards. Jurors didn't like boys who rape little girls. To make matters worse, the DA had won a motion to try him as an adult. If Vanessa didn't come up with something soon, Billy faced prison after a few years in juvenile hall.

The previous week, the defendant's mother, Sara Stangel, thought for sure that there were other boys involved. Vanessa had presented the theory to the DA who had promised to investigate. Her first order of business was to check how that was going. She took the stairs, forgoing the elevator, to give herself a moment to collect her thoughts. Facing his door, she exhaled long and slow before she punched in the security code on the key pad. The main door buzzed open. After a quick wave to the receptionist, Vanessa stood for a moment before she entered the office of Steven Adams, Lincoln County District Attorney.

"Are you busy?" Vanessa peered around the partially open door.

Steven looked up from his work and smiled. "I'm never too busy for you," he said, motioning for her to enter. At fifty-five, he was quite handsome. Dressed in a charcoal-gray suit, it enhanced his graying temples, but remnants of his blond hair and strong chiseled jaw were still evident. A likable sort, he was admired for his straightforward ethical approach to his job. According to his diploma displayed on the wall behind his desk, he'd graduated from Harvard a year before Vanessa.

He reached over and cleared files off a chair, but she felt too rushed to sit.

"Where have you been?" Steven asked. "I haven't seen you in days."

"Family business," she said. "What's new in the Welsh case? Did you find anything that will keep you from sending a boy to prison?"

Steven set his reading glasses down and rubbed the bridge of his nose. He pushed away from the desk and leaned back in his swivel chair, crossed his legs, and straightened the crease in his suit pants, buying time.

"He acted alone," he said. "The DNA confirms it. Why don't you save the taxpayers' money and have him plead out? The jury will fry him."

She leaned against the door-frame, staring at the floor, considering her options, which at the moment, were slim.

"I'm not ready to throw in the towel," she said, turning to leave.

"Vanessa," Steven said.

She looked over her shoulder.

"I'll...um...never mind, I'll talk to you later," he said.

She wondered what he wanted, but she had too much on hers to pursue it.

Greeted by her blinking message light when she returned to her office, she dialed her voice mail, sipped her now cold latte and listened.

"I found a place!" Michael said. "A cottage in Nye Beach. And I found a job! At the Chevron station on the highway. I can walk to work."

Vanessa hung up the phone and recalled the day before. The rain had battered the roof of her oceanfront cottage all day. With a roaring fire in the old river rock fireplace, she and her son had spent the day thumbing through old family albums, mementoes of another lifetime, chatting about years gone by.

Ten years had changed Michael. At the age of twenty-eight he stood six-two, with blond hair, the only one in the family to have such light-colored hair, a strong-set jaw, sad blue eyes, deep, too knowing for someone his age.

"Do you ever think of dad?" he'd asked, sitting next to Vanessa on the overstuffed sofa.

Stalling for time, Vanessa continued to leaf through the album. She had an urge to tell him all the miserable things Nicholas had done, but nothing would be gained by that.

"Sometimes," she said. "How about you? Ever wonder where he is?"

Michael stood and ambled to the window. He stared far out over the ocean before he spoke. He turned slowly and said, "He's in San Francisco."

Vanessa was stunned.

"You were all in San Francisco?" Her voice cracked, heavy with anger, hurt, disbelief. Speechless.

Now, sitting in her tiny office, she erased Michael's message. All these years without knowing where he was. Vanessa had always held the belief she'd see Michael again. Someday. And here he was! That had to be the important thing right now. He was with her. And, in some strange way, this helped Vanessa understand the devotion Billy's mother had for her son. In spite of the overwhelming evidence, she believed in her son. This made Vanessa all the more determined to find a way to help the boy.

Once again she plowed through the box of materials: Billy's statement taken at the scene; the victim's statement; police evidence; Billy's history; looking for something, anything she might have missed, that would assist in his defense.

Then it hit her! That screwed-up kid had lived with chaos and violence his whole life. Certainly that had affected him. If she could prove insanity, he just might have a chance. The idea of him in a hospital sounded better than a long prison sentence. He could get the help he needed. But insanity was hard to prove, a daring risk with this young man's life, but it was her only option. She dialed Billy's mother.

"Is something wrong with Billy?" Sara asked, hearing Vanessa's voice.

"No, Sara, he's fine. It's about the trial," Vanessa said, taking another sip of the ice cold latte. "I have an idea. It's a long shot, but frankly it's the only one we have. If I could show that Billy didn't have the capacity to know what he did was wrong, that he wasn't able to control his behavior," Vanessa struggled for the words to tell a mother she intended to prove her son was insane. "I need your permission for Billy to speak to a psychiatrist."

"What? My Billy's not crazy! He's a good boy."

"It's all I've got," Vanessa said. "Can you to come by this afternoon? I'm sorry, Sara, but the choice is insanity or I plead out and Billy goes to prison."

Vanessa searched the desk drawers for the aspirin bottle, hoping to fend off another headache, washing them down with the remainder of the latte.

She leaned back in her chair gazing out the window at the jailhouse roof next door, and recalled the first time she'd dealt with Billy Welsh and his mother.

Several years before, Vanessa had volunteered at the county juvenile retention program designed to help kids turn their lives around before they became habitually offenders. Billy had been referred after his arrest for shoplifting. It was evident that Sara could not control the boy and the county was ready to remove him from his home. He'd needed counseling more than legal aid, but Vanessa wanted to help.

She and Sara connected from the start. After a few meetings, Vanessa could see signs that Sara was a battered wife, and Vanessa feared for her safety. As they talked, the shy, frail-looking woman fidgeted with her key ring and tentatively began to reveal her life with her second husband, Ralph.

They met at the market where he worked. He befriended Sara and she'd confided in him about her first husband's abuse and drug use. Ralph told her she deserved better and that he'd be a good father to Billy. He'd kept it up until Sara got divorced. But once she married Ralph he became cruel and sadistic, far worse than her first husband had ever been. While Billy had only witnessed his father's cruelty to his mother, he was now a victim at the hands of his step-father. Vanessa encouraged Sara to report the abuse, but Sara was terrified he'd kill her and Billy if she did.

Vanessa asked a social worker to do a welfare check on the family. Enraged by the social workers visit, Ralph stormed into Vanessa's office. Drunk and almost incoherent, he'd threatened her. She reported the incident, but by the time an officer arrived at the family's apartment, they'd already moved. Vanessa hadn't heard from them until Billy's latest arrest.

Vanessa now scanned the ancient Rolodex resting on her desk, searching for the dog-eared card with the phone number of Dr. Catherine Sullivan, a renowned forensic psychiatrist who made a superb expert witness. One day she'd have to input all the numbers in her Blackberry, but that day would have to wait.

Unable to reach the doctor directly, Vanessa left an urgent message. There wasn't much time and, if all went well, the doctor would be her key witness.

3

Newport, Oregon

Something besides the Welsh case had caused that troubled look on Vanessa's face. Her usual stoic façade was crumbling. For the first time since Steven had known her, it revealed a vulnerable woman.

Several years ago after he'd unseated his long-standing predecessor, Wallace P. Winfield, for the job of Lincoln County District Attorney, he met Vanessa. It had been rumored that Winfield had been a Klan member in his native Baton Rouge, Louisiana. Steven had heard a story about Vanessa, who had been cited for contempt when she lost her composure over Winfield's crude remarks aimed at her client. Steven wished he could have been there.

Vanessa and Steven became staunch rivals in the courtroom, respecting each other's legal skills. On more than one occasion, he'd been amazed as she recalled an obscure precedent that was right on point, swaying the judge's decision. At other times, she'd rewarded his dry sense of humor with a hearty, genuine laugh. A playful tension kept them good-natured adversaries, competing for the brass ring while maintaining an easygoing friendship.

From the first, he'd had to restrain his attraction to her. It would have been political suicide to date the public defender. But seeing her that morning had changed that. Settling for an occasional lunch or a lingering chat in the hallway was no longer enough.

Earlier that morning, he'd almost suggested they meet for a drink after work. But he'd faltered. Now, fortified by his new resolve, he'd ask her out as soon as possible. Hang conflict of interest or ethical breaches. He needed to know what was behind those sad eyes.

4

Newport, Oregon

The wind whipped the rain sideways, battering the courthouse. Vanessa dreaded leaving the building, but if she didn't get lunch soon there probably wouldn't be another chance. And she was starving. She grabbed her coat and slung her handbag over her shoulder before she ran down the stairs, out into the winter storm. She zipped her raincoat, pulled up the hood, and set off for the Red Door Café, the closest restaurant to the courthouse. Once inside, she hung her dripping coat on a hook, while the hostess waited to seat her. Steven, sitting alone, smiled and motioned for her to join him.

"This is a terrible winter," Vanessa said, sliding into the opposite side of the red leather booth. She pulled back the checkered café curtain, to look out at the deluge.

"Do you have webbed feet yet?" he teased, taking a bite of his club sandwich.

"I believe I do."

"There it is," he said.

"What?"

"Your smile. It wasn't there this morning." He paused to take another bite of his sandwich. "You mentioned family business. I didn't even know you had family nearby."

"I don't," she said, scanning the menu she knew by heart. "Or, I mean,

I didn't until now. My son's visiting."

"I didn't know you had a son. Come to think if it, I don't know much about you outside of work."

"No. I guess not," she said, looking for the waitress.

"But I'd like to," he said.

"There's really not much to know," she said, signaling to the waitress that she was ready to order.

"How old's your son?" Steven continued his line of questioning.

"Twenty-eight."

"You're kidding! You're way too young!"

"Thanks," she said, unfolding her napkin and placing it in lap. "I haven't seen him for a while." She put a sweetener in her ice tea the waitress had just set in front of her, and stirred. "In fact," she said, avoiding eye contact, "since he was eighteen."

"Wow, that's a long time! Where'd he go?"

"San Francisco." She straightened her napkin.

"I'm making you uncomfortable."

"We've never talked about our personal lives before," she said.

"I guess I broke that unwritten rule."

Vanessa's salad arrived. She took several bites before she spoke.

"Did you see the article about the convention center?" she asked. "It looks like they've killed the deal."

Steven took the hint and contributed what he'd heard about that project. Then they debated how the court should handle the sudden flood of cases. Finally, Vanessa began to relax. This sort of banter came easy. When she'd finished her lunch, she searched in her purse for her wallet.

"Please, let me get this," Steven said.

"What's going on with you?"

"What? It's no big deal," he said. A wry smile crept across his face. "Tell you what. If I let you pay for your lunch, you can meet me for drinks later."

Vanessa laughed nervously, her brow furrowed. *What had brought on this sudden change?*

"Isn't that a conflict of interest, Counselor?"

"I've weighed that problem for...let's see...two years. We're ethical people. Surely, a drink won't compromise our professional relationship."

"This is a small town, people will talk," she said.

"Well, you have a point. We'll meet in the open, like two professionals, sharing a drink. Besides, we've had lunch occasionally and that hasn't caused a problem."

Steven was smart, fun, and attractive. She always enjoyed his company. Truth be known, she had fanaticized about him, but never had the impulse to act on that. Being friends had been enough. She wanted to keep her life uncomplicated. But, against her better judgment, she agreed to meet at the Embarcadero Lounge at eight that evening.

Steven glanced at his watch. "I've got court in ten minutes! You know how Judge Holloway is."

She hurried with him through the rain back to the courthouse. He ran down the flight of stairs to his office, while she took the flight up to hers. When she turned the corner, her door stood ajar. She'd forgotten to lock it and someone was in her office. The full-figured Dr. Sullivan was hunched over the desk, dressed in her traditional tweed suit.

"Oh! You startled me," the doctor said as Vanessa entered her office. "I was leaving you a note. Since I have a trial this afternoon, I thought I'd drop by early, hoping to catch you." She took a seat at the small conference table in Vanessa's office. "What's up?"

Vanessa briefly described the situation with Billy. "If I can show that he's a damaged kid as a result of the abuse he's endured, I've got a shot."

Dr. Sullivan scanned her appointment book. "I'll juggle a few things and see him in the morning. But right now I've got to get to court."

Stepping from the doorway as she left Vanessa office, the doctor almost ran headlong into Billy's mother.

"Oh, good. I was hoping you two could meet," Vanessa said, "Sara, I'd like you to met Dr. Catherine Sullivan."

Sara Stangel looked much older than her thirty-five years. Her hard life had taken its toll and this mess with Billy added to the burden.

Dr. Sullivan checked her watch. "I can give you five minutes."

Vanessa motioned for everyone to take a seat, hurriedly clearing boxes off the chairs.

"Sara, I'm going to be blunt," Vanessa said. "Dr. Sullivan is our only hope."

"I'm sure the other boys did it," Sara said.

"There were no other boys," Vanessa said. "The DNA evidence proves Billy acted alone."

"There may be a reason for Billy's behavior," Dr. Sullivan said. "I'll talk to him. If what Vanessa suspects is true, we may be able to get him help. Isn't that a better alternative than prison?"

Sara's eyes darted from Dr. Sullivan to Vanessa. "You want to put him in a hospital with crazy people!"

Hanging onto the table's edge, Sara pulled herself to her feet. She looked at Vanessa with pleading eyes. "You have to help my boy."

"That's what I'm trying to do," Vanessa said, producing a release form. "Sara, you've got to trust us. The doctor needs your permission to see him."

Sara looked from Vanessa to Dr. Sullivan. She pulled her shabby coat around her. Wordlessly, she brushed away the tears, and signed the paper before she fled.

5

Newport, Oregon

Sara Stangel plowed across the courthouse parking lot and climbed into the old, brown '75 Nova and turned the key. Nothing happened. She tried again and the car sputtered and coughed, before it died. On the third try, it started and she was on her way home. Since they'd moved from the apartment in Newport, home had been Siletz, a scruffy little town on the outskirts of Newport that stretched along a river of the same name.

Try as they might, the town elders couldn't seem to overcome the fallout from the high unemployment rate and poor living conditions that plagued many of their townsfolk. Sadly, those conditions seemed to fuel juvenile delinquency, drug labs, and other crimes. There, Ralph Stangel freed from nosy do-gooders and prying eyes, could wreak unfettered havoc on his family.

Sara drove down the rutted dirt road, stopping near the rusted green and white trailer. She sat in the car, gathering strength, struggling to suppress the choking fear that her life was a complete shambles. Finally, she dragged her tired body from the aging Chevy and knelt on one knee to pet Buddy, the only family member who returned her love. The dog lumbered to its feet and wagged its tail. When she got to the door, she took a deep breath as if diving headlong into a cold, foreboding sea, before she pushed open the door.

Her husband was waiting for her. Smelling like cheap whiskey and sweat, Ralph caught her by the coat collar.

"Where the hell have you been?" he demanded, his cigarette clenched between his yellowing teeth.

"I had to see Billy's lawyer."

"Well, you didn't leave nothin' to eat," he said.

"I'll have to go to the market."

He grabbed her hair, bending her head back. He spat out, "You were just out! Where did you go?"

"I told you."

"You were out fuckin' around, weren't you?"

"No, I swear."

Ralph seized a greasy frying pan left on the stove from breakfast.

"Beg me to stop, bitch," he said, hoisting the pan.

Raising her arms to protect herself, she cried, "Please, Ralph, don't."

He slammed the pan into the side of her face. She crumbled to the floor, numb and dazed. He threw the pan into the sink, pulled on a pair of dirty jeans, yesterday's rumpled shirt, and let the door slam behind him. When she heard the Nova pull out of the gravel drive, she said a pray of thanks.

6

Newport, Oregon

The afternoon flew by, consumed with reviewing cases. When Vanessa finally took a moment to breath, there was just enough time to go home and change before meeting Steven. The rain had let up and the rose-hued sunset cast a warm glow over her office. She absentmindedly fished in her handbag for her keys before remembering Michael had her car. At that moment, the phone rang.

"Hi, Mom. Did you get my message? I found a place not far from the beach," Michael said, his words tumbling over each other. "It's furnished, so I can move right in. Are you ready to go? I'll be right there."

Vanessa barely had time to say goodbye before the line went dead. She gathered her papers into her briefcase and packed her lap top before she hurried down to meet Michael in front of the courthouse. He soon arrived and they were off, driving through town, over Cape Foulweather to Vanessa's cottage by the sea. Michael chattered on as he drove, excited about his new job and new place. She listened to every word, pleased to see how he'd brightened.

Without a moment to spare, Vanessa changed her clothes, while Michael hurried around her place, packing up his few belongings. It wasn't long before they were headed back to Newport. There was no time to check out Michael's new place. She dropped him in front of his house and headed off to meet Steven, wondering, once again, what brought on the change in his behavior. She smiled to herself, she liked the change.

7

Newport, Oregon

The upscale Embarcadero Resort, located at the far end of Newport's historic Bayfront, had a nautical theme, reflecting the harbor just outside its expanse of windows. Steven owned a condo there and he moored his thirty-foot sailboat just steps from his front door.

When she entered the dimly-lit lounge, there was no sign of him. Unless threatened with the wrath of Judge Holloway, Steven was notoriously late. A tinge of excitement, added to the first-date jitters, sent Vanessa straight to the bar. *Was this a date?* Cigarette smoke billowed from a corner booth, but the occupants were too intent on their conversation to notice her. Other than the bartender, no one else was in the place. Not waiting for Steven, she ordered a vodka martini with a twist.

Just then two men, better suited for the local dives further down the harbor, appeared in the doorway. The tall, thin man, wearing a San Francisco baseball cap and a Newport Bay sweatshirt, led the way to the end of the bar. His short, stocky pal sporting a black Harley T-shirt, his massive biceps bearing a skull and cross bones tattoo, followed. She couldn't help staring. When they glared back, she put her head down and sipped her drink. Finally, Steven arrived.

"Don't you look pretty?" he said, looking very handsome himself, in an open-collar shirt and jeans.

He ordered a drink and steered her toward a booth.

The two men at the bar were joined by a third. They talked quietly, heads close, stopping from time to time to scan the room. Again they caught Vanessa staring.

"Why don't we get some dinner?" Steven asked, oblivious of the drama at the bar.

They picked up their unfinished drinks and moved into the dining room.

She whispered, "Did you see those guys at the bar? What do you suppose they're doing here?"

Steven first glanced over one shoulder, then the other before he leaned in, and whispered, "They're undercover CIA agents looking for international spies." He laughed at her serious expression. "You've been reading too many mystery novels. For all we know, they're corporate lawyers from Chicago, out for a holiday."

"Very funny."

After they ordered dinner and another drink, thoughts of the strange men faded while they teased and laughed, enjoying each other's company.

Finally Steven said, "I've want to know more out about the real Vanessa. Today I found out you have a son. What other secrets do you hold?"

"Why the sudden interest?"

"It's not sudden," he said.

"If you make me tell my life story, I'll make you tell me yours," she said, running her fingers through a long strand of auburn hair, leaning toward Steven.

"That's a deal," he replied, saluting with his glass.

She wasn't sure if it was the alcohol or his warm smile, probably a combination, but her carefully-crafted fortress began to melt. Years ago she would have sought out Kate, who always seemed to know how to handle things. But over the past ten years, Vanessa had no one to rely on, so she'd turned her feelings inward. Maybe she could trust this man. Maybe he'd be different. She took a sip of her second martini. Tentatively, she began.

"Okay. Here goes. I grew up in Winnetka, near Chicago. I joined my father's law firm after Harvard. If I'd stayed, I'd be a partner by now."

Steven interrupted. "When were you at Harvard?"

"Let's see, seventy-two through seventy-four."

"I graduated in seventy-three. How did I miss you?" he asked.

"Well, for one thing, I was married."

"So was I. But, I could swear we've met before." He drifted off for a moment before returning to the conversation. "I interrupted you. Please go on."

The waitress served dinner and hurried off. Ignoring the steaming plate, Vanessa continued. "My brothers and I were raised by nannies. Our parents were too preoccupied with business and social engagements to care about raising their children. We learned to take care of ourselves. My father's eighty now and he's still working." She took another swallow of the martini. "The way he sees it, you can never make too much money."

"Can you? Make too much money, that is," Steven said, with a mischievous grin.

"Yes, if everything else in your life takes second place."

"How long were you married?"

"Do you really want to talk about that?" she asked.

"You'll get your chance to grill me," he said, digging into the prime rib. "Please continue."

"Yeah? Hum. Okay. I married too young and picked the wrong guy," she said, pausing to taste the poached salmon. "I followed in my father's footsteps and became a workaholic. Nicholas was away a lot on business." She tried the rice pilaf. "This tastes good. I haven't had much of an appetite lately, but for some reason, tonight I'm famished. Where was I? Oh, yes. We finally ended it. My best friend, Kate, left Chicago for some reason around the same time, never knew why. I rarely heard from her after that. Michael fell apart. He ran away a few years after that." She finished off the martini and looked for the waitress for a refill.

"Vanessa, I'm sorry. I didn't mean to stir anything up."

"Don't worry, Michael beat you to it," she said. "While I was growing up, the only break I got from my otherwise dismal life back then was when I'd visit Kate's summerhouse." Tears welled up and her voice cracked.

"Vanessa, what is it?" Steven asked, reaching over to take her hand.

"The reason I missed work was because Kate died. Two days ago, in Florence. I hadn't seen her in years. And for some unknown reason my son was with her."

"That must have been difficult."

"To say the least." Vanessa bit her lip, then noticed the waitress had cleared away the empty dishes.

"So much is happening all at once. Kate's death, Michael's return, your sudden interest in my past. Why, after ten uneventful years has my past become so present?"

"This isn't the way I wanted the evening to go. It's just…what I meant to say…I just wanted to get to know you," Steven said.

"Well…look what you started," she said with a wry smile. "I've talked a blue streak," she said, releasing a nervous laugh, attempting to cover her embarrassment. "Did you put truth serum in my drink?" She smiled, but avoided his eyes.

"You know, we've had so many conversations, but you've never mentioned any of this. I promise to give you a chance at me," Steven said. "How about tomorrow night?"

Until tonight, she'd prided herself on keeping her personal life personal. Don't ask questions, mind your own business, keep family problems private. The Sterling family mantra. But she felt safe confiding in Steven, and she needed someone she could talk to.

As she drove home that night, the moon shone a bit more brilliantly over the ocean and the stars illuminated the sky. She fell asleep as soon as her head hit the pillow. The first good night's sleep she'd had in years.

8

Newport, Oregon

Michael thrashed about, fighting his way out of another gruesome dream. He awoke groggy and disoriented, unsure of his surroundings, before quickly recognizing his new place. He stretched his lanky body and stumbled into the kitchen where he retrieved orange juice from the fridge and drank from the carton. Leaning against the counter, he gazed out the window where storm clouds gathered on the horizon. Reflecting back over the past ten years, hell, even before then, he realized he'd done everything he could to screw up his life. Now he wanted a chance to make things right. He liked the Oregon Coast. A guy could do okay here. Screw San Francisco. Whatever waited for him there would have to wait.

Shaking himself free from his thoughts, he headed to the shower, wanting to impress his new boss by being early to work on the first day. Once dressed in his new uniform, he stepped out the door into the crisp morning air, feeling invigorated, ready for a new day.

The one-bedroom house sat on a quiet street in the middle of Nye Beach. Similar to San Francisco, this neighborhood had a mixed bag of new construction and refurbished buildings tucked next to dilapidated apartments and neglected cottages. It attracted the same mixture of people.

A mangy gray dog sprang to its feet, straining against its chain, which was attached to a metal post in the neighbor's yard next door. Startled, Michael scowled at the beast, and then crossed the street to continue on his way. And the day went downhill from there.

Shortly after he arrived at his new job, torrential rains blew in off the Pacific. Michael wore Gus' yellow slicker, several sizes too big, as he hurried from one pump to another. There must have been a hundred cars that pulled in for gas that day. And with Oregon one of the few states that still had attendants pump the gas, his right arm felt as if he'd worked out all day. He ran back and forth making change, trying to get a break, not even having time to eat his sandwich. And to top it off, his boss, Gus Anderson, sat inside all day, warm and dry, reading a paperback novel, drinking Coke, occasionally making change for Michael. At the end of the day, soaked, tired and hungry, he trekked back home, finally able to scoff down the sandwich he'd made for lunch.

He threw off his uniform and headed straight for a hot shower. By the time he was dressed, the rain-clouds had rolled back, leaving what should be a great sunset down at the beach. He pulled on his jacket and headed out. No sooner had he stepped onto the porch a late-model black SUV pulled up in front of the neighbor's. Two men clambered out and sauntered up the front walk. The mangy dog, still tethered to his chain, greeted them with a wagging tail. The skinny guy, who wore a San Francisco baseball cap, bent down to pet the beast. The neighbor opened his door and they disappeared inside, unaware of Michael.

Michael froze. His stomach tightened. Sliding back into the shadow of the porch overhang, he fumbled for a smoke. How did they find him? This can't be a coincidence.

"Yoo-hoo, Michael!" called Mabel Gaskin, his new landlord, strutting up the walkway. She lived on the other side of his house and had made it clear, when Michael signed the lease, she didn't go for any shenanigans, as she called it. He had no problem with that. He'd behave. There'd been enough trouble in his life already.

"Just seeing how things are going."

At eighty-two, she was a sight to behold. Her short, plump body was draped in a purple tie-dyed muumuu. Purple Birkenstocks were nestled on her gnarled feet. Defiantly a throwback to the sixties. As she walked up the path toward the house, she jammed a hand inside her dress sleeve to catch a runaway bra strap.

"Yeah, everything's okay," Michael said. He took a long drag on his cigarette.

Something set off the dog.

"I'd hate to see him off that chain," Michael said, nodding in the dog's direction.

Mabel rolled her eyes. "Gawd damn dog! Belongs to that Wade Mackey."

Michael's throat constricted.

She bent down to pluck a weed from a flowerpot on the front porch. "Damn riffraff!" She wiped some spittle away from her mouth with a dirt-stained hand, leaving a smudge.

"Yeah," he said, deciding to stay in for the night.

9

San Francisco
2004

Nicholas Thorne slammed down the phone, the fateful words still echoing. It wasn't unexpected, but the finality of it hit him hard. Kate was dead. It had taken her deadbeat brother a week to make the call, and by that time Kate had already been cremated and her ashes spread over her beloved Lake Michigan.

He felt a strange burning in his eyes, like when his mother died all those years ago. He'd loved Kate for as long as he could remember. Now she was gone.

Nicholas glanced at the crystal decanter. Not yet noon, but he needed a drink. He poured two fingers neat, and swallowed hard, then poured another. At almost sixty, his age was catching up with him. At one time or another, every bone in his body ached.

He stood by the mantel and looked wistfully at Kate's photo in its silver frame. It was beyond him why he'd ever let her go.

San Francisco
1994

Nicholas had been living apart from Vanessa for many years of their marriage, going to Chicago only when guilt pangs hit. There he'd avoid his wife by spending most of the time with his son, Michael. He'd told himself he'd put off the divorce because of the boy, but Vanessa's trust fund had played a part in delaying the inevitable. That was until he came into his own.

His marriage had not been a total bust. By marrying her, he'd been swept into the social life of the upper crust. He'd learned to soften the rough edges of his south-side Chicago upbringing; learned the value of dressing the part, choosing the best wines, and seducing the right women. He'd learned that a round of golf at his father-in-law's prestigious club meant more than making a birdie. It was where profitable friendships were cemented, corporate deals were discussed, and mega-mergers debated. The movers and shakers sealed deals worth millions, over scotch and cigars in the country club bar.

He learned the lessons well. No longer needing Vanessa, he finalized the divorce and didn't waste any time sending for Kate Remington. He'd fallen for Kate the moment they met. The playful, voluptuous blond was a direct contrast to tall, sleek, serious Vanessa. Kate and Nicholas had managed to be together that first night at Kate's summerhouse. In his brazen youth, he'd figured with two women in love with him, he had it made. He knew Vanessa would never play the mistress. She'd have left him flat. But Kate, sweet Kate, loved him enough to take the lesser role.

Floundering, his father-in-law found him a job selling corporate insurance, which kept Nicholas traveling all over the country. Nicholas had often wondered if that was the old man's way of trying to break up his daughter's marriage. He'd bought a townhouse in San Francisco, since much of his business was centered there and finalized the divorce. Now he was able to have Kate to himself. When he'd asked her to join him in San Francisco, at first she'd hesitated.

For years Kate had balanced being mistress to Nicholas and best friend to Vanessa. It was almost too good to be true that she and Nick could finally be together. That had meant severing all ties with her dear friend. But she knew in the end, she wouldn't be happy without Nicholas. She'd packed her bags and left Chicago without a word.

At first, it was everything she'd hoped for. But, as time went by, Nicholas seemed to spend more and more time away from home. And he never mentioned marriage.

With so much alone time, she would find herself mulling over the past. How she'd wasted so much of her life waiting for Nick. Oddly enough, she'd never been jealous of Vanessa. She'd loved her like a sister. Lying to her was just a way of protecting her. Being with Nick was like a dream come true. But lately she needed more.

At lunch one day, while Nick was out of town, a friend told her about a homeless shelter for kids. It was just what Kate had been searching for. She arranged a meeting with the director, Kenny Harper. Without hesitation, Kate began volunteering the following week.

When Nicholas returned, she could hardly wait to share her good news. She told him about it over dinner.

When she'd finished, he just stared at her. Finally he spoke. "I need you here."

"Don't worry. I told Kenny I would have to work around your schedule."

"Kenny! Who the hell is Kenny?" Nicholas said.

"He's the director of the project. Oh, Nicholas, don't be jealous."

Just then the maid entered.

"Will there be anything else, sir?" Josie asked, as she began to clear the table.

"Yes. We'll have coffee in the library," Nicholas said.

He threw his napkin down and rose from the table, bumping it hard enough to upset the wine goblets.

Kate caught up with him in the library. Josie poured the coffee and left, closing the door behind her.

"Nicholas, please don't be like this," Kate said.

"Like what?"

"I need to do something constructive. I love being with you. But, you're gone a lot, so I thought…"

"Did you think about me? What do you want? I can give you whatever you need."

"Money's not an issue here."

"Then what do you need?" he asked.

"Freedom to do what I want!"

He stood over her and for a moment she'd feared he would hit her.

"The matter is closed," he said. "Call tomorrow and tell him you won't be back."

She had no intention of quitting.

He sat at his desk, opened his laptop, and began to work, shutting Kate out.

Later, when he came to bed, she was reading. He climbed in, rolled over and without a word, turned out the light. She reached out to him. He took her hand and kissed the palm. He drew her close and kissed her hard.

"I'm sorry I lost my temper," he said.

He made love to her. But it was different, rougher and more demanding. Something had changed.

10

Newport, Oregon
2004

Vanessa couldn't seem to concentrate. She opened her narrow office window to let in the cool misty air. One date with Steven had changed the dynamics of their relationship, and that meant complications. There'd been chemistry between them right from the start, but until last night it had been channeled into playful banter. She liked the way things were. She filled her days with cases, took files home and worked most of the night. Sleep, if it came, was fitful. But work had been enough. She'd been consumed with the Welch trial and it still weighed heavy. And then there was Michael. She didn't need any more.

The wind shifted, blowing papers from her desk. She pulled the window shut and gathered the documents back into a neat pile. It wasn't like her to be so distracted. Forcing herself back on track, she scanned Billy's clinical evaluation that Dr. Sullivan had completed in one day. It proved what Vanessa had suspected, that the abuse throughout Billy's life had affected him, creating a precursor for a sociopathic personality disorder. The behaviors were all there: a complete and utter disregard for the rights of others. No regard for the rules of society. Those afflicted showed little anxiety and didn't have the capacity to feel guilt. No wonder Vanessa had felt uneasy interviewing Billy. She'd often wondered how a child could be so calm faced with such serious charges. Then, when he dealt with his mother, he could turn on her in uncontrollable rages, blaming her for all his problems.

With the trial just days away, she had to search for relevant case law, draft her opening statement and prep her only witness, Dr. Sullivan.

At six-thirty, she closed her laptop. Weary, but pleased she'd accomplished so much, she took off her reading glasses and rubbed her temples. Her second date with Steven was in less than an hour. Two dates in two nights. Not a good idea.

Unusually prompt, Steven stood at the door of Vanessa's cottage at the appointed time.

"Come in," Vanessa said, holding the door open.

He smiled broadly and handed her a bouquet of red tulips.

"They're beautiful," she said, cradling the flowers. "Please, make yourself at home. I'll put these in water."

He surveyed the living room with its over-stuffed sofas flanking the fireplace, an antique writing desk in the corner, piled high with files and reports. A large well-worn oriental rug covered the hardwood floors, and an explosion of books were crammed into the bookcases. A few spider webs hung from the beamed ceilings.

"I like your place," he said, calling into the kitchen.

Vanessa returned with the flowers arranged in a cut crystal vase and set them on the mantle. She noticed he noticed her clingy emerald green sweater. Her frequent walks up Cape Foulweather had paid off, keeping her slim and energetic, looking younger than her fifty-two years.

Steven helped her on with her coat and, once outside, opened the car door. It had been a long time since she'd had such attention.

The Side Door Cafe, a quaint place in Gleneden Beach, just north of Depoe Bay, greeted them with the aroma of seafood chowder and freshly baked bread. The dimly lit café was filled with locals and tourists, their voices melding into a low hum. Steven and Vanessa agreed on a bottle of Australian Shiraz and crab cake appetizers. Candles flickered on the table, and the lush green ferns, suspended from the ceiling, swayed in the breeze of the overhead fans. They sat on the same side of the booth. While they drank wine and chatted, the world around them seemed to fade.

Dinner was over far too quickly, so Vanessa invited Steven back to her place. *So much for taking it slow.*

The drive home took them past pristine beaches and thick forests. From every direction, Oregon had breathtaking vistas that drew thousands of visitors to the coast. This night, the full moon blazed a path across Boiler Bay. White capped waves roiled in the black ocean. Depoe Bay shops were shut; tourists were tucked into their hotel rooms; and few cars traveled the road as they continued south to Oceana Street. They were content to be quiet as they drove. The dark narrow lane where Vanessa lived appeared suddenly from around a blind corner. Steven's headlights illuminated the green street sign as he made the turn.

Vanessa lit a fire and retrieved a bottle of aged cognac from a kitchen cabinet. After pouring two glasses, she kicked off her shoes, settled in next to Steven on the sofa, and tucked her feet under her.

"It's your turn," she said, a smile spreading across her face.

"Oh brother, I'd hoped you'd forgotten." He sipped the warm liqueur. "Great cognac. So smooth."

"Nice defensive move, Counselor, but you're not getting off that easy." She laughed, tilting her head back.

"Okay. You win. Let's see. I was born in Weeds, Texas. But I grew up in Oklahoma City. I went to University of Oklahoma before going to Harvard."

"What were you like as a boy?"

"Like most boys, I guess. I liked baseball. My mother made me play the piano. She said balance in one's life was important, until she got tired of dragging me in from the sand lot to practice."

"Tell me about your ex-wife," she said, cupping her glass with both hands and taking a sip.

"Ouch, do you really want to get into that?"

"It's your turn, remember? I do the cross-examination this time."

"Okay. Okay. Let's see, we met on a flight to New York when I was a junior. She was the stewardess." He smiled. "She strolled those aisles as if she owned them. We got married about a year later, about the time I was going off to Harvard."

He downed the remaining cognac, and Vanessa refilled his glass.

"During the last year at Harvard, Chandler was born. We moved back to Oklahoma City, and two years later Candice came along. I accepted a position as a patent attorney; we bought a home and settled in for the long haul," he said, swirling the amber liquid in his glass. "At least I did."

Staring into the flickering flames, he said, "It's been years since I've talked about this. Julia had an affair. The kids were in school, so she took some classes at the university. I was pleased she wanted to continue her education. But she fell for her much-younger professor. I probably worked too much. She had too much time on her hands."

"Don't be so hard on yourself," Vanessa said. "Most likely the outcome would have been the same."

"Maybe," he said, taking another sip. "Anyway, the kids went off to college. That's when I moved to San Francisco where a buddy from Harvard got me a job as assistant DA. But I hated the rigors of a big city prosecutor's office. It was around that time, on an extended vacation, I visited the Oregon Coast and decided to stay. I set up a private practice. Later, I ran for DA."

Finally, reluctantly, they agreed it was time for Steven to go.

"When can I see you again?" he asked.

She laughed and said, "You see me every day at work."

"You know what I mean."

"Soon," she said.

He kissed her softly before disappearing down the path to the driveway.

11

Depoe Bay, Oregon

A warm, wistful smile crept over Vanessa's ruby lips. She leaned against the open door and watched until the tail-lights of Steven's car disappeared into the pines. His gentle kiss still lingered on her lips. She closed the door and made her way to the bedroom. There, she slipped on red silk pajamas, and climbed into bed. She leafed through a mystery novel, but after rereading the same paragraph several times, she gave up and set the book aside.

Thoughts of Steven sent a pleasant shiver through her body. Something she hadn't felt in years. *Get a grip.* It was sheer insanity. How seductive new love could be. Euphoria and passion, while exhilarating, blinded lovers to the faults and shortcomings of their loved one. But when she was young, self-assured and cocky, she plunged head-first into the cold waters of life unprepared for what she'd find.

University of Illinois, Champaign 1969

Over her parents' objections, Vanessa had begun her freshman year at less-than-prestigious U of I. She wanted something different from the private prep schools and Ivy League Universities. She wanted new experiences, diverse people and fresh challenges that would allow her to break free from her parents' stifling control.

It was the late sixties, a time of conflicting mores, the Age of Aquarius and war, an exciting time to be on a college campus. Servicemen were returning from Vietnam, unheralded and disillusioned, some going to college compliments of the government. They'd seen a world far removed from their classmates, who thought themselves revolutionaries as they paraded with anti-war placards across campus quads.

Vanessa's mother had accompanied her that first day, with a promise to leave as soon as she got Vanessa settled in. After one look at Vanessa's hippie dorm mate, her mother had rented Vanessa an apartment. It took Mrs. Sterling several days to get the apartment up to her standards. During that time she'd managed to quash the issue of a freshman living off campus by giving a sizable donation to the university.

At last, Vanessa waved goodbye to her mother, thrilled to be on her own. But instead of exciting new experiences, she settled into a routine of studying each night. She did attract boys' attention, but they seemed to be the same sort she'd met in private school: self-absorbed, spoiled preppies. Besides, her focus was on getting into Harvard Law School.

About two months into the fall semester, she hurried into the Ivy Café, a campus hangout, jam-packed with the lunch crowd. Waitresses, in short blue uniforms, breezed up to a table just long enough to take an order or drop off the food.

Vanessa was surveying the chaotic scene, when a friend from poli sci motioned for Vanessa to join her. Making her way around books and backpacks strewn on the floor, she noticed a dark-haired man a few years her senior. His coal-black eyes connected. She felt flushed and looked away. Once at the classmate's table, she looked over her shoulder just in time to see the handsome man disappear out the door.

Turning to her friend, she said, "Who was that?"

"Nicholas Thorne. A football jock," she said, scrunching up her nose in disgust. "He's here by virtue of the GI bill."

Vanessa couldn't stop thinking of those dark eyes. Later she was hurrying to her next class when she spotted Nicholas heading in her direction. She pretended to be checking her notebook.

"Hey, didn't I see you at Ivy's?" he asked.

"Yeah," she said, blushing.

"I'm Nicholas Thorne, but call me Nick."

She introduced herself.

"A freshman, right?"

"Is it obvious?"

"No. It's just that I hadn't seen you around."

They talked on, oblivious of the scene around them: students rushing by, campus trees ablaze with autumn colors, handmade posters announcing rush parties. A cool wind swept through the quad causing her to pull her cashmere cardigan tightly around her.

"I've got to get to class," she said, turning to leave.

"Wait!" Nicholas said, lightly touching her arm. "Have dinner with me tonight."

With a pounding heart, she agreed.

For the rest of the afternoon, her classes seemed to drag by. The professors droned on, but nothing got through. Finally her last class was over and she set off to meet Nick. She strolled along a boulevard of brilliant fall colors, orange and gold asters, red maple leaves under foot.

Nick was pacing outside Ivy's until he saw her approach. He waved and hurried to meet her.

"Let's go to Johnny's," he said, and quickly grabbed her arm to lead the way.

At six-three, with a linebacker's physique, he was quite imposing. His dark eyes were mesmerizing.

At Johnny's Bar and Grill, they devoured a large pepperoni pizza. Johnny's was the sort of place that was lax on checking ID, so Vanessa and Nick shared a pitcher of beer. By the second pitcher Nick became more talkative. He went on about the war, how he hated it, how he'd killed some Vietcong that were about the age of his younger brother. She'd been to Europe many times, once as an exchange student, but visiting galleries and cathedrals paled in comparison to his year in Vietnam. That experience made him a part of the world's hottest controversy, and as with other returning vets, shaped who he was. She felt an excitement she'd never felt before and just a little bit scared.

Unaccustomed to drinking, the beers hit her hard. Nicholas guided her as they made their way to Vanessa's apartment. Standing just outside her door, Nicholas kissed her, softly at first. When she didn't resist, he kissed her harder, more passionately. From then on they spent every moment they could together. Day after day, they strolled through campus, caught a movie, or hung out at Johnny's. All the while they barely noticed anyone around them, and the night always ended at Vanessa's.

He wasn't like anyone else she'd ever known. In spite of all their differences, she was hooked. When they made love, she could hardly catch her breath. Afterwards, he'd hold her and whisper how much he loved her. Mornings he'd be up early, making eggs and toast before they went off to class.

One night just before Christmas, they were at Johnny's. Nick always drank a great deal. But, then again, most young men on campus seemed to drink too much. He was leaning toward her, his arm resting on the back of her barstool, as he listened intently to her stories about her prep school days. Brandon, a young man from her lit class, whom she'd rebuffed several times, saw her with Nick. Brandon had already had a few drinks, he ordered another Bud, before swaggering up behind Vanessa. She was unaware he was standing there until he spoke.

"Well, what do we have here?" Brandon said. "A couple of love birds?"

Nick swung his powerful body off the stool and grabbed Brandon by the collar. Brandon dropped his beer. It shattered on impact.

Nose to nose, Nicholas said, "Get lost, smartass."

Trembling, Brandon tried to apologize, but Nick hung on, marching him through the door to the sidewalk, while Vanessa watched in disbelief. Nick released Brandon with such force, he stumbled and fell, then scrambled to his feet and ran off.

Nick threw some bills on the bar, grabbed Vanessa's arm and hurried her out the door.

"What was that?" she demanded. He pulled her into a doorway and he'd kissed her.

"That guy's a jerk! Don't worry, I've got everything under control."

"I've never seen you like that before," she said. But she let herself believe Nick and never mentioned it again.

Months flew by; her freshman year ended; and finals rolled around. Her grades had slipped, and her father had made it clear she'd be out of there if she didn't bring her grades up. She crammed for exams and managed to pull through. When summer finally arrived, she was off to Kate's grandmother's lake house in Wisconsin, as usual, just a few hours' drive from Chicago. That summer Nicholas was a frequent guest.

Kate, Nick and Vanessa spent the summer swimming in the choppy lake, sunning on the great expanse of lawn and, at night, when they were sure Kate's grandmother was fast asleep; the trio drank beer down by the dock.

All too soon summer's carefree days came to an end. Vanessa started her sophomore year, knowing she couldn't keep up last semester's pace. Nick left her little time to study and he often convinced her to skip a class. But it was impossible to give him up.

A few months into the fall semester, Vanessa met Nicholas at Ivy's for lunch. He was ready with his kisses and smart talk, but she pushed him back into his seat. She needed to be serious.

"I can't keep this up," she said. "I don't want to mess up my future."

He leaned in to kiss away her fears. "You don't have to worry about your future," Nicholas said. "I'm going to make plenty of money playing pro ball, and you'll have your trust fund. You don't have to be some big shot lawyer. I love you, Vanessa. Isn't that enough?"

"What are you saying, Nicholas?" she asked. "Are you asking me to marry you?"

"What...no...ah...I hadn't looked at it that way. But, sure, why not? Let's get married."

Vanessa threw her arms around him. "We can live in my apartment. My parents will pay for everything until I graduate. We can be together all the time and I can study at home, and keep my grades up. Oh, Nicholas, I'm so happy."

But her parents furious. They'd met Nicholas and saw him as an opportunist. They'd begged her to wait; even threatened to cut off her funds. She'd countered with a threat to elope. In the end, Vanessa and Nicholas were married during the winter break of her sophomore year.

12

Newport, Oregon
2004

Vanessa's last date with Steven had been a week ago, but with the Welsh trial closing in on her, she had little time to think about anything else. Billy's future lay in her hands. If she worked every waking moment until the trial date next week, she'd be ready. This was the worst possible time for her to be thinking about a new relationship. And the prospect of going up against Steven in court, if she let this go any further, was unimaginable. What was she thinking? It was not only unethical, but at odds with everything she stood for. Her first priority had to be her clients.

She headed down the hall and entered Courtroom Two. Since there was no trial in session, she was free to browse through the vast collection of law books housed there. Finding what she needed, she lugged several tomes back to her office, where they now lay strewn around her desk and conference table, opened to pertinent cases. She entered the Westlaw's website. The computer cut down research time, but reminiscent of her law school days, she always came back to the books.

Her deep concentration was broken when the phone rang. It was Michael. It had also been a week since she last spoke with her son.

"Hey. Where have you been?" He laughed and added, "And I thought you'd be the one bugging me if I moved here!"

"I've been swamped. How do you like your new place?"

"That's why I called. I want you to come and see it. Let me know what you think."

Years ago, she would have put work before her son. But that had to change. She'd been given an opportunity to make things right with him and she wasn't going to blow it.

"Sure, how about tonight at seven?"

She finished her call and replaced the phone in its cradle, before delving back in.

The next time she thought to check her watch it was seven. After packing her briefcase and laptop, she scurried down the back steps. She tossed her cases in the back seat of the Jeep, hopped in, revved the engine, and drove off.

Thick fog carpeted the street giving an eerie appearance to Nye Beach. She rolled to a stop in front of Michael's. A black SUV pulled up behind her with its high beams blazing. She turned off the ignition and stepped from her car. The SUV's lights went out, and the occupants exited their vehicle at the same time. There stood two of the men she'd seen at the Embarcadero the week before, looking as menacing as they had that night. She hurried up to Michael's door.

"Are those guys your neighbors?" she asked, scooting inside.

"Who?" he asked.

"There! Those two."

She watched through the window as the fog engulfed them. "They give me the creeps."

"Yeah, me too," Michael said. "Let me give you the grand tour."

She shrugged off the coincidence and followed Michael as he showed her the small one bedroom cottage.

"Very nice. I like Nye Beach. It has a special feeling about it," she said. "Have you checked out the coffee houses and art galleries?"

"I haven't had much of a chance, I've been working every day."

"Are you hungry?" she asked. "Let's get some dinner."

She drove the back streets, arriving at her favorite restaurant at the Bayfront. Along the narrow street, pungent fish packing houses intermingled with restaurants and gift shops. The port had a colorful history that went back a hundred years. Now, fishermen struggled to make a living amid mounting restrictions and catch limits. Even so, tourists and locals continued to flock to the picturesque harbor. Vanessa often bought crab or salmon right off the docked boats.

As she parked near the restaurant, the black SUV slowly drove by.

"Did they follow us?" she asked, turning to find Michael already out of the car and hurrying into the restaurant.

"What's with those guys?" she asked, taking a seat across from him.

Something was going on.

"Do you know them?" she asked.

Michael shrugged, staring at the menu.

She persisted. "How do you know them?"

Avoiding his mother's eyes, he said, "I knew them when I lived in San Francisco."

"How do you know creeps like that?"

"Mom, it's not a big deal. They probably don't remember me. Just drop it."

She went numb, her appetite gone. *This was no coincidence.*

They stared out the window, watching people hunch against the wind, making their way along the lamp-lit street.

"This will make you happy," he volunteered. "I found an AA meeting."

"That is great news! It must be tough to make a fresh start in a new town."

"Not really. No one here knows me and that's a good thing."

It was obvious she wasn't going to get anything more out of Michael tonight. It was almost a relief to drop him back at his place. The black SUV sat at the curb. She tried to imagine what connection Michael had with those men. She jotted down the license plate number of the SUV before she drove off.

13

Newport, Oregon

There was something mesmerizing about the power of the ocean. Michael shoved his hands deep into his pockets and braced himself against the wind, heading north on the rocky coast just below Nye Beach. He'd needed to clear his head after dinner with his mother. Things were not going as he'd planned. Hoping for a chance to forget about his past, of all the places on earth he could have moved to, he landed next door to Mackey.

He gazed out to sea. A crescent moon illuminated cumulus clouds, and as the wind blew the clouds took form. There was Kate with outstretched arms, calling to him. He bit his lip and looked away. Kate's death had been a devastating blow. Sand whirled at his feet. The winter tide would soon consume the beach. He turned, and trudged back.

Near the seawall by the steps up to the Nye Beach parking lot, three men stood smoking and talking, under a street lamp, their mangy dog straining at its leash. There was no way around the men. Michael hunched his shoulders trying to get by unnoticed.

"Well, if it ain't our old pal Mike," Wade Mackey said, turning to the bulky tattooed man standing next to him. "Now tell me, Bull, ain't this a small world?" He sneered, dropped his cigarette, and ground it out with the heel of his boot. "You left us a fuckin' mess, buddy boy."

Michael knew what would come next. He searched for an escape route. Nearby shops were all closed. The Visual Art Center stood dark and deserted, but the stairs next to it led to the street above. Just a block from his house.

"Who's the woman?" Bull asked, cleaning his nails with a pocket knife.

"Leave her out of this!" Michael said. He backed his way towards the stairs.

"Nice piece of ass," said Bobby Scarpelli, his lanky body taut and alert. Michael wanted to rip the man's heart out.

"Ya know, killin' Diego wasn't too smart," Bull said, closing the blade against his thigh. "Thompson's in jail for your murder rap."

"I didn't kill Diego!" Michael said. He made a break, running for the stairs. But, within seconds Mackey was on him. Gripping Michael's wrist, he spun him around, twisting his arm back, pinning him against the rough cement of the stairwell. Mackey grabbed Michael's hair, pulled his head back, and smashed his face into the wall. Blood gushed from his fractured nose.

Bull stood close enough for Michael to smell his rancid breath.

"Remember Diego?" he hissed. "Just before you shot him?"

"Oh, Jesus! Please don't kill me! I swear I didn't do it!" Michael said.

"Are you scared, buddy boy?" Mackey sneered through locked teeth.

Mackey kept Michael pinned, while the others pummeled him. The dog ripped at his clothes, sinking his teeth into Michael's leg. He screamed in pain, kicking and struggling, until a blow to his head knocked him cold.

"That oughta shake him up," Mackey said, stepping over the limp body.

At some point later that night, Michael came to dazed and disoriented. Still lying in the stairwell, he struggled to his knees. After looking around, sure he was alone, he slowly climbed the stairs. Crusted blood caked his nose and mouth. His head throbbed. Every breath sent pain ripping through his chest. Finding the streets deserted, he took a moment to rest, then made his way home. He locked the door, left the lights out, and crawled into bed. He passed out as soon as he hit the pillow.

Dreams invaded his sleep. Michael thrashed about, his legs tangled in the covers, as he tried in vain to out-run the all-too-familiar scene…

Gray afternoon light filtered through the high hung windows of the old San Francisco warehouse. Rhio Diego had set up his own shop in the derelict building, using it as a drop for Columbian cocaine. He had a flotilla of small boats that would come and go unnoticed through the bay. When word finally got out about his clandestine shop, Diego knew that was a death sentence.

Then, suddenly, he lay hog-tied and gagged on the dank cement floor, eyes pleading for mercy. Michael stood over him. A single shot reverberated through the cavernous building. Diego was dead.

"No!" Michael screamed. His eyes shot open. His body covered in sweat. He knew the beating was only the beginning. Mackey wouldn't rest until he'd avenged his friend's death.

14

Newport, Oregon

Fog cloaked the crest rising five-hundred feet above sea level along the main artery that led north and south along the coast. To Vanessa, the aura of Cape Foulweather seemed to lend itself to mystery and intrigue, as she drove over the peak each day on her way to work. Sometimes she'd devise corny movie promos: 'Torrid romance collides with murder and mayhem on the cliffs of Cape Foulweather!' But tonight the men in the black SUV occupied her thoughts. She'd seen their type before. They'd posture, strut, gesture, and glare, until it was time for the verdict. Then they'd be sniveling children.

Turning onto Oceana, the narrow road under a canopy of Juniper and Oaks, usually began to melt the day's tension. She rolled down the Jeep window to take in the fresh salt, pine scented air. But tonight she felt vulnerable and alone. Shadows took shape. Her headlights played off the bushes and vines along the roadside. She quickly rolled the window back up. Glancing in the rear view mirror, she made sure she hadn't been followed. She grabbed her cases from the back seat and hurried up the walk. Once inside, she fastened the door latch and checked every door and window in the house. She left the exterior floodlights on. She has always loved the isolation of living in the woods, high above the ocean, but tonight she felt uneasy.

She set her brief case and laptop on the dining room table, before going to the kitchen for a glass of Merlot. Probably not the best idea, since she had to work all night. But she needed to steady her nerves. Reaching for the cork screw, she noticed the red light of her answering machine. She pressed the play button.

'Vanessa. It's Steven. I...uh...we need to talk. Sorry I didn't see you today, I was swamped, and I'm going to be out of the office tomorrow. Since the trial starts Monday...it would complicate things...if we saw each other before then.'

She had already decided she and Steven could never go any further, but hearing it from him hit her hard. She sat in a dining room chair, feeling the weight on her shoulders, realizing she needed him. She needed to tell him about the guys in the SUV. And her dinner with Michael. She wanted him in the next room while she worked all night on a case. The realization sank in. She was no longer content to live alone. She wanted Steven in her life. She took a long swallow of the Merlot. This was a fine mess she'd gotten into.

15

Newport, Oregon

"Damn it!" Michael shouted at the walls.

He struggled to his feet and moved slowly to the bathroom. Bracing against the sink, he peered into the mirror. His almost unrecognizable face stared back. His lips were puffy, his eyes were black and blue, and his nose was swollen and misshapen. Every breath burned. He threw water on his face, washing away the caked-on blood, and gingerly dried with a towel. Stumbling through the house, he drew the shades, making sure the doors and windows were locked. He fixed an ice bag and veered unsteadily back to the bedroom. Sitting on the edge of the bed, he managed to pull off his blood-stained boots, which had luckily taken most of the dog's punishment. Every move was painful. He laid back on the pillow and put the ice pack against his nose.

He stayed in all day. Thankfully, he wasn't scheduled to work until the next day. He managed to get some soup down, but he wasn't really hungry. After dark, he turned on every light in the house. He found a metal pipe in the storage room, and kept it close. There was no getting away from Mackey and his men. He'd have to be prepared for his next attack. Michael's past had returned with a vengeance and slammed him to the mat. He fell asleep, sitting in the chair by the door, still grasping tight to the pipe.

When he awoke the next morning, still in the chair, he could hardly move. He managed to put on a pot of coffee and while it brewed, he showered. Bracing against the tile, he let the water cascade over him. He sucked in a breath as the hot water seared his wounds. After he stepped from the shower, he surveyed the damage. Compared to his face, his body didn't look too bad, but he was sure they'd broken a few ribs. Surprisingly, his appetite returned. He hadn't eaten at all the day before. Ravenously he consumed a peanut butter and jelly sandwich, along with a handful of aspirin that he washed down with a gulp of the coffee.

Still without a car, he hiked to work. By the time he arrived at the Chevron station, his shirt was drenched in sweat. It took every bit of strength to walk three blocks.

His boss, Gus, stared. "You've got a helluva shiner there, Buddy," he said. "What happened?"

"An accident," was all he said.

The day dragged. Even though there were few cars, Gus picked up the slack by having Michael stack oil cans and refill the soda machines. The pain was almost unbearable. By mid-day, he took a break out by the alley. He lit a smoke and took a deep drag. His head was beginning to clear and with it the desperation increased. He had to figure a way out. Going to the police was out of the question. He ground out his cigarette, convinced that there was only one solution.

Near closing, his mother pulled in. *Jesus, this is all I need!* He turned his back, trying to look busy.

Gus hollered, "Get that car!"

"I needed gas so I thought I would..." She saw her sons face and froze.

Before she could say another word, he went around the car to pump the gas. She got out and walked over to him.

"Michael, what happened?" She put her hand on his arm. His skin felt clammy.

"Nothing. I'm fine," he said, shrugging off her hand.

Their eyes connected. No longer able to contain it, his face contorted in pain.

"I need your help," he whispered, keeping his head down, pumping the gas. "I can't go back to my house tonight."

"Get in," she said. She hurried over to Gus, giving him a twenty to cover the gas. "I'm his mother," she said, trying to explain why Michael had just gotten into her car.

Gus replied, "Looks like he's in trouble. Seems like a nice kid. I sure hope you can help."

16

Newport, Oregon

"No way!" Michael said. "They'll ask too many questions."

"Well," she said, slamming the gearshift into park in front of the emergency room entrance. "They'll have to get in line behind me!"

Hours later, after an exam and x-rays, Michael emerged from the ER to find Vanessa reading a dog-eared magazine in the waiting room. Empty paper cups littered the table in front of her. He pulled up his work shirt to show his bandaged torso. He had two broken ribs, a broken nose, bruised kidneys and a prescription for Vicodin.

"The doctor looked suspicious when I told him I smashed up my car."

Michael hobbled to the Jeep and carefully settled himself in. After a stop at the drug store, to fill the prescription, they finally reached Vanessa's. Michael shuffled into the house and sank onto the sofa. While Vanessa put on some tea, he picked up one of the pillows and held it to his chest. She returned with an ice pack, along with two Vicodin and a glass of water. He downed the pills and held the ice pack to his face. She sat next to him, waiting for the kettle to boil.

"Did the guys in the SUV do this to you?"

"Yes."

"I knew it!"

"I can't lie anymore. I told you I knew them in San Francisco."

Here it comes. She closed her eyes and laid her head back on the sofa, her body flushed hot, her muscles tensed.

"They were part of a very big syndicate," he continued.

"As in drugs?"

"Yeah. When someone wanted to break away…they were killed to teach others a lesson," he said, removing the ice pack. He directed his piercing blue eyes at Vanessa. "I saw it."

"Saw what?"

"The murder."

"You witnessed a murder?"

"Yeah. Some low-life scum. They think I did it."

He saw a murder! Her mind whirled.

"You have to go to the police."

"I can't."

"But you have to."

"If I did, they'd kill me."

"You're just a witness, right?"

"Yeah. What do you think?" he said. "I swear I didn't do it." He made a sudden move and the pain shot through him.

The kettle screeched. She rushed into the kitchen to turn it off. As Michael's words sunk in, a burst of anger clutched her chest. Slamming the kettle down, she stormed back into the living room. "You didn't do it? Do you have any idea how many times I've heard that line? Give me one reason to believe you!"

"I could never kill anyone. You must know that."

"How do I know that? You've been gone for ten years. I don't know you anymore!"

He slid the pillow aside and leaned forward, grimacing from the move. Holding a steady gaze, he said, "I needed you when I was a kid, but you weren't there." He knew that would shake her up. "I need you now. I need you to believe me."

She stepped to the window and leaned her cheek against the cool pane. Crimson clouds hugged the horizon. She stood motionless until the light sank below the ocean.

"I believe you," she said, her voice cracked, weary from the weight of her words. She was not sure that was true. Not sure at all.

17

Depoe Bay, Oregon

The next day Vanessa drummed her fingers on the dining table, waiting for Michael to get up. She should have been at work, but last night's revelation made that impossible.

Absentmindedly she skimmed through the *Oregonian*, absorbing none of it. The night before, after Michael had delivered his bombshell, the Vicodin had kicked in and he'd gone off to bed, leaving her wide awake and full of questions. She'd turned the excess energy toward work and managed to get a considerable amount done on the trial. But sometime early morning, she'd made up her mind to stand by him, no matter what, and would put together a formidable legal team to defend him, if it came to that. He was her only child and, as he had pointed out she'd let him down in the past. But, not this time.

Now questions swarmed her mind. Somehow Kate was involved. Why else was Michael with her in the hospital? During one of the few contacts Kate had made with Vanessa during the last ten years, Kate had mentioned helping out at a homeless shelter for runaway teens in San Francisco. Michael had said she saved his life. That put her in San Francisco at that same time as Michael.

Michael startled his mother when he finally entered the dining room.

"I'm starved," he said. With rumpled hair and sleepy eyes, he looked sixteen again. But the fading bruises and bandaged ribs brought it all back. "I've hardly eaten in the last three days."

"I'll make you something in a minute," she said, pouring him a cup of coffee from the carafe on the table. "Look, I want to help you out. I want to believe you're innocent. But if other's think you're guilty, we may have to settle this in court. But let's not get too far ahead of ourselves. One thing for sure, I need to know the whole truth."

"I think I've said too much already." He added three hefty spoonfuls of sugar to the coffee and gulped it down.

"It's too late for that," she said, unmoved by his display. "First, I need to know how you became involved in this murder."

He tore off a piece of his mother's uneaten toast, popped it in his mouth, and brushed the crumbs from his hands.

"What do you want from me?" Michael asked. "If you get involved with this, you could be in danger, too. Not just me. We're not talking about petty thief. These guys have their tentacles everywhere."

Vanessa saw the uncertainty in her son's eyes. "I'll be okay. Right now I want to know how you got mixed up with these people. The only way this is going to work is if you trust me. I've been a defense attorney for some time now, almost ten years. I can help. You see me just as your mother, but I'm a capable attorney with good connections. Let me help you, damn it!"

"I may regret this. I've never told anyone what I'm about to tell you." His voice became raspy, foreign-sounding. "Rhio Diego worked for a guy that heads up a major drug syndicate on the West Coast. When Diego tried to take over part of this guy's territory, they killed him. They couldn't risk others getting any ideas about going out on their own."

She listened, her professionally dispassionate mind reading between the lines.

He continued. "After that, alliances were made. A guy named Max Thompson, along with a few others, defected with Diego. When Diego was killed, Thompson was framed for the murder. The whole thing got a lot of media coverage."

She took a moment to ponder the implications before speaking. "How do you know these people? How do you possibly know someone that heads a major drug cartel?"

Michael turned his attention out the window to the squawking gulls migrating inland. "It looks like rain," he said, grabbing his jacket off the back of the chair, where he'd left it the night before. "I need a smoke."

She trailed him to the deck where he lit a cigarette, took a deep drag and grimaced, his broken ribs still smarting. He exhaled through his nose.

"I can't take another Vicodin until I eat. And I'm starving!"

Vanessa was unrelenting. "I've had many clients facing drug charges, but none of them got anywhere near the top guy. This isn't adding up."

He took another drag before he sauntered to the cliff's edge where he flicked the butt over the steep cliff to the sea below.

Vanessa stared at Michael for a long moment before wordlessly returning to the house. In the kitchen, she began scrambling eggs and toasting English muffins.

Standing in the kitchen doorway, Michael's jaw set, he said, "That's all I can tell you."

When the eggs and toast were ready, she returned to the dining room with a steaming plate of food that she set before Michael.

Suddenly a winter storm was upon them. Rain struck the south-facing windows and hit the roof like thunder. Vanessa sat across from Michael, her patience growing thin. She refilled her cup and his, while he plowed through the eggs.

"So the head of the cartel did it, or had someone do it for him," she said, while Michael finished off the muffin.

His face flushed. "Mom, you don't know what you're getting into."

She'd hit a nerve. "Why is Thompson in jail if he didn't do it?"

"That's what I'm trying to tell you! That's how powerful they are! They planted evidence and the DA bought it." He pushed the empty plate away. "The murder was gangland style. The victim was hog-tied and shot. This guy Falcon, he can do anything he wants and he gets away with it."

She wasn't going to let him scare her out of getting to the facts. She forced herself not to react. "Falcon? I still don't understand how you know him. And why didn't you tell the police?"

"I couldn't," he said, leaving the room.

She followed. He sat near the fire, his shoulders hunched forward.

"Why?" she asked.

"I told you, they'd kill me if I did. Mackey must have defected with Diego and Thompson. Somehow, he's got it in his head I killed Diego."

"Who's Mackey?"

"The ringleader. He lives next door to me. The other two, in the black SUV, are his thugs."

Vanessa was stunned. It was obvious Michael had been, or still was, involved with the cartel.

"You've got to go to the police."

"I'd be dead for sure."

"I can't help you if you don't cooperate. You know who killed Diego," Vanessa said, beginning to pace. "From what you've told me, I can only assume that Falcon's involved. Why protect a murderer? I have contacts. They could put him away for a long time, and you'd be safe."

"Are you crazy? You don't know who you're messing with. Just help me get away."

"At some point, Michael, you've got to stop running and deal with this."

With that, Michael walked past her, down the hall, into the bathroom. The door slammed and shower turned on.

The unrelenting storm slammed thirty-foot waves into the cliff, shaking the house. A chill caught Vanessa and she added a log to the fire.

Michael reappeared, his hair damp, wearing his rumpled uniform.

"I want to do some checking on Mackey and this Falcon guy," she said. "There could be outstanding warrants, if we're lucky."

"Don't do this," he pleaded.

Unhearing, she continued, "Better yet, I'll go to San Francisco. I can contact the DA there. I have a connection through a friend of mine." She picked up her Blackberry and checked her schedule. "I can move some things around, but I'll have to wait until after the Welsh trial."

"Mom, listen to me! It's too dangerous! The Thompson trial will start soon in San Francisco. The media will be all over it. If you snoop around, they'll make the connection. Please…" His voice trailed off.

"I understand why you're scared, but you can't keep running. It's time to face up to your past."

18

Newport, Oregon

The steel gray sea reflected Vanessa's mood. It was after one before she headed to the court house. She held tight to the wheel as she maneuvered the twisted ribbon of road.

Michael slumped in the passenger seat. Unable to dissuade his mother from her venture to San Francisco, he decided to use what little money he left to check into a motel close to work. He couldn't stay with her and deal with her endless questions, and he couldn't return home.

After dropping him off at work, she continued to the courthouse. Loaded with her cases, purse, and coffee, she hurried into the building. In spite of her body feeling like dead weight, she opted for the stairs instead of the elevator.

When she arrived on the third floor, to her surprise, Steven was pacing in the hallway outside her office.

The minute he saw her he pounced. "What the hell is this?" He waved a report in the air, veins raised on his forehead. "A psychological profile on the Welsh kid. When exactly were you going to tell me you've changed his plea?"

"I thought you weren't coming in today?" she said, juggling her load while she unlocked the door, nearly spilling her coffee. "That's okay. No need to help me, I can manage," she sputtered sarcastically.

At that moment, jurors poured into the hallway from the waiting room, on their way to a courtroom. She ushered Steven into her office and shut the door. He sat stiffly in a chair opposite her desk.

She avoided his eyes while she set her things down and hung up her coat, buying some time, then sat behind her desk and took a sip of her coffee.

"Well?" he demanded.

"I sent you a copy of the report as soon as I had it," she said, folding her unsteady hands. "Yesterday you were too busy to discuss it. And you said you wouldn't be in today."

He tried to interrupt, but she held up her hand.

"This boy is too young to dispose of. Maybe, just maybe, he could get some help. I want him to have that chance. He'd be in a locked facility until the court determines he would not be a danger to himself or the community."

Steven rose and loomed over her.

"Well, Counselor, we'll see how this plays out in court."

Vanessa watched him leave, shutting the door firmly behind him. It couldn't have happened any other way. He had his job, and she had hers.

She leaned back in her chair, feeling the sun break through the clouds, and settle on her face.

A shrill ring intruded. She jumped.

"Damn!" she muttered, before answering the call.

"I've got to see you," Steven said, in almost a whisper.

"But I thought…"

"I know. Just dinner."

"I don't…,"Vanessa said, catching her breath.

"I'll pick you up at seven."

"No. Wait. We can't be seen together. I'll make dinner."

"I'll see you later at your place."

It was wrong on so many levels. Her hand shook so it took a moment to get the phone settled into its cradle.

19

Depoe Bay, Oregon

Later that day, following a quick stop at the market, Vanessa shot over Cape Foulweather, on her way home. Once there, she prepared her famous spicy chicken concoction, put it in the oven, then ran a hot bath. The aroma of lavender bath salts soon filled the room. Her business suit lay in a heap on the floor, after shedding it like a chameleon. She slipped into the hot foamy tub, where she laid her head back and allowed her shoulders to relax, feeling human again. Vanessa pulled on her slinky sea foam V-neck sweater, after a quick towel off, along with soft velour pants. She let her hair dry naturally, cascading around her shoulders, while she checked the chicken dish.

While putting the final touches on the dinner table, she heard the door. She wiped her hands on a towel she'd wrapped around her waist and dashed to answer it, with one last glance at the table set for a romantic supper.

With the descending sun as a backdrop, a silhouetted figure stood in the doorway.

"I hope you like garlic ginger chicken." She gasped. She didn't recognize the man. He opened the screen door and entered.

"Ms. Sterling," he said.

"Who are you?" she yelled. "Get out or I'll call the police!"

"Oh, you don't want to do that. I'd have to tell them all about Mike."

It was Michael's next door neighbor, Wade Mackey! She looked toward the phone. His eyes followed.

"I don't think you'd make it, do you?"

"Get out!" she screamed.

He lunged toward her, grabbing her arm. "I'll get out when I'm ready. First, I have a message to deliver."

She struggled to get free. Just then, Steven appeared at the open door, a bouquet and a bottle of wine in hand.

"What the...?" Steven said, unsure of what he was witnessing. But he soon sprung into action. He dropped the roses, grabbed the wine bottle by its neck, and charged into the house.

Mackey released his grip on Vanessa and spun to face Steven. Seeing the raised bottle, he shoved Steven and made his getaway.

Vanessa caught the blowing screen door and pulled it shut then secured the main door. She hurried over to Steven, who had managed to right himself.

"Unsatisfied client?" Steven asked. He straightened his sweater and ran his fingers through his hair.

Still shaken, she said, "Don't kid about this. I'm scared out of my wits. I don't know what to do."

"You call the police, that's what you do," he said, pulling out his cell phone.

"Wait!" She put her hand on his. "Please don't. Let me explain."

"Explain?! What on earth is there to explain? A man just attacked you."

"I need a minute to think!" she said.

"I'm the district attorney, for Christ's sake. I'm mandated to report this," he began to dial. "Oh my god, look at those bruises!"

Reddish-blue marks were appearing on Vanessa's arm.

"He just wanted to scare me. I shouldn't have left the door unlocked. I'll keep everything locked from now on. Just don't call," she said. "I'm sure he won't be back tonight."

Steven reluctantly ended the call. "You'd better have a very good reason for me to put my ass on the line here."

Letting out a deep sigh, she said, "I need a drink."

She hurried into the kitchen to check on dinner. As she basted the chicken, her hand trembled. *I'm not going to cry!*

Steven poured two glasses of wine, handing one to her.

"Look, we can't just ignore this," he said. "He could have killed you. I've got to report something. Trust me here."

She took a long drink of wine while he dialed his cell phone.

"Let me talk to Captain Williams," he said.

Vanessa started to object, but Steven motioned for her to be quiet.

"Earl, this is Steven Adams. Yeah, fine. Listen, there was a break in at Vanessa Sterling's home this evening. No, there's no need to send anyone. I was dropping some reports off and saw the guy run away. She's fine, nothing happened. I checked it all out and everything's fine. Just wanted a report on file, in case the guy comes back. Yeah, thanks. Okay. Goodbye." Then looking at Vanessa, he said, "I had to. I'm not going to lose my job over this. I promised Williams you'd file a report as soon as you had time."

"I'm not just worried about me. Michael's involved."

"Michael? What has he got to do with this?"

"He knows that man from San Francisco. There was a fight the other night," she said.

"What? When? Did Michael report that? Vanessa, what's going on here?"

"Even before the intrusion, I was going to tell you...I was going to wait until after dinner," she said. "But I guess I'd better tell you now."

"That's the least you can do," he said, setting his half-empty glass on the counter.

She told Steven about Michael's beating and about the other men. She omitted the fact that Michael had witnessed a murder. She wasn't sure how far she should go just yet.

"I don't want to put Michael in greater danger."

"You're already in danger. You both need protection," Steven said, taking her hand. "I don't want anything to happen to you."

That gentle gesture broke through her stoic façade. Tears welled in her eyes and she laid her head on his shoulder.

"I care about you, in case you were wondering," he said, brushing her hair back off her face. He took her chin and kissed her lightly. "You're very important to me."

She decided to go on.

"I'm going to San Francisco right after the trial to check out this Mackey guy and his buddies. When I get back I'll have a better idea what's going on. Then I'll make that police report."

"Oh, that's a great idea, Nancy Drew," he said, thrusting his hands in the air. "You could call it the San Francisco Caper. Vanessa, think this through. You can't get involved."

"I'm already involved. He's my son."

Steven picked up his glass and swallowed the remaining burgundy before refilling his glass, then pulled her to the sofa in the living room.

"If you insist on going, let me contact Dean Stanton," he said. "He's the DA in San Francisco. We're old friends. You can trust him."

She laid her head back on his shoulder. "Please...don't. Let me do this. I'll take his number and call when I get there."

The aroma of baking chicken wafted into the living room. As she rose to tend to dinner, Steven took her hand and pulled her onto his lap.

"Look," he said, staring deeply into her eyes. "I don't know what I'd do if anything happened to you."

They clung to one another. Steven laid her back on the sofa and felt the warmth of her body. Without a word, he scooped her up and carried her across the living room toward the back hall. Then he stopped.

"I have one problem," he said.

"What?" Vanessa asked, her arms around Steven's neck.

"Where's the bedroom?"

He slowly undressed Vanessa.

"You're so beautiful," he said, caressing her face, pulling her to him.

"It's been so many years, I hope I remember how," she teased.

"You will. It's like riding a bike, only more fun."

Her body tingled in anticipation. He removed his clothing, leaving them in an unceremonious pile on the floor. Intoxicated by her scent, he nuzzled her neck; his hand skimmed the contours of her body. Their passion grew, finally reaching an explosive climax. As they lay spent in each other arms, basking in the moment, the smoke alarm went off.

"The chicken!" Vanessa cried. She jumped from bed, running to the kitchen. The room was filled with smoke. She threw open the window, put on oven mitts, and pulled the charred remains from the oven. As she stood holding the disaster, Steven ambled in.

"Where's my camera when I need it?" he said. There stood Vanessa in the middle of the room, dressed only in oven mitts.

She threw the pan in the sink, tears streaming down.

"Oh, that's all right," he said, taking her in his arms. "We'll order pizza."

"That's not it. Well, not entirely. There's just too much happening."

He led her back into the bedroom and held her in his arms.

"I can usually handle whatever's thrown my way. But when people I love are involved, I lose it."

"Take it slow," he said, holding her close. "And Michael doesn't need his mommy. He can take care of himself."

"His words exactly!" she said. "But he left home so young. If he'd gone to college, had a career, met a young woman, you know, normal stuff. But he didn't, so I still see him as a child."

"My girls went off to college. Did normal stuff, as you put it. I still see them as children. It's hard to admit they're adults. Adults who really don't need us."

"Ouch! No longer needed. That's a hard one, isn't it?" Vanessa said.

"Well…I need you," Steven said, kissing her softly. "But for entirely different reasons."

He held her in his arms and, for the moment, made her forget about burnt chicken and her wayward son.

Later, snuggling into his neck, Vanessa's uncertainties about starting a new relationship began to fade. How wonderful it was to have this incredible man in her life. Their friendship, built over the last few years, would add substance and strength to their budding romance.

Vanessa appeared to be a woman of the world. But as far as relationships went, that was not the case. She'd had a few awkward adolescent experiences, but until this night, she'd had only one other man in her life. A man she'd been faithful to, although he'd given her plenty of reasons not to be. And there'd been opportunities, but that just wasn't her style.

Half-asleep, nestled in Steven's warm embrace, she remembered one night long ago and long forgotten. The one exception to her no cheat rule.

20

Harvard Law School
Cambridge, Massachusetts
1973

With finals out of the way, Vanessa was ready to celebrate. She and a classmate made plans to go bar hopping. Nicholas was away on yet another business trip, so she figured why not? When Nick was home he didn't like Vanessa to go anywhere without him.

The night started out at Wally's, a smoke-filled, dimly-lit lounge in midtown Boston. The jukebox wailed a soulful tune, and couples on the small dance floor swayed to the beat. Sally spotted some men she knew from the university and they joined the women at the bar. Introductions were made, but Vanessa missed the names and most of the conversation that followed. She didn't care, she wasn't out to meet men, she just wanted to unwind. Something she'd rarely done in the last few years.

The guys bought a few rounds, and several boilermakers later, the group moved on. While they walked to the next bar, Vanessa pulled her coat collar snug around her neck while she chatted with one of the men. A full moon illuminated the chilly night.

Charlie's Pub and Pool Hall was a slight improvement over the last dive. The group gathered around the bar and Vanessa's new companion ordered a round.

"Do you play pool?" the man asked.

"Sure," she answered, emboldened by the alcohol. "I'll beat your pants off."

"Sounds fun," he answered, flashing an incredible smile.

She slid off the barstool and joined him at the pool table. He won the first game, and she took the next three, each buying a round for the loser. She was enjoying the flirtation, but when she looked up from the pool table, she noticed Sally leaving.

"Well, there goes my ride," she slurred.

"Not a problem. I can take you home."

"Don't get any ideas," she said, holding up her ring finger. "I'm married, you know."

"So am I," he replied. "I'm just taking you home."

He helped her the few blocks to his car. She climbed in and gave him her address, then dropped off to sleep. When he stopped at the married students' housing, she was too groggy to make it on her own. He practically had to carry her into the building. He fished in her purse for her keys and opened the door, then guided her inside, hoping to avoid a confrontation with an irate husband.

He was in luck. The place was dark.

"Is your husband home?"

"No," she said, still groggy. "He's never home."

He turned on the lights and found the kitchen. "You need some caffeine."

He hunted through the cabinets until he found what he needed. Returning to the living room, he found no sign of her. A few minutes later she returned wearing a pink fleece robe.

They drank the fresh brewed coffee in silence. "Where's your husband?"

"He travels on business," she said, feeling a bit better.

"Don't you get lonely?"

"Yes. But I'm lonelier when he's here."

"Oh," he said, downing the last gulp. "If you were my wife, I'd never leave you alone."

She put her cup down and leaned close. She kissed him, then ran her hand through his soft blond hair, taking in his chiseled features and large blue eyes.

"I'd better go," he said, but didn't move.

"I said I'd beat your pants off. It's time to pay up."

She took him by the hand and led him into the bedroom. She wanted to be held, to be caressed, and made love to.

When she awoke in the morning, he was gone. She never saw the man again.

21

Depoe Bay, Oregon
2004

Vanessa emerged from a deep sleep, Steven still next to her. She snuggled in close and he awoke with a smile. Over her shoulder, he caught the time on the bed-side clock and shot upright. He had a trial in an hour and he couldn't be late again. He hurriedly dressed and with one last kiss, he was out the door.

She couldn't seem to get herself motivated, so she moved outside to greet the day. Dressed in her robe, she stretched her slender body the length of the redwood lounge. Things were far from perfect in her life, but at least she didn't have to face her problems alone.

For so many years, she didn't allow herself to dwell on the past, being a workaholic helped her avoid that. But now, her past reemerged: the mistakes she'd made, the people that had hurt her. All she could do now was learn from her mistakes and not jump into anything too fast. While Steven was like no other man in her life, she had her doubts. After all, in the beginning, she'd truly loved Nicholas Thorne.

Chicago Illinois
1945-1977

Nicholas Augustus Thorne was born post World War II into a working class family on the south side of Chicago. By the time he was ten, his two older brothers were already in gangs, one had been in jail a few times. But Nick's mother protected him, keeping him out of harm's way until her sudden death. He was only twelve. He floundered and by the time he entered high school his only interests were football and girls. He drank too much and had sex with every willing girl in school by the age of sixteen. A few months after graduating, he was drafted. When his tour in Vietnam ended, he enrolled in college, rekindling his dreams of playing pro ball. He earned a place on the varsity football team and, during his senior year, a scout had been so impressed with him that he signed with the Detroit Lions. Then tragedy hit. During his last game, in the fourth quarter, an over-zealous linebacker slammed him to the ground. His knee gave way on the hard turf. With his dreams dashed at that decisive moment, he lost his passion for everything, including Vanessa. By then she was in law school and they'd been married five years.

After that, she'd taken the abuse he heaped on her, believing one day he'd be his old self again. She handled the disappointment the only way she knew how, by burying herself in work. After law school, she worked for her father's law firm, using her high-powered job to bring her respect, admiration, and money. And it helped her ignore the fact that her private life was an abysmal mess.

22

Depoe Bay, Oregon

Squawking gulls broke through, as a southerly breeze blew across the deck. There was a rustling sound by the house and, remembering Mackey's attack just the night before, she darted back into the house. She bolted the door shut just as the phone rang.

"I can't go to work," Michael said, calling from the motel. "They'll find me there."

"Just stay in your room," she said, making her way to the bedroom. "Have your food delivered. If you lose your job, you'll find another. Meanwhile, I'll send over some money. You should be safe until I get back. We'll get Mackey. I promise."

"I'll go nuts by then," he said. "You can't fix this mess. These men are not like the losers you deal with."

"Mackey looks like the same kind of punks I deal with every day."

"Mackey! When did you see him?" Michael asked.

"He...um...broke into my house last night."

"What! Are you okay?" Michael asked. "That does it! I have to leave before you get hurt. Mom, please, don't go to San Francisco."

"I'm staying with your uncle in Berkley. No one will find me there. I'll be fine. When I return, I think I should have enough on them to get Mackey and his buddies shipped back to California."

That bluff may work with Michael, but she had no idea what she'd find in San Francisco. She'd never dealt with guys like this without the protection of the court.

23

Newport, Oregon

Later that morning Vanessa darted up the steps of the courthouse, her hair still damp from the shower. She grabbed the files she needed for the hearing and entered the courtroom just as her case was called. She smiled lamely at her client as a silent apology, and faced the judge.

The hearing ended in her favor around noon. After returning to her office, she checked her blackberry for other appointments for the day. Vanessa wondered why she hadn't heard from Billy's mother. Sara Stangel would have been interested in the outcome of Billy's evaluation, surely Vanessa would have heard from her by now.

She thumbed through the transcript from Sara's deposition. Sara had been living in Siletz for the last few years. Maybe a field trip was in order. It would give Vanessa added ammunition for Billy's trial, if she could see how Billy had been living.

She dialed Sara's number.

"I haven't heard from you in a while," Vanessa said after Sara answered the phone. "I'd like to see you." There was no reply. Vanessa continued. "How's today?"

"Um...I...I don't know," Sara said.

"I'll come out to your place, save you a trip to town."

"Oh?"

"Sara, are you okay?"

"Uh huh."

"What's the matter?" Vanessa said, annoyed with the evasiveness.

"Nothing," Sara whispered.

"So, I'll see you in a few hours."

"Who the hell was that?" Ralph demanded. He sat in a well-worn leather Laz-e-boy permanently fixed in the reclining position. The TV blared from the corner.

"No one."

"Whaddaya mean, no one?" he demanded.

"It's not important."

Ralph sprang to his feet and was on her in a split second. He grabbed her hair and spat out his words. "Listen, bitch. Don't lie. Who the hell was on the phone?" he demanded. It was still morning, but his breath smelled of alcohol.

She knew it was futile to evade his questions.

"Vanessa…she's coming out here today."

"Gawd damn it, woman! I told you I don't want nobody out here, especially her!" he snarled. "When ya gonna learn?"

His blow sent her flat onto the mattress of the pull-out couch. She covered her face with her arms, trying to protect herself, to no avail. He pulled her arms back, put his knee on her chest and punched her face. His rage escalated.

"And that bastard kid of yours! If he gets off, I'll make sure he's dead before he comes back here."

It was pointless to fight back. He undid his belt, pulled it from his trouser loops, and whipped her legs until they were bloodied. Exhausted, he threw the belt down and collapsed back into his recliner, turning up the volume on the TV to drown out her moans.

Sara dragged herself off the bed and scurried to the bathroom like a frightened animal. He was done, for now. She wet a washcloth with cool water and held it to her face, then washed down her legs. When she rinsed out the cloth, the water ran red. She sank down on the lumpy narrow mattress in the back bedroom. There would be nothing to live for if Billy went to prison. She had to talk to Vanessa, but Ralph would never let her answer the door looking this way. He always went for her face. It would keep her in for days. She held her knees to her chest and rocked herself to sleep.

24

Siletz, Oregon

Just past Toledo, Vanessa turned onto Highway 229, bound for Siletz. A mile from town, she slowed, looking for River's End Road. She found the narrow rutted lane that cut through a thicket of spruce, and ended at a rusted trailer. The old dog that lay in the dirt was not interested in announcing her arrival, but she gave him a wide berth nonetheless and knocked on the frayed screen door.

Ralph Stangel, foul as ever, appeared.

"What the hell do ya want?" he said, a cigarette clenched between his teeth, one eye shut to avoid the smoke.

"I have an appointment with Sara."

He rubbed his stubbled chin, looking puzzled. "The ol' lady ain't home."

"Well..." Vanessa hesitated. She was alone on this deserted road with a man who had threatened her several years ago and regularly beat his wife. Heart pounding, she began to back away.

"Sorry. My mistake. I'll call Sara later," she said, hoping to make a safe retreat.

"Ain't no problem. Ya kin wait in here," Ralph said, motioning for her to come in. "She'll be home real soon."

"No, that's okay," she said.

He stepped from the door and sauntered toward her, with a tobacco-stained grin.

She continued backing up until she reached the car door. She jumped in, slammed the door, and locked it. He stood, leering, as she turned the Jeep around.

A flutter of movement from a small window caught Vanessa's attention. Framed by a faded, striped curtain was Sara's bruised and battered face. She was almost unrecognizable. Vanessa's glance connected with Sara's, as she backed the car out. She watched in the rearview mirror until Sara's pitiful face was no longer visible.

When she reached the main road Vanessa exhaled. She had to do something. *He could be killing her right now.* She dialed her cell phone. Thumping her fingers on the dash while she waited for the connect. A car approached River's End Road. It slowed and made the turn. It was the familiar black SUV. Fortunately, Mackey didn't notice her.

"Hayes, here," Sheriff Ben Hayes answered his direct line.

"Ben! This is Vanessa Sterling," she said. "There's an emergency at the Stangel trailer. You've got to come immediately."

"What's wrong?"

"I was just there," she said. "Ralph's beat Sara up again. And a known drug dealer just turned toward their place. Wasn't Ralph arrested on drug charges recently?"

"Yep, had a meth lab out there. We busted up the lab, but he was released until his trial. Just don't have enough money to keep all those guys."

"Ben, please, get out here fast! I'm afraid for Sara."

"I'll get some of my men and be right out. Meanwhile, you get outta there. Those guys are too much for you."

Vanessa waited. Thirty minutes passed. Her anger escalated with every ticking minute. Still no sheriff. She gripped the wheel and closed her eyes. Years ago she'd been the victim, too afraid of Nicholas to stand up for herself. Now, she couldn't wait any long. Years of pent-up frustration overrode reason.

She sped back down the dirt road and parked far enough from Sara's not to be seen. She pulled the car off on the shoulder, into the trees. *Why didn't I stand up to Nicholas? I let him tear me down, bit by bit.* Her jaw tightened. That's why Sara stayed! Bit by bit, too terrified to leave. Vanessa's pulse quickened. Her silk blouse clung to her sweaty back.

She stepped from the Jeep, traded her heels for running shoes, and pulled on her coat. Going around the back way, she cut through the bramble of blackberry vines. Leafless and bare, they tore at her legs. She didn't let that slow her down.

Drunken voices rose over the roaring Siletz River that ran alongside the trailer. Surely the sheriff will be there any minute. She hid behind a large spruce and waited. Through the open window, Vanessa heard Sara pleading, followed by a scream. That was it. She couldn't wait for the sheriff. Vanessa's fists tightened, digging her nails into her palms. She ran to the door and knocked.

"What the hell?" Ralph said.

"I forgot to tell you Billy's court date," Vanessa called through the screen door.

Suddenly, Mackey was there.

"Well, lookie here," he said. Shoving open the screen door, he grabbed Vanessa by the arm and dragged her inside.

Dirty dishes piled high teetered on the edge of the sink. A rank odor turned Vanessa's stomach.

Sara was sprawled on the bed, trying to cover her nakedness with a blanket.

"Leave her alone!" Vanessa's fury gave her incredible strength, enough to shake free of Mackey's grip. "Get off me!" she yelled. Her shove sent him toppling over onto the floor, sputtering a drunken laugh.

"Vanessa...help!" Sara cried.

Every muscle in Vanessa's body tightened.

"Sara, let's get out of here!"

"Over my dead body!" Ralph said.

"I shoulda finished ya off last night!" Mackey sputtered, trying to stand.

"You made a big mistake coming to my house!" Vanessa fumed. "That was the district attorney you shoved. What do you think he'll do to you in court?"

Vanessa grabbed for Sara. At the same time, Ralph lurched forward, but only managed to catch the blanket, pulling it off Sara. Vanessa had the terrified woman by the arm and pulled her out the door.

"The sheriff's on the way," Vanessa said, stepping out of the door. "You're in enough trouble; you don't want to mess with me!"

Where was the sheriff?

Caught off guard, the men backed off just long enough for Vanessa and Sara to make their escape. Standing in the dirt yard, Sara began shaking and crying uncontrollably. Vanessa flung her coat over Sara's naked body.

Mackey and Ralph charged out the door. They froze, then ran back into the trailer. Two squad cars, lights blazing, churned up dust as they ground to a stop. As he sprang from the patrol car, the sheriff couldn't believe his eyes.

With scraped legs and tangled hair, Vanessa marched up to the sheriff, with the bruised and battered Sara Stangel in tow.

Ben motioned for two of his men to go around the back.

"What on God's green earth are you doing here?" he asked, amazed at the sight before him. "Are you crazy?"

Vanessa was as surprised as the sheriff. She'd never put herself into such a precarious situation before. If the men hadn't been drunk, they could have killed both of the women. But now her energy soared. She felt strong and powerful.

"They're all yours, Sheriff," Vanessa said. "They raped and beat Sara. They threatened me. I'll be happy to give you a report and testify at trial. Put them in jail and keep them there!"

Ben beat on the trailer door. "Don't get me mad, Ralph!"

The door slowly opened. The sheriff, along with two more officers, disappeared inside. Vanessa could hear the duo protesting, but one look at

Sara had convinced Ben. Mackey and Ralph were handcuffed and put in the squad car. Ben tore the trailer apart, finding meth, pot, unlicensed guns, and blood-splattered floor and bedding. He had enough evidence to send Ralph and Mackey away for a long time.

Vanessa drove Sara to the emergency room. The poor woman was so disoriented she needed a wheelchair.

"You're going to be okay," Vanessa said, brushing Sara's damp hair off her face, after being admitted to the hospital. "I've arranged for you to go to a safe house when you're released. Don't worry about the hospital bill; it's taken care of. And I don't think you'll have to worry about Ralph again."

Drowsy from a sedative, Sara mumbled, "Thank you." She squeezed Vanessa's hand.

Vanessa wiped away the tears trickling down Sara's face and held her hand until she fell asleep.

25

Depoe Bay, Oregon

Vanessa awoke from a deep fitful sleep. Her legs stung from the briar patch and her body ached from the encounter with Ralph Stangel and Wade Mackey. She staggered to the bathroom and splashed cold water on her face. Leaning toward the mirror, she examined the dark circles under her eyes. She needed a break, but playing hooky wasn't an option. The trial was only three days away. Strange as it seemed, the whole mess with Billy's stepfather, provided material for a powerful closing argument. And she needed to tell Michael about Mackey. He caught the phone on the first ring.

"I'm going crazy! I can't live like this," he said.

Vanessa went on to relate in detail what happened with Mackey and Stangel.

"Mom, you could have been killed!"

"I couldn't let them hurt Sara," she said.

"Great news about Mackey being in jail. I'm heading back home, but first I'll stop and have a talk with Gus."

Vanessa took a quick shower and hurriedly dressed. On the way out the door her cell phone rang.

"What am I going to do with you?" Steven asked. "I just talked to the sheriff."

"Good morning to you, too," she said.

"What were you thinking?"

"I had no choice. What would you have done? Ralph had gotten away with battering poor Sara long enough. I couldn't stand by and do nothing. Mackey was just an added bonus."

"Honestly, Vanessa, you have to be more careful. What were you doing out there, anyway?"

"I had some bright idea about the trial."

"Now that you mention it..."

Here we go. He's going to be like every other man she'd been with.

"I hate to bring this up," he continued, "but I...er, we got carried away the other night. Now's not the right time with the trial coming up...and..."

Do I really want to put myself through this again?

"Let's sort this out after the trial," he said.

"Sort it out? Like laundry?" She ended the call. As far as she was concerned, Steven Adams could take a flying leap at the moon.

26

Newport, Oregon

Michael immediately checked out of the hotel. The forced hibernation had actually been good for him. Gave him a few more days to heal. He was sure Mackey's flunkies didn't make a move without him, so he figured Scarpelli and Bull would leave town, before they were swept up in their boss's legal troubles. Maybe his mother could work miracles after all, but she was crazy to think she'd have the same success in San Francisco.

Michael managed to convince Gus to give him a second chance. But Gus made it clear that was the only time he'd make an exception. Michael put in a hard day's work before he set off for Nye Beach. He was right about one thing, Mackey's men were gone. No SUV at the curb, the dog was nowhere to be seen, and Mackey's house was closed up tight.

Michael entered his house and flicked on the living room lamp, then made his way down the hall. Throwing his backpack onto the bed, he kicked off his boots and stripped off his grimy work uniform.

He looked in the full-length mirror, on the bedroom door. His bruises were fading. He unwrapped the bandage around his rib-cage. He looked much better. He flexed his biceps. In the last few years, he'd put on twenty much-needed pounds and had worked out at the gym in San Francisco most days. He'd been a skeleton when Kate found him.

Sweet Kate. A bittersweet smile crossed his lips. The first real smile since…since Kate died. Guilt swept over him. *Had it only been two weeks?*

He threw on some jeans and a sweatshirt and made tracks down the beach, the only place where he could think. He ran until he couldn't run any further, then bent forward, resting his hands on his knees, his chest throbbing from the exertion. He drew in long, deep breaths. *Why did life have to be so damn complicated?*

He grabbed a fistful of stones and flung them into the breakers. He couldn't shake Kate from his thoughts. He owed her so much.

San Francisco
1999

Kate's eyes adjusted to the dim light filtering through the grimy window. She'd been volunteering at the teen shelter for a few months and most days she and the director, Kenny Harper, searched abandoned buildings for runaways. It still unnerved her. But Kenny, with his imposing physique, made her feel safe.

Buildings, such as this dilapidated row house, were havens for addicts and runaways. Kate and Kenny would search each room, finding lost souls, filthy and forlorn, and offer them food and shelter. Some kids were ready, while others weren't willing to leave their life on the streets. She would never get used to leaving children, some as young as thirteen, in such squalor. Kenny would do his best to get help for them. He'd call county protective services with hopes they would rescue the children. But like everyone else in the field, the social workers were overworked and underpaid. There weren't many like Kenny, a dedicated man who worked tirelessly with little pay, committed to helping kids. The agency was so small he handled the roles of director, counselor, and fundraiser, relying on volunteers to fill the gaps.

Kate peered into the dark. The room was littered with old sleeping bags, trash, and discarded needles. A figure moved into the light, illuminating his haggard face. Kate gasped.

"What's wrong?" Kenny whispered.

"I know him!"

"From where?"

"Chicago," she said.

The young man turned toward her, staring with blank eyes.

27

Newport, Oregon

The sun set and the wind shifted. Michael zipped his jacket and shoved his hands deep into its pockets. He meandered near the cliffs, avoiding the incoming tide, retracing his steps back down the beach and up the ramp to the parking lot. Tonight it stood deserted. Streetlamps illuminated a bright green-and-pink painted Victorian that had been converted into a coffee house. It was still open.

The small café was warm and inviting. Dog-eared magazines and the daily paper lay strewn on the countertop. Colorfully-wrapped hazelnut candies filled a large ceramic bowl and sat among other handmade confections. A glass case, filled each morning with freshly-baked muffins, cookies, and hot bagels, was almost empty by this time of night.

At the far end of the counter, a young woman in her early twenties straddled a stool, her long multi-colored tie-dyed skirt hiked up over her knees revealing strong, trim legs. She had a small butterfly tattoo on her right ankle.

When he entered, a broad smile brightened her face.

"You're new around here," the waitress said.

"Do you know everyone?"

"Everyone except tourist and you're no tourist." Her unruly mop of blond curls bounced as she slid off the stool. "What can I get for you?"

"A double espresso."

"I guess caffeine doesn't keep you awake."

"I don't think I'll be getting much sleep tonight anyway," he said.

"A good-looking guy like you must be kept up often," she said with a sideways glance, turning to the espresso machine.

He was mesmerized, watching her start the process, grinding the beans, and waiting the few seconds while the machine hissed and steamed, finally emitting the dark liquid.

"Two-fifty," she said, handing him the cup.

He pulled a five from his pocket and told her to keep the change.

"You're either rich or crazy. Either way, that's too much." She handed him two dollars.

"Have a seat, wherever," she said.

Her slender hip slid back onto the stool. She resumed thumbing through the magazine, while he took a seat at one of the wrought iron tables. Two young women entered.

"Hi Jenny," they called out in unison. "How's it going?"

"Pretty slow," she said. "The usual?"

Jenny chatted with the women while she made two mochas with soy milk, then joined them at their table. He couldn't keep his eyes off her. She gestured broadly as she spoke, laughed out loud, making her large blue eyes sparkle. Her orange T-shirt stretched across ample breasts. He noticed it all. And she noticed he noticed.

He finished his drink and strolled toward the door.

"Good night," she called to him. "Hope you get some sleep."

"Yeah, thanks."

After he walked out the door, she leaned in and said something to her friends. They giggled like school girls.

28

San Francisco, California

Cruising at thirty-thousand feet, Vanessa absentmindedly gazed out at the blue expanse, cushioned by billowy white clouds. The first-class attendant refilled her glass and she took a sip of the cool white wine. Funny how money had become so irrelevant to Vanessa since she'd left Chicago. But when she'd gone on-line to make a plane reservation she'd checked first class. The huge trust fund her mother left her had been invested by the family's attorney-of-record. He received monthly and annual reports of the growing funds and he'd send a formal letter at least twice a year asking if she needed any of the money. She ignored him, for the most part.

She'd left for San Francisco as soon as the trial ended, without a word to Steven, needing time to sort things out, as he had put it. The way she felt right now she wanted nothing more to do with him. It had been a huge mistake to think their relationship wouldn't interfere with their work. It had been more difficult then she'd imaged facing him at trial. She'd always enjoyed the challenge, but so much more was at stake this time.

Newport, Oregon

Running late the first day of the trial, Vanessa shot the Jeep around the corner, heading for the courthouse parking lot, only to slam on the brakes, nearly causing a rear-end collision. There stood media vans from local and national stations lining the back parking lot. Their satellite dishes thrust into the air, as if it were a Star Wars invasion.

Reporters, hoping for breaking news, and curious citizens wanting a free show, flooded the gallery. The victim's family huddled together in the front row. Sara Stangel sat in the back, dabbing her eyes with a damp handkerchief. A victim's advocate from the battered women's shelter sat next to her, attempting to provide some comfort.

The jury shuffled in between the rows of jury-box seats, cautiously eyeing Billy Welsh, who was intent over his notepad. Six men and six women solemnly took their seats. The bailiff directed everyone to rise as Judge Matthew Randall O'Riley entered the courtroom. Standing well over six feet tall, he made a formidable presence. He settled his bulk at the bench, his neckless red face bulging from his black judicial robe. He'd been the presiding judge in Lincoln County for twenty-five years, making it clear throughout those years, he wouldn't tolerate any 'tomfooleries.' But he was fair and just, and Vanessa had been pleased he would be hearing the case.

With a rap of the gavel, the judge called court in session. Steven gave a tug to his navy-blue striped tie while making his way to the jury box. His conservative dark brown suit would play well to the working class people and retirees who made up the jury.

His opening statement provided an overview of the case, emphasizing the calm, calculating method Billy had used to commit the crime.

He concluded his typically terse opening, addressing the jury, "This is going to be an emotional trial, but you must remain above that. Fully weigh all of the testimony and evidence. Listen closely to the victim and make your decision based on facts, not emotions."

Steven returned to the prosecutor's table, while Vanessa rose from the defense table. She buttoned her black gabardine suit jacket and picked up her legal pad. Her breeding, education, and poise were not lost on the jury or the press.

"I'm asking you to consider what Billy did," she said, making eye contact with each juror as she spoke, "in context of what drove a boy of sixteen to commit such a crime. I will show that Billy had endured sexual, physical, and emotional abuse throughout his life, at the hands of the very people who should have protected him. It left him a seriously disturbed child, acting out his vengeance, oblivious of the consequences."

Feet scuffled, and a chorus of whispers broke the silence. A sharp rap of the gavel quieted the courtroom.

"I will show that, at the time of the crime, Billy Welsh was criminally insane, rendering him incapable of understanding that what he did was wrong, leaving you, the jury, no recourse but to find him not guilty by reason of insanity."

The emergency operator was the first witness for the state. She played a very damning tape of the victim's hysterical mother. She was followed by the first officer on the scene, who testified that Melissa told him Billy Welsh had raped her. The officer had immediately obtained a bench warrant and arrested Billy later that night. And on it went. The physician's assistant on duty that night at the emergency room, who administered a rape kit, testified the child was hysterical, inconsolable. *The same person that tended Sara just a few nights before! Sometimes this town was too small.* The forensic medical examiner confirmed Billy's DNA was found at the scene and in the rape kit.

The seemingly endless morning's testimony came to a close sometime around twelve. Vanessa muttered quiet thanks when Judge O'Riley adjourned for lunch. The courtroom cleared, and the bailiff took Billy to the holding cell, where his court-provided burger and fries waited, the same fare the jury would be served.

Vanessa dashed across the hall to her office and locked the door behind her. She'd learned early on reporters would hound her every step if she attempted to leave the building. Seated at the small conference table, she unwrapped her bag lunch and popped open a soda can. A spasm grabbed her shoulders. She ran her hands along the nape of her neck. Feeling the lumps and bumps of tension, she rotated her head from side to side, then took two aspirins, swallowing them down with the cola. The sandwich lay uneaten.

When court resumed, Billy sat slumped in his chair. He'd taken off his sweater and thrown it partially inside out onto the defendants table. His shirttail hung untucked, and his hair stuck up in random spikes. *How could Steven try this boy as an adult?* Vanessa sighed. Billy picked up a pencil and resumed his doodling. The afternoon dragged on, not going any better than the morning session. In response to Billy's psychiatric evaluation, Steven had his own expert, a tall statuesque psychologist with impeccable credentials.

After a lengthy review of the evaluation she had conducted, Steven asked for the doctor's conclusion.

"Billy Welsh is a disturbed boy," Dr. Brown said. "But under the legal definition, he is not insane. He understood what he did and shows no remorse."

"Just to make sure the court understands, you're saying Billy knew his acts were wrong?"

"Yes."

"Thank you. That's all."

"No questions," Vanessa said, as she had for all of Steven's witnesses.

Billy kept at his scribbles. Finally Judge O'Riley swung the gavel, calling an end to the first day.

With few objections and no cross-examination, Vanessa had let the testimony ride. The evidence had been persuasive, but it would have been even more damaging if she'd kept the witnesses on the stand longer. She'd play her trump card soon.

29

Newport, Oregon

Rain clouds hung low in the sky the second day of the trial. The depressing bleakness of the day permeated the courtroom. Steven continued to call witnesses, including Melissa's mother. By noon the jury sat slumped in their chairs, exhausted from the onslaught of graphic testimony. There was obvious relief when the court called for a recess.

Promptly at one o'clock the trial resumed. Steven's star witness, ten-year-old Melissa Durbin, was called to the stand. When she entered the courtroom, the spectators let out a collective gasp. Until this moment she'd been protected from the media. Her dark hair hung in ringlets around her cherub face. The hand-me-down frock she wore was inches too long. The bailiff had to provide several thick law books to boost her up so she could be seen over the rail of the witness stand.

"Melissa," Judge O'Riley said, leaning over his bench toward the child. "Do you know the difference between telling the truth and telling a lie?"

She raised her shy brown eyes, looking toward the judge. "Yes, sir. When you lie, you go to hell."

Judge O'Riley stifled a smile and told Steven to proceed.

Steven slowly led the child into her testimony by asking her name, age and where she went to school. When he sensed she was ready, he asked, "Was Billy Welsh your baby-sitter?"

"Yes."

"Could you tell me about him?"

"I hate Billy!"

"Tell me some of the things Billy did when he babysat?"

"One time he let me watch a grown-up TV show. He gave me candy for sitting on his lap."

"Did you like that?"

"It was creepy," Melissa hesitated, looking at Billy.

Billy stopped doodling to glower back. She gulped down a sob.

"It's okay, Melissa. Take your time," Steven said. He repositioned himself, blocking Billy from view. "No one can hurt you here. See, there are policemen, there and over there."

She covered her nose with a tissue and blew. Her large inquisitive eyes wandered around the courtroom. Steven handed her a cup of water and she took a sip.

"Now, Melissa, tell the court what happened on the night you were hurt," Steven said.

"Objection!" Vanessa said. "Leading the witness."

"Withdrawn." Steven rechecked his notes. "Melissa, tell the court what happened the last time Billy babysat for you."

With a shaky hand, Billy resumed doodling.

"My mom had to work. She has to work a lot."

Mrs. Durbin's hands covered her guilt-stricken face.

"My mom called Billy," she said. A sob escaped, her chin trembling. "He brought me a teddy bear. He said I could have it when I went to bed. I didn't want to go to bed. But I didn't want to get in trouble." She stopped and took a deep breath. Tremors shook her slender shoulders and tears flowed down her bright pink cheeks. She gasped for breath.

Judge O'Riley called a fifteen-minute recess. Steven led Melissa off the witness stand and, along with her mother, went to a side conference room.

During the break, an officer took Billy to the bathroom, while Vanessa reviewed her notes. Melissa's testimony captivated the audience. To make matters worse, next to Melissa, Billy looked older than his years.

The few spectators who had left during the brief recess shuffled back to their seats. Billy was busy with pad and pen when court resumed, scribbling pages of nonsense.

"Melissa, you're doing a great job," Steven said. "You were telling the court you didn't want to go to bed that night. Please continue."

"I didn't want that stupid bear! I didn't want Billy in my room!" Melissa said, taking in a large gulp of air, twisting the tissue in her hand. "Do I have to say what happened?" She scanned the crowd.

"We're just about done," Steven said. "Remember, look at me. Tell me the story."

"Oh…okay," she said, daubing her nose with the Kleenex. "He said the bear was tired. He…um…pulled the covers back!"

Melissa looked for her mother. Their eyes connected. Mrs. Durbin's lips contoured into a feeble smile.

"Please go on," Steven said.

"He touched my tummy. It's bad when people do that!" She gasped. "He told me…to…to shut up. He was mad. I didn't do anything! He held me down so I…I couldn't move!" Melissa struggled to catch her breath, but she managed to tell the court what had happened. She'd been well coached.

Jurors, reporters, and the public sat in stunned silence, except for her mother's quiet sobs. All eyes were riveted on this tiny figure. Only Vanessa noticed Billy's hand was steady now.

When Melissa finished, Vanessa said, "No questions."

Steven helped Melissa off the witness stand. He held her hand and walked her to her family. Aunts and grandparents, each gave her a hug. Mrs. Durbin held Melissa, and the child buried her face in her mother's shoulder.

Steven finally closed for the state.

It didn't look good for Billy.

"Court will resume at nine in the morning," said Judge O'Riley, adjourning early.

Reporters tripped over each other, running from the courtroom. Melissa's testimony would be tomorrow's headlines.

The flight attendant startled Vanessa by setting her lunch down on the extended tray. The seafood salad sat uneaten while Vanessa continued to stare out the plane's window. Her life was nothing but loose ends. She released a long sigh, attempting to calm her churning stomach. *What did she hope to accomplish in San Francisco?* The uncertainty rattled her nerves. But she couldn't get the replay of the courtroom drama out of her head.

The last day of the trial, bits of blue sky peeked through the gray clouds, promising a better day.

Vanessa called her one and only witness to the stand, Dr. Catherine Sullivan.

The plump doctor strolled into the courtroom with an air of confidence. With numerous trials to her credit, she passed the prosecutor's table without so much as a glance, and took her place on the stand. Dressed in a rust-colored tweed suit and low-heeled pumps, her graying hair gathered neatly into a bun, there was no question, she was all business.

The doctor began by going over the tests she'd administered to Billy and their relevance to his case. She assured her assessment was based on accredited techniques and proven methodology.

When Vanessa felt sure the jury was satisfied with her witness's capabilities, she asked, "Dr. Sullivan, based on your examination of Billy Welsh, what is your diagnosis?"

"Billy has conduct disorder and reactive attachment disorder, a precursor for an anti-social personality disorder," Dr. Sullivan said, looking directly at the jury. "Those with this disorder demonstrate a lack of regard for others' basic rights. They manipulate their victims to gain their trust and use them for their own benefit. Billy's psyche had long since found a way to detach from the abuse he'd endured as a child. This detachment not only blocked his emotional and physical pain, but also the abuse he rendered to others. At the time of the crime, I believe Billy Welch did not have sufficient mental capacity to know and understand what he did was wrong."

"Please tell the court the root cause of this disorder."

"Typically a violent, demeaning, erratic family with an ineffectual mother and an abusive controlling father," Dr. Sullivan said. She took a sip of water before continuing. "Billy grew up in such an environment. Child protective services removed him several times, only to return him home again and again. From what I can see, the system failed Billy Welsh."

"In previous testimony, it was stated that Billy showed no remorse. Is that symptomatic of your diagnosis?"

"Yes, individuals with anti-social personality disorder are incapable of feeling other's pain. They feel justified in doing whatever it is they want to do."

"Is this disorder irreversible?" Vanessa said, surveying the twelve-member panel.

"Caught early, as in Billy's case, intense psychotherapy has provided some success."

"What would be the outcome if Billy goes to prison?" Vanessa asked.

Steven jumped to his feet, "Objection. The witness has no way of knowing what prison would do to the defendant. And it's immaterial."

"Withdrawn. Dr. Sullivan," Vanessa said, resting her hands on the railing, her eyes fixed on the jury. "In your professional opinion, what would be the results of this disorder if left untreated?"

"Someone with this disorder would most likely develop full blown anti-social personality disorder. Our prisons are filled with such people. The disorder becomes more difficult to treat the older the individual becomes. At sixteen, there's still a chance."

"What is your recommendation?" Vanessa asked

"Billy should be sent to the State psychiatric facility for treatment."

"Thank you, doctor. No further questions."

Steven stood. He reviewed the legal pad in front of him before approaching Dr. Sullivan.

"There are many inmates who were abused as children. Should we put them all in a psychiatric hospitals to see what would happen?"

"That probably would be a good idea," Dr. Sullivan said.

Laughter rippled through the gallery. The thunder of the gavel brought them back to order.

"So your conclusion is that Mr. Welsh should not be punished for the crime he has committed, but simply reside in a psychiatric facility for some undetermined time."

"Your Honor, does the District Attorney have a question for my witness?" Vanessa said.

Steven bristled and shot a glare Vanessa's way.

"No further questions," he said.

Vanessa asked for redirect.

"Dr. Sullivan, what happens to individuals once they are sentenced to a psychiatric facility for the criminally insane?"

"They are held in a secured locked area in the hospital that has limited access. They never leave the facility, they are under constant supervision, they must participate in counseling, testing, psycho-pharmaceutical treatment and the release date, if any, is set by the court when they are satisfied the person has met all the requirements of the hospital."

Vanessa closed for the defense, leaving Billy's future with the jury. Oblivious of the gravity of the moment, he continued his manic scrawls in the legal pad Vanessa had given him at the onset of the trial.

"Billy Welsh committed a terrible act that is apparent." Vanessa began her closing statement, pacing in front of the jury box. "But let us put that in the context of his disorder. He has been a victim his entire life. His father and step-father regularly beat him, sodomized him, humiliated him and berated him. Living in squalor and constant fear, his mother, battered by the same men that abused Billy, was powerless to stop these violent men. His step-father was recently arrested on domestic violence charges, as well as, manufacturing and selling drugs."Vanessa stopped and looked at the jury. "Not only did his family fail him, the very system that was put in place to protect such children failed him, as well. Dr. Sullivan provided clear and convincing evidence that Billy Welch lacks the capacity to appreciate the criminality of his conduct. If Billy gets the help he needs, there's a chance. Hospitalization is not a slap on the wrist. It's an alternative sentence in a locked facility until he makes significant improvement. He's only sixteen. Your decision will determine the direction of this child's life."

Vanessa walked slowly back to the defense table. Her glance at Steven was not returned. His gaze was buried in his notes as he mentally prepared for his closing.

"Ladies and gentlemen," Steven said, approaching the jury. "The evidence you've heard over the last few days leaves no doubt that Billy Welsh raped Melissa Durbin. He carried out a deliberate, premeditated act. The defense claims his early abuse caused his behavior and, somehow, if he goes to a hospital he'll be miraculously cured. Do not take that chance!

He's being tried as an adult because of the gravity of the crime. Melissa Durbin's life has been irrevocably altered. It's her life that should be considered first. This crime calls for the strongest sentence the law provides, and that sentence should be served in prison. Hold him accountable!"

Vanessa's hope sank.

The judge provided last minute instructions and the jury filed out of the courtroom for deliberations.

An officer approached the table to take Billy to the holding cell.

Vanessa wandered back to her office. She pulled off her suit jacket and slung it over the chair back. She opened her lap-top. *This was the worst part. The wait.* She wanted to drown herself in vodka martinis, but she'd sit right there until the verdict came in. She busied herself working on the lap-top, nibbling the sandwich she hadn't touch at lunch, until the phone rang. The jurors had reached their decision in just two hours. Not a good omen.

The courtroom was abuzz with reporters. Vanessa avoided Steven's eyes and took her place next to Billy. The jury glanced at Billy as they entered, their feet shuffling between the jury box rows. The judge settled into his chair and rapped the gavel. The sound reverberated around the room.

"Has the jury reached a decision?" the judge asked.

"We have, Your Honor," the foreman said.

The room was still. The air, thick and warm. Steven balanced on the edge of his chair. The minutes ticked away. Vanessa could feel her heart beat. And Billy doodled.

"We, the jury, find Billy Welsh guilty except for insanity."

Sara Stangel sat in stunned silence. Mrs. Durbin sprang to her feet, yelling something at Steven. Spectators whispered to their neighbors, and reporters grabbed their notebooks, readying to file their reports. Judge O'Riley demanded order.

The final blow of the gavel sent everyone flowing out into the hallway. Vanessa tried to convey to Billy what would happen to him now. He listened over the din before being lead away. Vanessa had no idea if he understood a word she said. She threaded her way through the congestion. Steven had been captured by a hoard of screaming reporters. *Oh, no! The interviews!* She squeezed through the crowd and ran for the stairs. By the time she reached her car, she remembered her purse was locked in her desk drawer. *Damn!* She'd have to run the gauntlet again.

Vanessa learned later that day that Billy's stepfather had made a deal with the DA in return for dropping the battering charges in exchange of a ten year sentence. Sara Stangel would, for the first time in her life, live in peace. Vanessa assumed Mackey met with the same fate. She'd be sorry she made that assumption.

30

San Francisco
2004

Before the plane was secured at the gate, passengers leaped to their feet, grabbing bags and lining up, impatiently waiting to deplane. Finally, the hatch opened and the passengers streamed out. The chaos continued inside the Oakland terminal. A mass of humanity scurried headlong in every direction. Vanessa joined the flow, swept into the hoard headed to the luggage pickup area.

Standing there, eyes searching the crowd, was John Sterling. He'd insisted on picking her up. Ten years had passed since she'd last seen her older brother. He'd put on a few pounds and had lost some hair, but otherwise looked pretty much the same. His wire-rimmed glasses and tweed jacket over a faded T-shirt and jeans, gave him the look of a quintessential college professor. For the last thirty years he'd taught English Lit at his alma mater, Berkeley. In the sixties, she'd spotted him on the nightly news, a straggly haired student carrying a placard denouncing the war. Later, in graduate school, he'd met his wife, Melinda. Thirty-five years and three kids later, they'd managed to stay married. Unlike Vanessa, once divorced and their oldest brother, Mark, who was on his second divorce.

As much as the siblings had bickered and fought as children, the three of them had formed an alliance. Their parents had not been easy to deal with. Their mother had been more concerned with her bridge club than raising her children. She'd left that task to nannies. Their overbearing father had rarely been available, unless something displeased him, such as his sons' vocational choices. Vanessa had hoped to avoid her brothers' pitfalls by choosing to become an attorney, hoping for her father's approval. But even that hadn't altered his cool and distant demeanor.

John waved, grinning broadly, and hurried to meet her. After he gave her a hug and a peck on the cheek, he said, "Hi, Squeaky."

She cringed. Still the kid sister.

"It's good to see you," he said.

Together they wedged themselves into the crowd around the luggage carousel. Finally, the bags slowly made their way to them. John grabbed the bags as she pointed them out. Finally, they were on the way to his car.

A brisk hike led them to John's Volvo. They piled the luggage in the back and drove from the parking structure. At the toll booth, John fished in his pocket for a couple of crumpled singles to pay the fee. With a quick glance over his shoulder, he merged with traffic, and headed to the freeway.

"Your phone call was a surprise," he said. "What brings you to Berkley?"

"Just some business in San Francisco," she answered, vaguely. "And a chance to see you and Melinda."

John accepted her explanation and talked on about his children's achievements, each having finished graduate school, married with children. John was relaxed and content with his life. Something Vanessa greatly envied.

31

Berkeley, California

Arriving at John's charming home, Vanessa was transported back in time. Through the years, she'd spent many holidays there. The nostalgic aroma of vanilla scent was everywhere, from candles to Melinda's perfume. Entering the living room, Vanessa could picture her nieces and nephew playing a board game with Michael, warmed by the roaring fire, giggling and teasing, eating decorated holiday cookies—orange iced pumpkin shapes for Thanksgiving, white-edged gingerbread men for Christmas.

The house was quiet now, except for a sonata playing softly in the background. The old Victorian house that John and Melinda had meticulously restored over the years suited them. Oversized contemporary paintings dominated the wall space, a counter-balance to the fussy details of the woodwork, clearly her sister-in-law's passion.

Melinda, with her fuzzy graying hair and her 'Kiss the Cook' apron, sprinted from the kitchen just long enough to embrace Vanessa and welcome her, before dashing back to add the final touches to one of her famous meals.

"What'll it be, Squeaky?" John asked, poised at the thirties-era bar.

"I can't believe you still call me that."

"It fits," he teased.

"I'll have a vodka martini," she said, pretending to be annoyed. "I don't remember how that nickname got started."

"Of course not," he said, his hands clutching each end of a stainless steel shaker, as if playing a rhythm instrument in a Latin band. "When you were born, instead of crying, you squeaked. At least that's how it sounded to me, and your name was difficult to pronounce. Anyway, Mother hated the nickname, so I couldn't resist."

Laughing and talking, John was caught up in the festive moment, blurting out, "We should have a family reunion."

The conversation halted when Melinda called them to dinner.

The pungent aroma of the veal scaloppini, garlic bread, and winter squash, mixed enticingly with the sweet fragrance of fresh cut flowers. It all sat center stage on an antique Irish linen cloth. John and Melinda had always enjoyed gracious living, a holdover from their privileged upbringing. The setting sun filtered through the French doors, casting a rosy glow on the room, completed the scene.

John raised a crystal goblet. "Here's to my beautiful sister. Glad you could visit after all these years."

"Thanks, John," Vanessa said, with a wry smile. "Everything looks great, Melinda."

Vanessa filled her plate, her appetite piqued. Melinda had outdone herself.

They chatted while they ate, enjoying a full-bodied burgundy, and the camaraderie. Just like old times. But all the while Vanessa felt a tightening in the pit of her stomach. She knew it was just a matter of time before Michael's name would be brought up. The strange thing was she wanted to confide in them.

Melinda cleared the table. They lingered at the table, finishing their wine, when Vanessa decided it was a good time to tell them about Michael.

"I have some sad news," she said. "Kate died about three weeks ago."

"Vanessa, I'm so sorry. Kate was a dear, sweet person," Melinda said.

"I drove to Florence and was able to spend the last few minutes with her. But to my absolute surprise Michael was there."

"Michael!?" Melinda said goblet frozen midair. "Where had he been?

I'm still mad at him for putting you through all that."

"Strangely enough, he ended up here, in San Francisco. With Kate."

"What was he doing with Kate?" John asked, obviously having a hard time taking it all in.

"Why didn't he call us?" Melinda broke in. "He must have known we would have helped." Sweet, uncomplicated Melinda.

"He was in pretty bad shape. He's doing okay now, but," Vanessa said, tucking a wayward tress behind her ear, "he...ah...was addicted to heroin."

"Heroin! What on earth was he thinking?" John said.

John and Melinda were stunned into silence, absorbing the fact that someone in their family could be a drug addict. *If that shocked them, how would they handle the rest?*

"He's been sober for some time now. But there's more," Vanessa said. "Michael's in serious trouble. It seems he witnessed a murder." A hot flush raced up her neck, splashing onto her face. She'd gone too far. These gentle people didn't deal with the harshness of real life. Academics, often insulated from reality, dealt in ideas and ideals. But it was too late. The words were out.

"Witnessed a murder!" Melinda gasped. "How could that be?"

"Surely there's some mistake!" John said.

"How do you know this? Did Michael tell you?" Melinda continued.

"Yes. I guess the story was in all the papers, but, thankfully, it didn't mention Michael," she said.

"What a mess he's made of his life," John said, shaking his head in disbelief.

That was true. Nevertheless, her brother's remark hurt. Vanessa folded her linen dinner napkin and laid it on the table, her fingers lingering on the fringed edge of the cloth.

"You're right," she admitted. "But I've got to help him. The trial is this week. They have a man in custody, but Michael says they have the wrong man. I thought if I could find out more, maybe I could keep Michael out of it, but tell the authorities who I think did it."

"Is that why you're here?" John said. "Michael should handle this himself. You of all people should know that!"

She drained her glass.

"I don't like any of this," John continued. "Michael suddenly reappears and you're treating him like a kid. He's old enough to take care of his own mess."

"I'm sorry you feel that way," Vanessa said. "But I'm going to do this for him."

Silence. Each looked away. John stood and gathered the napkins. Melinda picked up the empty goblets. Vanessa wasn't sure what she'd wanted from them, but she hadn't planned on alienating them.

"Why don't we have dessert in the living room," Melinda said, appearing thankful for the momentary respite the kitchen would provide.

"Can I help?" Vanessa asked, having no appetite for dessert.

"Oh, no thanks," Melinda called back over her shoulder. Hands filled with glasses, she bumped open the swinging kitchen door with her ample hip and disappeared.

A short time later, she joined her husband and Vanessa in the living room. Looking more composed, she set the tray down and went about serving dessert.

Following an old family tradition when things got tense, Melinda changed the subject. It's amazing what you can ignore, buried under the rose-colored carpet. Melinda talked about her artwork and garden while Vanessa nibbled at the strawberry torte. Finally, when the appropriate time arrived, Vanessa said good night and headed down the hall to the familiar guestroom.

Her bags sat in the middle of the floor. Too tired to unpack, she knelt and searched for her pajamas and toothbrush. She ran a bath, pulled off her traveling clothes, and climbed into the claw-foot tub. Her head resting against the cushion at the edge, she settled into the steaming water.

While she lingered in the tub, she thought about this guy named Falcon, furious that he'd dragged her son into his filthy life.

32

San Francisco, California

Early the next morning, Vanessa drove her brother's aging Volvo over the Oakland Bay Bridge, along with the rush hour traffic. By the time she neared the city, the morning fog had burned off, revealing the city's dramatic skyline.

Parking was impossible, so she settled for a four-story parking structure and hiked the two blocks to the courthouse. When she entered the lobby it was already abuzz with the day's activity. Two stern-looking armed security guards were on duty at the metal detectors. As she approached, dressed in her salmon-colored silk suit, tailored to perfection, they both seemed to brighten some. Nevertheless, she was relieved when she made it through security. She grabbed her purse and briefcase off the conveyor belt and hurried to catch the next elevator.

The fourth floor appeared deserted. Fluorescent ceiling fixtures barely illuminated the cave-like hallway. Cracked green linoleum cut a pathway to Room 411. She waited a minute, mustering her courage, adjusting her jacket, nervously fingered her pearl necklace, before rapping on the door.

A deep voice called through the door for her to enter.

William Rowan sat framed by piles of folders on the cluttered desktop. As he stood to his full six-foot-two, he struggled to button his suit jacket around his bulging middle, before he extended his hand. He motioned for her to take a seat. From her vantage point, the room overlooked the heating system on the roof next door.

"I'm pleased to meet you, Ms. Sterling. But, to be honest, I'm not sure why you're here. What exactly is your interest in the Diego murder?"

"I couldn't go into it over the phone, but I think I can help," Vanessa said. When she'd called the assistant DA to make an appointment the week before, she'd been purposefully vague.

"I've been in contact with someone who claims to be an eye witness to the murder."

"What!" Rowan said, eyes widening. "Who is it?"

"I'm not at liberty to reveal his identity at this time, but he claims Falcon framed Thompson, the man you have on trial."

"Well, well," Rowan said, as he leaned back in his chair, shaking his head, chuckling, "So you think Falcon…"

"Mr. Rowan," Vanessa snapped. "Please don't take that condescending tone with me! And I'm here at great personal risk and that of my client."

"Sorry. But you have to understand we've been trying to get Falcon for the last ten years. If he killed Diego, he's covered his tracks pretty good. To be honest, I'd suspected him at first, him or one of his men, but all the evidence points to Thompson. We've got his prints on the gun and witnesses placing him at the scene."

"Thompson was set up."

"It's clear you're mistaken. We have no reason to…"

"Did you completely miss my point?" Vanessa said. "I have an eye witness!"

"I can't do anything unless you tell me who the eye witness is," Rowan said. "And I have a chance to interview him."

"As I said, his life is in danger. If Falcon is charged with the murder, I can get the witness to testify."

"Oh sure, I get Falcon. No one even knows what the guy looks like. Then there's the problem of evidence. I don't think you understand."

"I've been an attorney for twenty-five years! I don't appreciate the implication."

"What would you do in my shoes?" Rowan asked. "A total stranger tells you she's got an eye witness. Would you act on the words of a nameless eye witness?"

"Let me talk to him again. He's scared, but he can identify Falcon," Vanessa said. "Just think what nailing Falcon would do for your career."

Rowan brightened. "This is big!" No longer able to contain his excitement. "If you're right, we could get the biggest drug kingpin on the West Coast! We'd cripple the industry, at least until they could reorganize. I need to talk to the DA. In fact, let me call him right now." Rowan picked up the phone.

Her gut tightened. Steven's friend. She suddenly regretted talking to Rowan.

"No! Don't do that!" *Too emphatic. Calm down.* "Let me talk to my witness first."

"Okay," Rowan said. "But you'd better get back to me soon. If you have evidence that Thompson's innocent, we should not proceed with the trial." Then he added, with a smile. "Why don't you come to court this morning? Afterwards, we can get some lunch and discuss how to proceed."

She'd bought some time. "Okay," she said, trying to sound enthusiastic. "I'll see you in court."

Key West, Florida
1987

Falcon had arrived on the Key West scene ready for a change. He found what he was looking for in Key Largo. It was his kind of town. Hot, sunny days and wild, sultry nights.

On such a night, Falcon swung the rented Mercedes into the Palms.

After the valet took the car he strolled into the smoky lounge. It was a lively place that attracted the right kind of people. Most of the tables were packed, so Falcon slipped the maitre'd a fifty to ensure a table near the stage.

Tall, shapely Amanda had been dating Falcon for the last six months and worked at the Palms. She made her way over to him, balancing a tray of drinks on one hand. She stopped to give him a kiss on the cheek before continuing on her way. It was a pleasure watching her glide between tables. He liked women, but, at the moment, he especially liked Amanda. She was great in bed. But, more important, he liked who she knew.

Falcon followed the maitre'd and, once seated, looked around for familiar faces. It was a large room but the tables were crowded close together, barely an elbow width apart. Right next to Falcon sat four men he hadn't seen before. One of them looked over and for a moment stared at Falcon, then looked away. Again, Falcon caught the man looking his way.

"What's up?" Falcon asked.

"Sorry," the man said.

Having finished her shift, Amanda headed toward Falcon's table. But before she could join him, the short, heavily built man at the next table, put a hefty arm around her waist and pulled her to his lap. She laughed, then playfully slapped his hand away. The man who had been staring moments before asked Amanda a question. She turned toward Falcon before answering.

Once seated with Falcon, he pulled her close and left his arm around her shoulder.

"What the hell was that?" Falcon asked. "Why's that guy so interested in me?"

"He says you looked familiar."

"From where?"

"Vietnam."

"Jesus!"

"He says if you're the guy he thinks you are, you saved his life." She whispered. "He's one of Fontana's guys. Fontana's the one with the cigar."

"Jesus Christ!" Falcon said. "He works for Fontana?"

"Yeah. Fontana owns this club."

"That's not all he owns. He owns the whole East Coast."

"Keep your voice down," Amanda cautioned.

Falcon looked over and nodded. Just as Amanda was going to make the introductions, the midnight show began. By the time it was over, Fontana and his men were gone.

Several nights later Falcon was again at the Palm's. Fontana stood at the bar with Amanda. She hurried over to Falcon and took his arm.

"Fontana wants to meet you!" she whispered.

Falcon took a table and lit a smoke. This was just the break he'd been looking for. He was tired of working for people who didn't appreciate his talent, but he'd let Fontana come to him.

"Fontana," he said, extending a beefy hand. "Mind if I sit?"

Without waiting for a response, he pulled out a chair. The minute he sat, a waitress rushed over.

"The usual, Mr. Fontana?" she asked.

"Yeah. And bring my friend another of whatever he's drinking, sweetheart." Fontana pinched her behind. She blushed and hurried away.

"Amanda's been telling me you're looking to make some connections. What brings you to Key Largo?"

"Some business, some pleasure." Falcon kept an eye on Amanda, as she joined them at the table. He smiled her way and said, "A whole lot of pleasure."

Amanda smiled in return and pulled her chair close to Falcon's.

"A guy by the name of Tony Portello works for me," Fontana said. "He thinks you're the guy that saved his life back in Nam. You that guy?"

"Could be."

Fontana looked over his shoulder just as Tony ambled into the club. He motioned for Tony to join them.

"This the guy?" Fontana asked Tony.

"I don't friggin' believe this!" Tony said. He gave Falcon a wholehearted handshake. "I wasn't sure last night. But, yeah. Great to see you, man. How you doin' after all these years? I never knew your name, but always wondered if you made it out. I owe you, man."

"Take a load off, Tony." Then Fontana said to Falcon, "Amanda's told me about you. And with Tony here being in your debt and all, I got a proposition. If you're interested."

"What do you have in mind?" Falcon asked.

"Not here. Come to my office tomorrow. Amanda knows the way."

As abruptly as he'd arrived, he left. Tony followed.

"So that's Fontana," Falcon said. "I thought he'd be taller. What does he want with me?"

"You'll see," Amanda said, with a knowing smile. "Let's have some champagne to celebrate your new job."

The waitress moved a little faster since Falcon had been seen with Fontana. He leaned back and lit a cigar. Things were beginning to look up.

"Fontana has more business than he can handle," Amanda said, her long red hair whipping in the breeze of the convertible as it cut along the highway, heading south to Sunset Point the next day. "He's having a tough time finding people he can trust."

Amanda was unusually chatty; filling Falcon in on Fontana's far flung enterprises and his connections in Colombia. Falcon didn't miss a word. He wanted to know everything there was to know about this man who ran the biggest drug syndicate in the states. He wasn't going to mess up this opportunity by shooting off his big mouth or doing something stupid. He'd messed up before, but this time he'd get it right.

They turned up the palm-lined drive that led to a three-story office building. The Gulf of Mexico lay beyond.

Fontana sat at the head of the large mahogany table, a Cuban cigar clutched between his teeth.

"Falcon, come on in," Fontana said. Then turned to the men sitting with him. "This here is Ruiz, and that fat slob is Bear. And you remember Tony." He pointed to an empty seat at the conference table. "I'm a man of few words. Let's get down to business. Falcon, I've got a job for you."

Once seated, Falcon crossed his arms. "What kinda of job? I don't even know who any of you are."

The other men froze and looked at Fontana.

"What the...? I'll tell you who I am!" The fierce words raised the veins on his temples and drew spittle to his lips. "Someone who'd just as soon put a slug in you as continue this conversation. I'll tell you once, don't mess with me, capiche?"

Falcon backed down. "You won't get any trouble from me."

"Okay," Fontana said, straightening in his chair. Everyone relaxed, and Fontana chewed on the stogie. "I need a new face. You got a record?"

"Hell, no. I'm a fuckin' war hero, for Christ's sake. I got a medal for saving your boy Tony here."

"Jesus. Listen up,' Fontana said. "Trust is everything in my business. If you do okay with this job there could be more. There's a shipment coming in next week."

It was a balmy, starless night the following week when Falcon pulled onto a dock behind an old fish packinghouse, north of the Key West airport. Bear was along to supervise the rookie, which made Falcon very uneasy. Too nervous to sit, he climbed from the truck to scan the area.

He'd just lit a smoke when the signal came from the darkened sea: one long and two short flashes. Bear flashed the truck lights in response. Falcon's stomach tightened. He flicked the Pall Mall into the water, and hurried to the dock's end. Two Colombian nationals and an American hurried up the wharf ladder. Bear labored his girth out of the truck cab and joined the men. He opened a canvas gym bag he'd hauled with him. After the American checked the contents he nodded and the men silently loaded 250 kilos of pure grade cocaine into the paneled truck. Falcon stood guard, his eyes darting, straining against the dark. Just as the last kilo was loaded a security car rounded the corner by the warehouse.

"Fuck!" Falcon said under his breath. Teeth clenched he nodded to his compadres, locked the back of the van, then discreetly pulled a revolver from its holster nestled in the small of his back. The car's spotlight caught Falcon strolling over.

"What's going on?" said the guard. "This is a private dock."

He started to open his car door, but Falcon slammed it shut.

"What the hell?" the guard said.

Without so much as a blink, Falcon aimed and pulled the trigger, putting a slug between the man's eyes. With the look of surprised still frozen on the dead man's face, the men pulled him from the patrol car and hauled him onto the boat. His body would be dumped at sea. Falcon drove the patrol car to the dock's edge, jammed a brick on the gas pedal, and put it in gear. It sailed off into the water, where it sank in minutes.

With the boat's motor fading into the distance, Falcon scanned the area one more time before he climbed into the truck. He gripped the steering wheel until his knuckles turned white.

Bear punched him in the arm. "You did good."

Falcon started the truck and he released a long, slow breath.

Across the street from the warehouse, the occupants of a white van peered through their night vision binoculars. The job went off just as they planned with the exception of the security guard. Fontana would be happy to know, Falcon handled himself just fine.

It had been almost a year since Falcon started working for the syndicate, making his way up through the ranks, when he was summoned to Fontana's house. Luis escorted him up the marble staircase. Falcon had rarely been to the house, he hoped he hadn't screwed up.

"I need someone out on the West Coast," Fontana said, offering Falcon a cigar. "You're not like the other friggin' yes men around here. I trust you. So here's the deal. West Coast gangs are working with the Columbians to take over the trade. We've got men in San Francisco, but there's a problem. A Spick named Diego. Get him in line. Know what I mean?"

"I can handle it," Falcon said, lighting the cigar, smiling to himself.

"Great. I need you out there pronto. I'll start you at twenty grand a month. You straighten things out and I'll double it. I can make you a very rich man, Falcon."

33

San Francisco, California

When she finished the meeting with Rowan it was nine, leaving her a half an hour before the trial began. Since she hadn't eaten breakfast, she went in search of a café. She'd walked about a block when she spotted Annie's coffee shop. By the looks of things, she'd just missed the morning rush. She flung her coat over a chair at the only clean table, sat down, and searched her briefcase for her notebook. That had been a close call in Rowan's office. She didn't want to inadvertently involve Steven. She needed to go slower, more methodically, plan it out, as she would any other case.

She had begun to jot down some ideas when a tall solidly-built waitress sailed up to her table, blond corkscrew curls bouncing, coffee pot in hand.

"What'll it be?" she asked, still in rush-hour mode. "Do ya wanta hear the specials?"

"No thanks. Just scrambled eggs and a bagel," Vanessa said.

The waitress shrugged, filled Vanessa's cup, and hurried off to fill her order.

It was always a wonder what a full stomach did for the thought processes. She had several pages of questions to ask Rowan at lunch.

She located the courtroom on the second floor, entered, and took a seat toward the back. Morning light filtered through the tall narrow windows, illuminating the dust particles in the air. The room was quiet, except for the bailiff's hushed whispers to the court clerk. Max Thompson entered with his court-appointed lawyer, looking around uneasily.

Vanessa turned her attention to the only other people in the room, three men sitting just behind Thompson, several rows ahead of her. Her jaw dropped. *It couldn't be!* There sat Wade Mackey with his buddies. *How stupid! What was I thinking?* Mackey looked around. When he spotted her he nudged the big guy next to him, then he reached over the bar and tapped Thompson on the shoulder.

Vanessa was planning her escape when William Rowan entered the court room. Noticing her, he smiled and nodded. *Could this get any worse?*

Mackey whispered something excitedly to the other men. She took the opportunity to run from the courtroom. She ran all the way to the parking structure on her four-inch heels. After she clambered into John's car, she sped back over the Oakland Bay Bridge to the safety of her brother's house.

Melinda knelt in her garden, planting petunias when Vanessa drove up.

"I'm glad you're home early," she said, walking toward Vanessa as she removed her green polka-dot gardening gloves. Her smile crumbled when she noticed Vanessa's ashen face.

"What's the matter?" Melinda asked.

Vanessa grabbed Melinda's elbow and steered her into the house.

"The guy that beat up Michael was in the courtroom this morning! I thought he was in jail."

"Who? Michael was beat up? When?"

"A few weeks ago."

"You saw him in the courtroom today?" Melinda said.

"Yes."

"Do they know who you are?" Melinda asked, setting her gloves on the arm of the chair.

"Yes. When I saw them I ran from the courtroom," Vanessa said, her pulse slowing. "They didn't follow me."

"Are you sure?" Melinda said. "Vanessa, this is scary!"

"We're okay, I'm certain of that."

Neither of them noticed the black SUV slowly driving by.

34

San Francisco, California

Later that same day, Falcon strolled into Sal's Bar and Grill in North Beach. Sal's had been at that location for over thirty years and, while it lacked the panache of trendier places in this upscale part of town, it had a certain old-world charm.

Sal stood behind the bar, his foot propped on a case of booze, a white apron tied around his narrow waist. A hands-on restaurateur, he practically lived at the place. It was between the lunch and dinner crowds, so it was quiet for now. His elbows rested on the bar, spectacles balanced low on his nose, while he perused the daily *Chronicle*.

"How ya' doing, Sal?" Falcon asked, stepping inside.

Sal peered over his specks and smiled. "Not bad. Good to see you."

Falcon threw a leg over a barstool and hoisted himself up, while Sal reached for a bottle from the antique hand-carved back-bar, and poured Falcon his customary scotch.

"Listen, Sal," Falcon said, taking a sip. "I've got a meeting in a few minutes. I'd appreciate a little privacy. I'm sure they'll be thirsty when they arrive."

"Sure thing."

Falcon pulled five one-hundred-dollar bills from a silver money-clip and placed them on the bar. Drink in hand; he strode into the dining room, positioning himself at a table at the back of the room where he could watch the door.

Outside, people scurried by, their images backlit by the midday sun. Falcon sat nursing his drink until Antonio Molina and Javier Hansen arrived. Sal waited until the men entered before he turned the 'open' sign to 'closed' and locked the door.

"Tony, Javier." Falcon rose and shook hands with his two best men.

Hansen, standing six-foot four, two hundred and fifty pounds of solid muscle, coal black hair and blue eyes, reflected the mixed parentage of his Scandinavian father and Brazilian mother. The CIA had trained him for a covert operation in Central America twenty years ago. An ace sharpshooter, he could hit a man between the eyes at a hundred yards. He'd led thirty trained militia deployed to a steamy Colombian jungle to take a guerrilla stronghold. In just forty-eight hours, he'd lost twenty men. Seeing it was hopeless, Hansen radioed for the remaining men to be picked up, but was told they were on their own. When he emerged from the jungle three months later, he was the only one left. He came back into the country through an underground connection, went directly to his commander's house, and shot the entire family, leaving his commander for last. Presumed dead, Hansen was never suspected. Now, working for Falcon, he was a member of the inner circle. Hansen could be trusted, as long as he knew his back was covered.

Molina was dwarfed by Hansen's burley build. Growing up in the gang-infested neighborhood was tough enough, but when he was twelve, his mother had thrown him out because her new boyfriend didn't like kids. A local gang became his family. He still bore gang tattoos from his days in South Central. Living on the streets had taught him how to survive by his wits. There, many had made the mistake of sizing him up as an easy target. They quickly discovered he was no one to mess with. At twenty-nine, Molina was the youngest in Falcon's troop. He'd quickly worked his way up the ranks, proving himself many times, but Falcon had really been sold when Molina alerted him about Diego's defecting.

Sal approached the table. "What'll it be, gentlemen?"

As soon as Sal returned with their drinks, Falcon got down to business.

"I got a job for you two. There's twenty grand in it for each of you." Making sure Sal was out of earshot, he said, "I need you to eliminate Max Thompson."

"He's in jail, for Christ's sake!" Hansen hissed.

"How do we pull this off?" Molina asked.

Falcon's jaw tightened. "Tomorrow morning they'll take him from the county jail on his way to court. He's shackled, but he's wearing a vest. So you gotta aim for his head. Javier, you'll only have time for one shot. They take him out the west door and down four or five stairs to the alley where the police wagon picks him up. There's two cops with him and two more in the wagon. You'll have your chance while they're on the stairs."

"But I'll need at least a full day to…"

Falcon rolled his eyes. "I've got it covered. You'll drive a white panel truck that looks like a million other trucks. No one will notice. Tony, you'll pull up to the curb just west of the alley. Get there early so Javier can line up his shot. There's a hole drilled in the side of the truck. After you get Thompson, shoot out a tire on the wagon. Get outta there during the confusion. Drive east. Turn up the first alley. Dump the truck between Polk and Larkin."

Hansen looked at Molina.

"We want thirty grand each, half up front," Javier said.

Falcon nodded. With business almost over, he raised his arm, signaling Sal.

"They have the best friggin' lasagna here," Falcon said. "Javier, there's one more thing…"

35

Berkeley, California

Vanessa's description of the day's events did little to help John's already jangled nerves. It'd been a mistake to involve them. She would leave in the morning.

After an uneasy dinner, John suggested turning on the news. But instead of a distraction, CNN was discussing the Max Thompson trial.

That was all Vanessa could take. She padded down the hall to the guest-room. The four-poster bed with its wedding-ring quilt and fluffy white pillows invited sleep. Before turning on the lights, she peered through the curtain at the deserted street. She checked the window lock, pulled down the shade, and climbed into bed. About an hour into her book, her eyes grew heavy. She set aside the novel, turned out the light, and quickly fell asleep.

Around midnight a loud thud startled her awake. Still groggy, not sure what she'd heard, her pulse quickened. She sat up and listened. *This is crazy.* No one could break in without setting off the state-of-art alarm system John had installed following several burglaries in the neighborhood. She rested her head back on the pillow. *John or Melinda must be up. Stop worrying!* She pulled the covers to her chin and slipped into a fitful sleep.

She struggled to breathe. Something was covering her mouth. She tried to sit up, but couldn't move. *Oh, dear god! It wasn't a dream!* Her eyes shot open. A dark figure bent over her, holding her down, his large gloved hand covering her nose and mouth, suffocating her. She grabbed at his hand, but he held tight. He bent close to her face and whispered, "You're causing problems. A real pain in the ass."

Adrenaline pumped through her body. She forced her legs free and kicked him so hard he stumbled backwards. She tried to yell, but her voice froze. With her body freed from the weight of his body, she struggled to get up. He regained his footing and grabbed her arm, twisting it behind her, sending a shooting pain through her shoulder. He shoved her face-down onto the bed. She managed to turn her head and, finding her voice, let out a piercing scream.

"Shad up!" he hissed. Grabbing her hair, he pressed her face into the pillow. She gasped for air.

John burst into the room, pointing a small revolver.

"What the…?" John said.

From there it became a blurred, slow motion nightmare. Melinda appeared at the door behind John. The intruder drew a gun, turned to John and fired. Melinda screamed. John fell back onto his wife. Another shot skimmed Melinda's cheek as she went down. They crumpled onto the hall floor.

Vanessa lunged at the man and grabbed for his gun. She was no match for the intruder, he easily knocked her to the floor. The barrel of the gun was now pointed at her. The light from the hall illuminated his face. Their eyes connected for a split second. He lowered the gun ever so slightly.

John, barely able to move, raised himself onto his elbow, and got off a shot; the intruder lunged toward the window. The bullet missed its target. The man broke through the window and ran as the alarm shrieked to life.

Vanessa hurried to John. Melinda had passed out, but was still breathing. Vanessa ran to the bathroom for towels, hoping to stop the bleeding of the gaping wound in John's arm. She handed him a couple of towels and held one to Melinda's face. Melinda came to, looking bewildered. The phone rang. Vanessa turned and stared.

"It's the alarm company! Answer it!" John said.

Barely able to speak, Vanessa picked up the phone.

"Security! Is there a problem?" the caller asked.

"Yes! Break in. Two people shot! Hurry! Please."

Vanessa returned to the hallway. It looked like a war zone.

"Vanessa," John whispered. "I don't have a license for the gun. I never registered it. I didn't think I'd ever use it."

She took the gun from her brother, wiped the red stains from the handle, and shoved it in her purse, it was the least she could do.

Within minutes, three patrol cars and an ambulance arrived. The cars formed a semi-circle in front of the house; search-lights streamed through the windows. Police spread out, checking the surrounding properties. Vanessa unlocked the front door. Once the police secured the house, the paramedics streamed in, rushing down the hall toward John and Melinda. They immediately set to work on each of their patients, applying pressure to their wounds to stop the bleeding, taking their pulse and blood pressure before beginning IVs. Gurneys were set up. John was rolled onto one, Melinda on another. Vanessa bent over John.

"I'm so sorry," she whispered, tears streaming down, just before they were whisked away.

The ambulances sped off, sirens blaring. Neighbors huddled in their doorways, wrapping their dressing gowns around them, watching, disbelieving anything bad could happen at the Sterling residence.

Vanessa, bruised and shaken, but otherwise unharmed, stood frozen in the bedroom doorway. She'd refused medical treatment. Flashes of what had just happened rushed in; her stomach churned. She hurried to the bathroom to lose what was left of the previous evening's dinner. Standing on wobbly legs, she looked in the mirror: red-rimmed eyes, the start of a nasty bruise around her mouth, red marks down her neck. She splashed water on her face and patted it dry. She became aware of her blood splattered nightgown. She looked around the guestroom, and spotted the jeans and turtleneck sweater she'd draped over a chair the night before, and pulled them on.

Police helicopters circled overhead, searchlights blazed as dawn broke; the media arrived bringing more helicopters, and vans were parked everywhere. Someone appeared to board up the broken window.

A tall young detective, not much older than Michael, stood in the entry hall. A police photographer was documenting the crime scene.

Seeing Vanessa, the detective directed her towards the kitchen.

"I'll make us some coffee," he said.

She followed the detective through the dining room into the kitchen. She flicked the switch. The room flooded with light.

Vanessa went through the ritual of pulling cups from the pantry and cream from the fridge, while the detective filled the coffee maker. Her movements felt stilted and mechanical. She seated herself on a stool by the breakfast bar.

"Can you tell me what happened?" he finally asked, pulling a stool by the bar, so he could look directly at her.

"It's a blur. I woke with the intruder's hand over my mouth," she said, the coffee maker gurgling in the background. "I don't know how he got in. There's an alarm."

"These guys know how to bypass alarms," he said. "Could you describe him?"

"Big...six-two-three, with broad shoulders. He had an accent. Spanish, I think, although he spoke English."

"He spoke to you? What did he say?"

"I...don't remember. I couldn't breathe. Somehow I was able to fight him off."

"Are you going to be okay? I can get a medic to take a look at you."

"No...thanks. I'm fine."

She could handle the pressure of a courtroom, but this was personal, and it took her way outside of her comfort zone. And what could she say? That she was here investigating a murder that her son may or may not have been involved in? That she got her brother and sister-in-law shot? She'd have to deal with it all soon enough. But, not now.

"This is my brother's house. I'm just visiting."

"We'll add this house to our patrol," he said, jotting something in his notebook. "We've had a number of break-ins in the area, but this is the first time anyone's been hurt. Most of the burglars are on drugs looking for stuff to sell. Too bad you didn't see the vehicle or his face."

He continued his questions, took notes, and completed his initial report. She repeated what she'd already told him until he'd heard enough. By the time the interview ended, it was after nine in the morning. She sat motionless, staring out at the garden Melinda so loving tended.

Vanessa packed her bag, called for a cab, and then dialed the hospital. John was so medicated he could hardly speak. Melinda was resting comfortably. Vanessa's eyes stung. What a mess she'd made of things.

The cab driver honked to announce his arrival. Stepping gingerly over the blood-splattered Persian rug, around the yellow crime-scene tape, Vanessa left her brother's house.

36

San Francisco, California

The cabbie wanted to chat on the way to the airport, but Vanessa was in no mood. She ignored him until he was quiet.

How naive, thinking she could come to San Francisco and solve Michael's problems. He'd been right. *I've really screwed things up!* She couldn't leave everything unresolved.

"Driver, I've changed my mind. Take me to the Sir Francis Drake."

The cabby made a quick U-turn and headed to the Oakland Bay Bridge. Vanessa gazed out at the steel-gray water of the bay. As they approached the hotel, the seasoned driver maneuvered through the congestion of Union Square up to the busy hotel and pulled to a stop. The bell captain scurried over and blew his silver whistle. A bellhop grabbed her bags from the trunk, and the traditionally-attired Beefeater doorman ushered her in.

It had been twenty years since she'd last visited, but the hotel had held onto its timeless elegance. Marble staircases anchored with elaborate wrought iron rail led to the mezzanine. Crystal chandeliers hung suspended from gilded ceilings. Huge palms grew in copper urns, amid silk sofas and Louis XIV chairs.

She approached the front desk, and for the first time that morning thought of her appearance: the crumbled turtle neck sweater covered the marks on her neck, but not the bruise by her mouth. Her bed-flattened hair was pulled back into a haphazard pony-tail. She wore no makeup. Despite her appearance, when she asked for the presidential suite, and produced an exclusive titanium American Express card, the clerk was more than happy to accommodate her. They were used to eccentric clients.

The elevator left her on the sixteenth floor. She tipped the bellhop for depositing the luggage in the suite's bedroom. Finally alone, she collapsed onto the sofa. From her resting place on the down-filled sofa cushions, she scanned her temporary domain. Original art work hung everywhere. She lay on one of two red and yellow Oriental print silk sofas that flanked the marble fireplace. Double doors led to the master bedroom. It had been a long time since she'd enjoyed such elegance.

Vanessa glanced at her blood encrusted nails. In twenty-four hours, she'd fled Mackey and his thugs, fought for her life with a barrel-chested intruder, and nearly gotten her brother and his wife killed, not to mention lying to the police. This was bigger than anything she'd ever handled before and she couldn't do it alone. She pulled her cell phone from her cluttered handbag and dialed the number Steven had given her.

A youthful female voice answered, "San Francisco County District Attorney."

"This is Vanessa Sterling. Steven Adams, a good friend of Mr. Stanton's, suggested I call. Could I speak to him, please?"

"Just a moment, please. I'll connect you to his personal assistant."

"This is Jayne Monroe. May I ask your business with Mr. Stanton?"

The lion at the gate. Vanessa repeated what she had told the receptionist and, a moment later, Stanton was on the line.

"Hello, Ms. Sterling. Steve's friend, huh? How's that old duffer doing? Hope his golf game has improved with age," he said, with a laugh.

The good ol' boys' club, alive and well.

"He's fine. He sends his regards," Vanessa said, hunting in her bag for a notebook and pen. "I need to talk to you about a serious matter."

"Oh?"

"I don't know how to begin, so I'll just jump right in. I've been in touch with an eyewitness to the Rhio Diego murder. He tells me you have the wrong man on trial."

"You spoke to Rowan yesterday, right?"

So much for giving me time. Thanks, Rowan.

"Yes, I did."

"Where are you right now?" he said.

Why would he want to know where I am?

"I'm at the airport," she said. She was getting good at lying. "My plane leaves in a few minutes."

"Would you mind postponing your flight? I'll have someone pick you up and drive you to my office. I think the sooner we discuss this, the better."

"Let me see if I can change my flight and I'll get back to you."

"No, wait!" he said. "That won't be necessary. We'll arrange a later flight for you. My men are on their way. What airline are you..."

Now she was sure. She turned off the phone and stared at it, disbelieving what had just happened. When it rang, she jumped. Hurrying to the balcony, she hurled the cell phone over the rail. It hit the street below, shattering on impact.

How deep did this go? Rowan said no one knew what the guy looked like, but this Falcon character seemed to own the city.

There was no one she could trust. She locked the door to the suite. Called the front desk to notify them she didn't want her name or room number released to anyone.

She felt safe enough for the moment to take a much-needed bath. She kicked off her shoes and undressed while she filled the Jacuzzi tub.

The hot bubble bath slowly loosened the knots in her neck and shoulders, but the frightening series of events kept running through her mind. The intruder did not match Mackey or his friends' descriptions. Where did he come from? Why the hesitation when he pointed the gun? He could have easily shot her if that's what he'd intended to do. He just wanted to scare her off. Somehow she'd gotten too close.

Vanessa rested her head on the edge of the tub, plotting where to go from here. Kate had to know who Michael was involved with. Or at least knew why Michael was running. Michael and Kate had kept in close touch, it seemed. But Vanessa had rarely heard from Kate over the past ten years. What wedge had split their friendship apart? They'd always been close, never had any secrets from each other. Kate had been Michael's confidant, too, when he was a child. Kate always shared those secrets with Vanessa, often during visits to the lake house.

Lake House
Kenosha, Wisconsin
1984

Lake Michigan lapped the shore, white caps danced atop the waves. Michael's laughter could be heard over the other children, splashing and swimming during the waning days of summer. The water raised goose-bumps, but the hot humid air eased the chill. Michael waved his skinny ten-year-old arms in the air and Kate and Vanessa waved back from the white-wicker porch chairs.

"Michael told me the cutest thing," Kate said, refilling their glasses with gin-spiked lemonade. "He liked Lisa Ferguson, but he'd been afraid to tell her. So he wrote her a note. The teacher caught him and made him read it to the class."

"Poor Michael. No wonder he had stomachaches the last few days of school."

The phone had rung, and Kate jumped up, running into the house, letting the screen door slam behind her. Vanessa heard Kate's muffled voice. Someone she knew. She was laughing and cheerful with the caller. Vanessa closed her eyes, intending to cat-nap while Kate chatted. Sometime later Kate reappeared, handing Vanessa the phone.

"Nick's on the line," she said.

37

Sir Francis Drake Hotel, San Francisco
2004

The water had grown cold, but Vanessa continued soaking in the tub, lost in her thoughts. Kate must have mentioned someone, in her rare phone calls and emails. Someone who could have known them both. Of course! Someone at the shelter! She sprang from the tub and pulled the hotel's white terrycloth robe on over her sudsy body. Still dripping, she prowled through the desk until she found the phone directory. She scanned the yellow pages. *There it was!* She dialed the hotel phone.

"Shelter from the Storm," a male voice answered.

"May I speak to the director?"

"Well," he chuckled, "you're talking to him. Kenneth Harper. How can I help you?"

"This is Vanessa Sterling. A friend of mine, Kate Remington, worked there a few years ago."

"Sure, I remember Kate. I heard she was pretty sick."

"Yes, well, she died a few weeks ago," Vanessa said.

"Oh, that's too bad," he said. "She was great with the kids. They just seemed to..."

"Mr. Harper..."

"Most people call me Kenny."

"Kenny, sorry to interrupt, but I was hoping you could help me. I was trying to find someone who knew Kate. We were good friends for many years, but the last few years we lost touch. I believe you may also know my son, Michael."

"You're Michael's mother! Wow! Did Kate and Michael get back together? She was devastated when he left."

She dropped the phone. She heard Kenny say, "Hello?"

"Yes, I'm still here," she said, picking up the phone, her voice stilted. "I was wondering if I could meet with you today."

"Well, I don't know if I can be much help. But, heck, sure, come on over."

38

San Francisco, California

Later that day, a cab pulled up to an aging two-story red-brick building on Turk Street. Once a thriving neighborhood, now most buildings stood abandoned and neglected. Drug addicts and dealers roamed the streets, causing the few remaining residents to stay behind locked doors and pulled shades.

Vanessa exited the cab. The storefront appeared vacant, except for a small sign that read 'Shelter from the Storm.' Pulling her black trench coat around her, she rang the bell, and watched the cab disappear into the afternoon fog. She glanced uneasily up and down the street, and shifted from one foot to the other until the door swung open.

Kenny, a tall, athletic man with massive shoulders and luminous dark skin, introduced himself while he ushered her in. They passed through the deserted reception area with its hand-me-down sofa and chairs into a narrow hallway. Several doors stood ajar, revealing tidy rooms with bunk beds lined up along the walls.

"It's not much," he said. "But we're able to help about eighteen kids at a time. They're on an outing; otherwise, it would be a zoo around here. This way." He motioned down the hall.

He opened the door to a brightly-lit office. One of the colorful posters on the wall read 'Hang in There.' Windows, shielded by iron bars, looked out onto the back parking lot where a lone oak stood sentinel in an otherwise desolate scene. His desk was a jumble of phone messages, files and reports.

Kenny was warm and friendly, with a ready laugh.

He offered her a seat near the desk. She pulled off her coat, letting it fall onto the chair where she sat.

"There's always more than a person can do," he said, attempting to straighten his desk. "The receptionist quit two days ago and I need two more counselors. But you didn't come to listen to my problems."

"That's all right. It's a worthwhile project," she said.

Kenny seated himself behind his desk.

"You're Michael's mother," he said, chuckling quietly. "You look more like his sister."

"Thank you," she said, hating that she blushed. "I understand from Kate and Michael…"

"So Michael was with Kate. I'm not surprised. Sorry, please go on."

"I understand she helped him."

"That's true, but not that simple," he stopped, realizing he was about to say too much.

"I'm aware of confidentiality," Vanessa said. "I'm an attorney. I assure you Michael told me he was here and went through rehab. He's gotten into some serious trouble and he needs our help. There are so many unanswered questions. Please, what happened when Michael came to the shelter?"

"That was one troubled boy. The last time I saw him, well, he was in pretty bad shape. I may regret this, but here goes. We usually don't take anyone over eighteen. But for Kate's sake I made an exception. She had been so generous with her time and money. We wouldn't have those bunk beds if it weren't for her, heck, we wouldn't be here at all. Anyway, Michael obviously needed help and that's what we do here." He stopped and turned toward a stained coffee maker resting on a small table behind him. "Could I pour you a cup?"

"No, thank you." Vanessa said. She just wanted some answers.

While he poured, his biceps bulged under his tight sweater. When he turned back, a broad smile brightened his rugged features. Had he noticed her watching?

"You were saying?" Vanessa said.

"Oh, yes. One day Kate spotted this straggly kid. How she recognized him is beyond me."

San Francisco
1997

It hadn't been easy, but Kate had convinced Michael to come with her and Kenny. They were not far from the shelter, so they walked the short distance. Once there, Kenny escorted Michael to the boy's bathroom. He followed the usual routine. Kids had to be stripped and scrubbed down to avoid infesting the shelter with all manner of pests.

Kenny helped Michael, still disoriented and groggy, into the shower, while Kate put his old clothes in the trash bin around back. Kenny noticed the telltale needle tracks, leaving no question this one was a heroin addict. His tangled hair, beyond combing, had to be shaved, which left his face looking even gaunter. His skeletal body with protruding ribs and sunken stomach, left Kenny little hope for his survival. Kenny found clean clothes from the storage closet and showed Michael to his room.

Michael lay down on the bottom bunk and Kenny drew up a chair.

"When was your last fix?" Kenny asked.

Michael peered through hollow eyes, "Whatta ya mean?"

"The jig's up," Kenny said. "I saw the needle marks. I'm not going to narc on you. Level with me. I just want to help."

"This morning, I think," Michael said, figuring he didn't have much more to lose.

"I hope you stay. The doors aren't locked. But from what I see, I think you'll be dead soon if you don't kick it." Kenny stood to leave. "It's going to be a rough few weeks. Someone will stay with you through the worst of it."

For days Michael had been delusional, then belligerent, cursing everyone and everything. He'd wanted to leave many times, but Kate talked him out of it. She rarely left his side. When he was able to keep food down, she made him eat. She bought him new clothes. He began to look like the Michael she remembered, but with an edge. Nevertheless, he began to smile a little more and, occasionally, the twinkle in his eye returned, usually when he was about to make a smart remark. His boyhood crush on Kate rekindled. She really cared about him, and that felt good.

He begrudgingly fell into the routine of attending AA meetings, lectures, and group counseling. It was a teen program, but where else could Michael go? At that time Kenny had no idea that money was not the issue that kept Michael at the shelter. Kate wanted him there.

During the time Kate volunteered at the shelter, she and Kenny had become good friends. They relied on each other on the streets, and the counseling sessions with the kids left raw nerves and reopened old wounds for both of them, so they'd meet in Kenny's office after work processing their thoughts and feelings. If she wanted Michael to stay, it was okay with Kenny.

Several months into the program at the shelter, Michael finally had had it. He was shoving his few belongings into a plastic bag when Kate walked into his room.

"I'm outta here," he said.

"Where will you go?" Kate asked.

"I don't know. Anywhere but here. I'm sick of Kenny and the other do-gooders trying to drum stuff into my head."

"I think it would be a good idea to stay a little longer," she said.

"I've stayed long enough."

"If I can't talk you out of leaving, I want you to come home with me."

Michael's heart raced. *Maybe she cares about me the way I care about her.*

"But first I have something to tell you," Kate said, sitting next to him on the lower bunk, looking down at her hands. After a moment she continued, "For the last five years I've been living with your father."

"What the fuck!" Michael yelled. His chest tightened. His eyes narrowed and burned. He gripped the bed rail. She knew where his father was? How long had *that* been going on? How could this be?

"Michael, please. I know this is a shock. But he loves you. I love you."

"Oh, yeah! Some love. You're both liars!"

"I know this is difficult. Please, come home. Let us try to make it up to you."

She pulled her cell phone from her pocket and pushed speed dial. After speaking quietly into the phone for a moment, she handed it to Michael.

"Hello, son," Nicholas said, his voice distant. "Kate tells me you're ready to come home."

39

San Francisco
2004

"Michael had nowhere else to go." Kenny stopped to take a swig of coffee.

"His father! Nicholas was in San Francisco? And Kate was with him?"

All those years ago, he'd walked out, leaving her to deal with Michael and the devastation of the divorce. Vanessa had no idea where he'd gone.

"I can see this is all news to you."

The betrayal cut deep. She felt herself stand. *Kate and Nicholas together! How could that be?*

"Thanks for your time. I'd better go."

"Yeah, sure. Are you okay?" he asked.

"I'm fine," she said, but was anything but fine.

Looking at his watch, Kenny said, "I'm leaving in a few minutes. Can I give you a lift?"

A cab would be hard to get during rush hour, and she didn't relish waiting for it in this neighborhood after dark.

"Yes, thanks."

"No problem. Just give me a minute and I'll be ready to go." With that, he disappeared into the hall, amid the clamor of returning residents.

She planted herself back in the chair. He knew more about the people in her life than she did. Kate and Nicholas and Michael. How cozy. They'd all lied to her! What had she done to deserve that?

"Ready?" he called in the door, bringing her back to the moment.

She grabbed her coat, shouldered her handbag, and followed Kenny out the back door. The cool night air refreshed her.

Kenny's 1985 Toyota looked as disorganized as his desk. "I'm used to traveling alone," he said, hurrying around to the passenger side to snatch up his briefcase overflowing with files and a red plastic cooler that sat on the floor. He threw the armload in the trunk, climbed into the driver's seat, and turned the key. The motor spurted, but turned over. They were off, hitting every pothole in the parking lot.

While Kenny drove through heavy traffic, Vanessa's curiosity grew.

"How long have you worked at the shelter?"

"About fifteen years. After I finished my PhD I wanted to make a difference. I worked on research projects and planned to write a book. Research wasn't enough. I needed hands-on experience, so I volunteered for a summer at the shelter and stayed on."

"Whatever happened to the book?"

"Well, it got published," he said, a bit of pride showing. "Several universities keep it on their 'must read' list. It's in its fifth printing."

She sat back and tried to relax as he maneuvered the hilly streets. Even though what Kenny had told her was unsettling, he was proving to be very helpful. Very helpful, indeed.

40

San Francisco, California

Trolley cars clanged along Powell Street, jam-packed with passengers heading to the Embarcadero. Union Square was alive with throngs milling about, waiting to catch the next available cable car or just to people-watch. Limos and luxury cars lined up two-deep by the hotel entrance. Kenny inched his antiquated car towards the curb.

"I'd like to buy dinner, to repay you for your help," Vanessa said.

"That's not necessary."

"Actually, I would enjoy the company," she said.

"Are you sure? This is a very expensive place."

"It's okay," she said, shoving at the car door. The bell hops seemed to be busy with the other guests. The door finally popped open, and Vanessa stepped out.

Kenny drove several blocks before finding a parking place, then hoofed it back to the hotel. Vanessa stood amid rowdy conventioneers and brightly dressed tourists who filled the lobby. He joined her there, and they headed toward the restaurant.

The maitre'd gave Kenny a look of disdain as they approached the Bistro.

"Excuse me, sir," he said, before they asked for a table. "Starting at six, we have a dress code."

Kenny looked down at his pullover and jeans. "Oh, sure. No problem."

They moved away from the dining room and stood in the lobby, contemplating what to do.

"I know a good restaurant in Chinatown," Kenny said. "It's close enough to walk."

Unfortunately, as soon as they headed toward the main entrance, people came rushing in, fleeing a sudden downpour. It looked like a walk was out.

"We could drive," Kenny offered.

"Why don't we have dinner in my suite?"

"Are you sure? You really don't know me," he said.

"I'm a fairly good judge of character," she said, smiling.

They rode the elevator to the sixteenth floor, stepping out onto the marble hallway.

"Sweet!" Kenny said, as the door to the suite swung open.

"Make yourself comfortable," Vanessa said. "What would you like for dinner? As I recall, the prime rib is excellent."

She called in their order, before stepping behind the fully stocked bar.

"Would you like a drink?"

Kenny strolled over to the wall of windows that looked out over the city.

"I'll have a beer," he said. He opened the French doors and stepped out onto the covered balcony.

"Let's sit out here," he called to her.

She slipped her coat back on and joined him. The city lights twinkled through the raindrops. A cool breeze caught Vanessa's hair as she handed him his beer. She sat opposite him at the black wrought-iron table.

"I love the rain. I guess that's good since it rains a lot here. Cheers," he said, tilting the glass toward Vanessa, then lifting it to his lips. "Sure tastes good."

They sat quietly for a moment, admiring the view of the city and the Bay Bridge.

"It rains a lot in Oregon, too," Vanessa said. "The storms are incredible. Waves break against the rocks, sending spray up a hundred feet in the air. It reminds me of fireworks. The smell of pine trees after a rain is intoxicating." She took a sip of wine. "I grew up near Chicago, so moving to a small town was quite an adjustment."

"I'd miss the city. Its diversity, the entertainment, restaurants."

The clouds parted and a full moon appeared. The temperature dropped and their breath made small clouds in the cold air as they talked.

"Have you lived in San Francisco long?" Vanessa asked.

"Yeah. I'm from LA. I moved up here to go to school and decided to stay."

"You mentioned you're used to traveling alone. You're not married?"

"That's right," he chuckled. "Came close a few times."

"A smart, good looking man like you, I thought you'd be married with a couple of kids."

"Thanks," he said, his flushed face shadowed by the night. "The timing wasn't right or the woman wasn't right. I've always wanted children. Someday, maybe."

"It sounds like you made work your life," she said.

"Yes, I guess I did," he said, sipping the dark ale.

"I did, too," she confessed. She felt comfortable with Kenny. Talk came easy. "I spent too many years trying to make partner. At my mother's funeral, I remembered how my brothers and I were shuffled off to boarding schools, so my mother could spend her time fundraising for needy children. Ironic isn't it? Without intending to, I did the same thing to Michael."

Kenny drained his glass.

"Would you like another?" Vanessa asked.

"One's usually my limit. But what the heck," he said, standing up. "I'll get it."

"I'm coming in, it's getting a little too cold for me."

As they stepped in, Kenny stood behind her. A whiff of expensive perfume hung in the air. Her auburn hair cascaded around her shoulders. His hand lingered a moment before slipping off her coat. A knock at the door startled them both.

Vanessa opened the door to a waiter with a pushcart filled with silver-domed dishes. The aroma filled the room while the waiter set the table. Vanessa went to the bar to pour a second round. Kenny started the gas fireplace. She set the drinks by their gold-rimmed plates, each filled with prime rib topped with tangy horseradish sauce and wild mushrooms with cilantro. A chocolate torte was set aside for dessert. She signed the tab, and the waiter left.

Kenny pulled her chair out before he seated himself.

"Thanks, again," he said, smiling broadly. "This sure beats takeout in front of the TV."

With the fire flickering in the background, they chatted through dinner about incidental things, sharing life's foibles.

When the conversation ebbed and the plates were empty, they moved to the sofa. The break in the action had given Vanessa time to absorb what Kenny had told her earlier. She felt ready to dive back in. There were still so many unanswered questions.

"It's really hard for me to believe Kate and Nicholas were together," she said. "But I should have suspected something when she left Chicago so abruptly and virtually cut off communication."

"Perhaps they wanted to keep their relationship a secret to protect you," Kenny said. "This must be hard for you. From the looks of that bruise on your face, you've had some hard knocks recently. If it helps any, they weren't getting along. She mentioned a few times Nicholas was difficult."

"That's putting it mildly!" she said. "What happened when Michael went to Nick's?"

"As I recall, Michael was angry, at first. But, as I said, he didn't have much choice."

41

San Francisco
1997

Michael chain-smoked all the way to his father's house to annoy Kate. Since she'd joined forces with his father to deceive him, he hated them both.

She maneuvered the sporty BMW through San Francisco's street maze, while he sank deep in thought. There was a time when Michael and his dad played football in a park near their home in Chicago. As a boy, he hadn't had the natural aptitude for sports that his father had. But, nevertheless, Nick was patient with Michael, watching him drop the ball time and again, until Michael would finally catch it. "That'a boy!" His dad yelled. "Hold on. Now charge me. Try to take me out." Michael ran, head down, ball tucked under his skinny arm. He tackled his father with all his ten-year-old might, and they tumbled onto the grass. Michael had loved his father then.

Closer to the marina, the neighborhood turned upscale. The waning sun cast long shadows off the stately oaks that lined the promenade. Lush green lawns lay captured behind ornate wrought-iron fences. Kate pulled the car up to a three-story brick townhouse. Its black enameled shutters hugged leaded-glass windows and spiral topiaries rose from burnished copper pots next to the main entrance.

Michael smirked, flicking his smoldering cigarette onto the manicured lawn. Since arriving in San Francisco, he'd lived in the gutter just a few miles away.

Kate unlocked the front door and Michael stepped into the foyer. His eyes followed the curving mahogany rail up the stairway to where his father stood.

"Welcome, Michael," Nicholas said.

Swept into the surreal moment, Michael felt as if he had a starring role in some bizarre movie, but was unsure what role to play.

His father's dark hair now fringed with gray, a hesitant smile deepened the creases in his once-smooth face. Five years had made a difference. However, he was still trim and fit, dressed in dark blue athletic wear.

Michael stood in place. Nicholas, still with a spring in his step, quickly descended the stairway, and engulfed his son in a fatherly hug. Kate and Nicholas exchanged a glance. She remained in the foyer a moment longer, watching the reunion, before turning towards the kitchen to check on dinner.

Nicholas led Michael up the stairs and directed him into the library where Josie, the maid, had left a tray of turkey sandwiches. Déjà vu. As a child, Roberta, his mother's housekeeper, made him the same turkey sandwiches each day after school. Always his favorite. Back then, he'd rush into the penthouse after a long bus ride home, the front door slamming behind him. His navy-blue tie askew, rumbled shirttails hanging out, he'd tear across the granite floor to the bathroom, his books scattering where they dropped.

Roberta would yell, "You don't live at the zoo. Don't be coming into this house like an elephant, slamming doors and throwing books. You mind your manners, you hear?"

He'd slide onto a tall kitchen stool where he'd munch on a sandwich and tell Roberta about his school day. Not his mother or father, mind you, but the maid. Roberta was more like a mother to him then Vanessa ever was. Finally they'd shipped him off to prep school, where he was conveniently tucked out of sight.

Now, Michael sat on the sofa across from his father and wondering if anything had changed. He doubted it.

"Have something to eat. We've got to fatten you up. You're too skinny,"

Nicholas said. "Josie's made up a room on the third floor. There's a private bath. You should be quite comfortable. You're welcome to stay as long as you like."

Michael reached toward the sandwiches. Ignoring the plates and napkins, he held one in his hand. He hadn't uttered a word since he'd arrived. Unsure how he felt, he let his father do the talking.

"You're probably wondering about Kate and me," Nick went on. "Well, I'll be honest. I've loved her for a long time. It's…well, it's complicated. I loved your mother, too. You need to know that. But, we grew apart. Things changed. Kate and I didn't live together until the divorce was final. She didn't want to hurt you or your mother. She loves you like a son."

Like a son! He tossed the sandwich back on the tray.

"I was wondering," Michael said, brushing crumbs off his hands. "While you and Kate were living it up, did you ever think about me? Did you give a flying fuck what happened to your only son?"

"Watch your language!" Nicholas said. "I didn't know where you were."

"I had no idea where *you* were. I would have moved in with you, if you'd given me the chance. Mom just buried herself in work, so I left."

"I can't change the past," said his father. "But I want to make it up to you now. You won't have to worry about anything. You can live here. You can even work for me if you want. For now, have fun, go out, get laid, do whatever you want. Just stay out of trouble."

42

San Francisco
2004

Vanessa expended nervous energy by clearing the dinner table, putting dishes back on the cart while she listened to Kenny.

"As time went by," Kenny said. "Kate came to the shelter less and less, until she finally stopped. She made a sizeable contribution, probably out of guilt. But she kept in touch. I guess there was no one else to confide in."

Another jab. She was near her limit, yet she felt compelled to forge ahead, to hear every detail. The pain of not knowing was far worse. To think that all those years *she'd* felt guilty, that somehow *she'd* driven *them* away. Could she ever forgive them for their deception?

"One day Kate called, she wanted to talk," Kenny said, breaking into Vanessa's thoughts. "We met for lunch."

San Francisco
1999

Two years had gone by since Michael moved into his father's house. He was spending as much time as he could with Kate; he could never stay mad at her. They visited museums, attended concerts, and sailed the bay on Nicholas's yacht, renewing the playful relationship they'd had all those years before. Nicholas continued working long hours, so Kate enjoyed the company.

Michael had been working part-time for his father for about a year, at that time. He had taken to the business and Nicholas paid him well. If he continued to gain his father's trust, he knew he'd soon be making a lot more money. He envied his father's lifestyle and wanted what he had, which included Kate. And Michael was growing impatient. He wanted Kate to know how he felt. The opportunity finally arrived when Nicholas had to be in Bermuda for a few weeks, and Kate had some family business in Chicago. She invited Michael along, and he went with his father's blessing.

The Lake House
Kenosha, Wisconsin
1999

Kate had contacted Bert, the grounds keeper, to get the house and boat ready for their visit. Bert was almost seventy-five, having stayed on after Kate inherited the house from her grandmother. His wife had died a few years before, but he still lived in the small cottage on the grounds he'd shared with Greta all those years. Where else would he have gone?

Once Kate had finished her business with the attorneys in Chicago, she and Michael drove out of the city along Lakeshore Drive in a rented Porsche, top down, hair blowing. They sped north through crowded suburbs, quaint villages, and open countryside. Elegant vacation homes, used only for a month or two each year, dotted the lake as they approached Kenosha.

A smile spread across Michael's face when they turned into the familiar drive. The stately five-bedroom, two-story, yellow clapboard house brought back fond memories of summer vacations spent there with his mother and Kate, as a child. He could picture his mother sipping lemonade on the white-railed porch that wrapped around the house, its wide stairway descending to an expansive lawn that led down to the lake. Sturdy oaks dotted the property, providing blessed shade from the humid Midwestern summers. At the end of the pier, stood the Lily I.

The vessel, purchased by her father some twenty years ago, still looked grand. He'd ordered it from a shipyard near Boston. When it was delivered, he and his wife had hurried to the lake house to get a look. It had been named for Kate's mother. They took one look at the imposing boat and were too intimated to step aboard. But Kate fell in love. She learned to sail under the tutelage of an old salt from Racine, and spent many hours exploring the waters of Lake Michigan.

That first night, Michael sank into the bed where he'd spent many childhood nights. The next day he planned to tell Kate how he felt, once they arrived at Angler's Cove. He slipped into a deep sleep, dreaming of the last sail they took on the Lily I.

43

The Lake House
1990

When the divorce became final, it further damaged the already-fractured relationship between Vanessa and Michael. Kate had invited Vanessa to visit for a month at the lake house; time to recoup from the trauma. Michael was sixteen and had insisted he was old enough to remain in Chicago. He'd told Vanessa he'd much rather stay with his city friends, but his mother insisted a month was too long to leave him alone, even with the housekeeper there.

Once at the lake house, he accepted his fate. He swam and horsed around with the neighbor kids he'd known his whole life, but what he loved best was sailing. Since Vanessa didn't like to sail, in fact she was terrified of the treasonous lake, Kate would take Michael along for company. Over the years he had become an able-bodied seaman. She'd taught him to navigate, set the jib and masts, tie sailor's knots, but she'd never let him take over at the wheel of the forty-two-foot sailboat.

As they finished breakfast one day, Kate glanced at Michael with a sly smile. "How about sailing to Angler's Cove today?"

"You bet!"

"For your sixteenth birthday, you can pilot the boat part of the way."

Michael jumped up to his newly sprouted six-foot height and pulled Kate to her feet. They danced around the dining room.

"Honestly!" Vanessa laughed. "It's like having two kids. You'd better be careful out there."

The Ketch with polished teakwood decks, fully batten main and misen, stood in stately splendor at the end of the dock. Following a hearty breakfast, and gathering needed supplies, they tramped down to the dock and climbed aboard. The vessel could hold its own in the choppy waters of Lake Michigan. The forecast called for clear and sunny skies, winds at twenty knots. Perfect.

They waved goodbye to Vanessa and set sail. Finally underway, as promised, Kate let Michael take the wheel. She strolled to the deck where she removed her T-shirt and shorts, like she always did, so she could sun in her red floral bikini. But this time it was different. This time he noticed. Michael tried not to look, but he couldn't resist admiring her voluptuous breasts. He'd hoped she wasn't aware of his stares as she bent over to secure the lines or raise a sail. He gazed longingly at the curve of her inner thigh that rose to the dark mystery that lay at her depths. He remembered how he and Tommy Thurston had studied his father's *Playboy* magazines every Saturday morning for months.

As the wind died down, Michael helped Kate lower the sails and drop anchor. She spread a towel on a deck lounge, lying stomach down. With one hand, she reached around and untied her top. Michael stretched out on the lounge next to her.

"Would you rub some oil on my back?" she asked.

As he touched her tanned skin, tracing the slender white lines left by her bikini straps, he felt a stir. He was getting hard. It was pleasant, but embarrassing. He put a towel over his lap so she wouldn't notice. When he couldn't stand it any longer, he stood and dove into the cool lake. Ever playful, Kate secured her top and jumped in after him. They took turns dunking each other, then, laughing and breathless, they hauled themselves up the swim ladder. He lay down on the deck to dry off in the sun. Kate sat next to him. The nearness of her body left him lightheaded. He closed his eyes and wished he could touch her.

When he opened his eyes, she bent close. Her blond curls framed her angelic face, her azure eyes flashed. Her ample breasts pressed against him and she kissed him fully on the mouth. She pulled away and laughed.

"You're becoming quite a man," she said.

At that moment, Michael fell in love.

44

The Lake House
1999

Michael awoke from a deep pleasurable sleep and crawled from bed. Standing at the window, he scanned the cloudless sky. The windsock down by the dock blew gently in the southerly breeze. The Lily I stood at the ready. He took a quick shower, drew on his jeans over his swimsuit and pulled on a gray crewneck sweater, before joining Kate in the breakfast room.

"Do you remember the last time we sailed here?" Kate asked, rising to get Michael's breakfast.

"How could I forget? You gave me my first real kiss."

"The kiss! I thought piloting Lily would be the big deal," she called from the kitchen. She returned with a plate piled high with blueberry pancakes covered with maple syrup. "You were just sixteen. That's usually an awkward age, but you were tall and handsome."

"I dreamt about that last night," Michael said, with a mouthful of pancakes.

He was famished. He had slowly regained the weight he'd lost during his drug years. Working out at the gym made him feel physically and mentally stronger and more self-assured. His eyes flashed now, back to his old self. He was ready. He wanted Kate more than ever and he wouldn't wait any longer. The age difference never occurred to him.

As he finished off the pancakes, Kate's hand rested on his shoulder while she refilled his cup. Michael's stomach tightened.

They packed lunch, gathered towels and extra clothes, and climbed aboard the Lily I. The boat had been in dry dock, which had taken its toll. But, for the past thirty years Bert had polished and fitted the old sloop. He assured Kate everything was ready.

The sleek craft skipped across the water, the warm sun glistened off the polished deck. The smell of lake air mingled with new varnish and, with the sun beating down, it couldn't get much better. Michael set course north to Angler's Cove.

He kept an even keel while Kate stood on the deck and removed her sweater and jeans. A black bikini clung to her trim, ageless body. She smoothed suntan lotion on her legs and arms, lay on the deck chair, and soon fell asleep. She looked so beautiful. He could have sailed on forever.

Several hours later, traveling at ten knots, they neared the cove. The gentle breeze had suddenly turned northerly, churning up threatening waves. Clouds obscured the sun, dropping the temperature. Kate woke and wrapped a towel around her chilled body.

The vessel rolled with the rough water. Michael held tight to the wheel, intent on reading the weather change and keeping on course.

Kate went to check the cabin for safety lines. They weren't there. She pulled on a sweatshirt and pants, then donned her rain-gear and life jacket. She gathered Michael's gear, climbed up to the wheel, and took over while he donned the storm gear.

"Bert didn't put the life lines back!" she shouted over the roar. "Said they needed repair. Must have forgotten." Looking north toward the darkening sky, she turned the wheel back to Michael. "I'll ready her for the storm."

Michael knew a storm over the lake had to be taken seriously. It was a huge body of water, more like an inland sea. Storms often came out of nowhere and had been known to take down large ocean-going vessels that had made their way through the St. Lawrence Sea Way from the Atlantic, on route to Great Lakes ports. The Lily I had been through some pretty good squalls, but he knew he had to be prepared for the worst.

As the skies grew darker, his prickling skin forewarned of something threatening. It took his full strength to hold the wheel steady as he tried to outrun the storm.

Kate set the storm jib and lowered the main and Genoa sail. The storm hit with wind gusts up to fifty knots blowing across the deck with such force that the old boom vang snapped. As it cracked off, the boom began flailing about. Fearing more damage, she grabbed for it. But she missed. It swung back around, catching her off balance, and, with no life lines securing her to the boat, she was knocked over the starboard side into the ten-foot crests.

She hit the choppy waters hard, but resurfaced quickly and screamed for Michael. He could barely see her through the blinding rain and huge crests. He brought the Lily I about, then swung into action. He'd watched Kate heave-to in the past, but he had to act fast. It took skill to balance the rudder and the remaining sail to prevent the boat from continuing forward. His first impulse had been to jump in and save her. If he had, they'd both be watching the boat sail off.

Michael tossed the life ring into the foam. Her vest kept her afloat, but the turbulent waves washed over her again and again. She resurfaced, gasping for air. She couldn't last much longer. She grabbed for the ring, just missing it. Exhausted, but determine to live, she swam for it.

"Grab the ring!" Michael screamed into the wind.

Battered and tossed, she made another grab. This time, she caught it. She wrapped her arms around it and held on. Michael struggled to pull her through the choppy waters back to the boat. As she neared, he laid his body flat on the deck and stretched his arms over the swim ladder. He grabbed her lifejacket and dragged her up the ladder onto the deck where they both collapsed. He rolled toward her and encircled her in his arms.

"I'd die if anything happened to you," he said.

They staggered to their feet. Too weak to make it on her own, Michael helped her below. He returned to the deck and lowered the remaining sail, then started the motor. About an hour later he maneuvered Lily into the safety of the cove. There, he anchored and joined Kate below.

She was lying on the bed, still dressed in her wet clothing, her teeth chattering. After starting a hot shower, he walked back into the tiny bedroom and sat next to her.

"I meant what I said. If you hadn't made it, I don't know what I would have done," he said, taking her hand and holding it to his pounding heart. "Kate, I love you."

Without a word, he began to undress her. He helped her to the shower. A moment later he stepped into the shower with her, where he pulled her to him. With the rain beating on the deck above, the steamy shower pelting their bodies, they made love. His young, hard body pressed against hers, throbbing and reckless. He was frantic, fearing it would end as suddenly as it had begun. He turned off the shower and wrapped a towel around her, after that he led her into the cabin. They lay on the berth, where he held her tight.

"Kate, tell me you love me. I know you love me the way I love you."

"Michael, this is so complicated."

"No! No, it's not. Just love me."

"I do, Michael. I do love you."

She buried her face in his smooth chest. They spent the night cocooned in the small cabin below deck. In the early morning hours, the storm passed. He woke her to see the light of the new moon illuminating a path on the water. He made love to her again, but this time slower, sweeter, softer. She belonged to him now.

45

San Francisco
2004

Vanessa froze, silverware in hand.

"I can't believe anything came out of a fling with Michael."

"Well…you'd be wrong. According to Kate, they had a kid."

Vanessa knocked over a glass. Scarlet-red wine flowed down the tablecloth onto the white carpet.

"That's not possible!" she said. "There has to be some mistake! You're lying!"

"Lying? Why would I lie?"

"You're in on the whole thing. They're trying to get back at me for something."

"Vanessa, stop!" Kenny said. "I have nothing to gain. You called *me*, remember? I didn't know you existed before that phone call."

She took hold of the back of a barstool, then sat down.

"You're confusing him with someone else. You've worked with so many people."

"There's no mistake," Kenny said.

"This doesn't make any sense!"

Kenny waited patiently for her to regain her composure, hovering nearby, trying to comfort her.

"Where's the child?" she finally asked.

"Last I heard, with Nicholas."

"Nicholas!" she said. "How could Michael keep this from me?"

Her resolve to help Michael was crumbling.

Kenny had broken his cardinal rule: never fraternize with family members. Even sharing a meal blurred the lines.

"I'd better go."

She put her hand on his.

"Please, don't."

He hesitated. He knew better.

"I don't know what else I can tell you," he said.

A crash of thunder shook the windows. Vanessa grabbed Kenny's arm.

"I should leave," he said, but didn't.

"I don't want to be alone," Vanessa said.

She sighed, letting her shoulders slump. They sat on the sofa staring into the fire. Soon, her eyes felt heavy. She laid her head on Kenny's shoulder. He snuggled her into the crook of his massive arm, where she nestled her cheek. Feeling safe and exhausted, she floated off to a dreamless sleep.

Sometime later she awoke in bed. Through the double doors, in the darkened living room she could see Kenny lying on the sofa. She rose from bed and tiptoed over to him. As if sensing her presence, he awoke. She took his hand and led him into the bedroom.

46

San Francisco, California

Cable cars rumbled sixteen floors below while traffic pounded the streets around Union Square. Sounds of a city rising from its slumber. The new day's crimson rays splashed across the bedroom walls and his Old Spice lingered on the pillow. Vanessa pushed the crumpled sheets aside. The night with Kenny had only momentarily eased the pain. He'd left sometime in the early hours. Now she lifted her head, feeling groggy, as she struggled to her feet, plodding to the bathroom for a shower. Just when the steamy flow began to revive her, Steven crept into her thoughts. She lingered in the hot spray, hoping to wash away the guilt.

Wearing the thick terry hotel robe, and a towel twisted around her damp hair, she was in the kitchenette making coffee when the phone rang.

"How are you this morning?" Kenny asked.

"My head's spinning," she said. "Too much wine."

"Well, you had a pretty rough day."

"Ironic. I always thought I was the one that screwed everything up. It never occurred to me that Kate and Nicholas were having an affair. Looking back…I guess I was too trusting. But Kate and Michael! That really threw me. And a child!" she said. Saying it made it seem more real. "It's too much to digest!"

"One of the things I do in my job is blow the whistle on family secrets. Most of the kids blame themselves for what went wrong with their families.

That's often why they leave home. I hope you know you're not to blame for choices your family made, but I'm sorry to have been the one to tell you. Let me make it up to you. Are you free for lunch?"

"Um…I'm not sure. I've got a lot to do today," she said.

"I wanted to see you one more time before you left town," Kenny said.

Her head throbbed. She needed to erase the last month of her life.

"Sure, okay," she said, certain it was the wrong thing to do.

"I'll pick you up by the hotel entrance at one."

She hung up. Her hand lingered on the phone. What shocked her most, of all the things Kenny told her, was the child. She pulled her laptop from its carrying case and turned it on. After entering the Internet she found the San Francisco County web site and clicked on birth records. She calculated her grandchild must be about four. Checking the year 2000, she scrolled through the records. She'd almost given up when, bingo! Madison Katherine. Born to Katherine Lynn Remington and Michael Joseph Thorne on December 24, 2000. A Christmas Eve baby.

She felt compelled to find the child. Nicholas' address was unlisted. Undaunted, she pulled up real estate tax records, starting with the year of their divorce. Nothing. Going back year by year, she finally found he'd purchased a four-bedroom townhouse in 1985. *Five years before the divorce!* She printed a map and put it in her handbag before calling the front desk for a car.

At ten-thirty that morning, she turned onto North Point Street, near the Presidio. She spotted the address and parked within view of Nicholas's house.

She sat staring at the house for several hours. *This is crazy. Would a glimpse of Madison be enough? What if Nicholas found me stalking his house? I don't need any trouble from him.* She turned the ignition key and put the car into drive. If she waited much longer, she'd be late for her date with Kenny.

At that moment, a black Lincoln town car pulled to a stop. The chauffeur got out, hurried around the car, opening the curbside passenger door. Out jumped a little girl in bright red pants and a yellow floral jacket with red and yellow ribbons tied in her long curly blond hair. She held a crayon drawing. The child skipped up to a flower that had escaped the wrought iron fence. Still clutching her drawing, she put her button nose near the petals, while the chauffeur ambled to the steps to chat with the maid.

Madison looked so much like Michael at that age. Vanessa recalled his downy soft curls that she couldn't bear to cut, until one day he was mistaken for a girl. He was in the barber's chair the next day. She had watched each ringlet hit the floor, saving one that she pressed in his baby book.

Against her better judgment, she wanted to watch until Madison went into the house. No sooner had she put the car in park a van roared up and stopped behind the Lincoln. The sliding door flew open, and a thin wiry man sprang out. The chauffeur went for his shoulder gun, but it was too late. A single shot took him down. The maid screamed. The shooter grabbed Madison and leaped back into the vehicle. The sliding door slammed shut and the van peeled off. The crayon drawing, caught by a breeze, glided down to earth.

The frantic maid screamed for help.

"No!" Vanessa yelled.

She threw the car into gear and set chase. The kidnappers turned onto Divisadero and careened through traffic. With little thought for her own safety, she followed. They traveled several miles before they made a sharp right turn onto a dead-end street. The blue van was swallowed up by an underground garage. The electric door slamming shut behind it.

She was pretty sure they hadn't seen her and parked a few doors down. Seemingly deserted houses and jacked-up cars were interspersed with small businesses along the derelict street. She'd hardly taken a breath since the nightmare began. She hunted in her purse for her cell phone, remembering just the day before she'd thrown it over the balcony at the hotel. With no pay phones in sight, and the shops closed or vacant, she had no choice but to handle things alone. She couldn't waste another minute. As she moved her purse to hide it under the seat, the weight reminded her she still had her brother's thirty-eight. She hadn't handled a gun since hunting with her father as a teen.

Slowly withdrawing the weapon, she laid it in her lap. She hardly dared to think what they could be doing to Madison. At that moment, she'd do anything to protect the child. They left her no choice. She snapped the chamber open. Three bullets. She prayed she wouldn't need them.

47

San Francisco, California

The revolver weighed heavy in her coat pocket. She tramped through the overgrown backyard of the neighboring house that had been converted into a beauty salon. Like all the other buildings on the street, it sat dark and deserted. From that vantage point, she had a good view of the house where Madison was being held. She scanned the area to make sure no one could see her, and stealthily crept behind the kidnapper's lair.

Staying low under a window, she took a deep breath and quickly looked inside. A tiny kitchen led into a narrow hallway. No one in sight. She crouched back down and made her way up the back steps. There she tried the doorknob. Finding it locked, she quickly moved back down the steps and hid in the bushes.

A few feet away, beyond the shrubbery, lay the entrance to the root cellar of the old house. Vanessa crept over to the slanted wooden doors and gave them a tug. They opened and she climbed into the cavern. She tried to close the heavy wooden doors by bending low on the ladder rungs, but she lost her grip. They slammed with a loud thud over her head. She held her breath, heart racing, for what seemed like an eternity. Finally, satisfied no one had heard, she began her descent down the steep ladder into the dark cellar.

The dank, windowless cavern smelled like rotting garbage. Slowly her vision began to adjust. A shaft of light came from beneath an interior door at the top of a stairway. Her first tentative step entangled her in a thicket of webs. She suppressed a scream and swatted them away from her face. Finally, her foot hit the bottom stair rise. When she neared the top, she heard muffled voices approaching the cellar door.

"He'll come around as soon as he knows we've got the kid. When he gets Thompson off, he'll get her back. Make sure nothing happens to her. I'll pick up some pizza. This is gonna be a long night," he said. Footsteps echoed off the wood floors.

"Hey, Bobby," the other man called out. "Get some beer."

"No, Bull! We've got a job to do. Just make sure nothing happens to the kid."

Bobby Scarpelli and Bull! Mackey's guys! They'd taken Madison to get Michael to confess to the murder!

Relieved that Madison was safe for now, Vanessa heard Bobby go out the front door, pulling it shut, and locking it with a key. Bull turned on the TV.

She slipped out of her shoes, leaving them on the top step, and opened the door a crack, peering into the hallway. Momentarily blinded by the bright sunlight streaming through the glass in the front door, she listened for the direction of the TV. She drew the pistol from her pocket and crept into the hallway where she took position behind the open door to the TV room. Through a crack of the doorjamb, she spotted Madison lying on a small cot, with duct tape crudely plastered across her mouth and eyes; it bound her wrists and ankles. *What cowards. Binding a small child, as if she were a threat.* Bull stared at the tube, his beefy back to the door. Bobby could return any minute. She might be able to handle one guy, but not two.

Vanessa adjusted her position to get a better view. She bumped the door. Bull turned, grabbing his gun from his shoulder holster.

"Who's there?" he yelled.

Vanessa stiffened against the wall.

"Lay still, you little brat!" he yelled at Madison. He returned to the TV, checking the ammo in his weapon before holstering it.

That gave her an idea. She bumped the door again, this time harder.

Bull grabbed his gun and came toward the hall. At the right moment, she shoved the heavy oak door with all her weight, catching his ungainly body off-balance. He smashed into the far wall, dropping his gun.

"What the hell!" Bull lay sprawled on the floor.

Charging from her hiding place, she kicked his gun, sending it skittering down the hall. She steadied the thirty-eight with both hands and took aim.

"Lie face down, flat on the floor!" she ordered.

Hearing Vanessa's voice, Bull rolled over and sat up. "Well, well," he smirked. "Where the hell did you come from? Your son's the killer. You'd never have the guts to pull the trigger."

"Stop right there!" Vanessa shouted. The revolver still aimed at his chest.

He worked his way up the wall. "Give me the gun!" he shouted, moving towards her.

Fearing for her life, she lowered the gun slightly and pulled the trigger. Blood sprayed from the hole ripped in his thigh. He fell back against the wall and slid to the floor.

"You god-damned bitch," he snarled, grabbing his leg. He slid along the floor, smearing blood, his outstretched hand nearing his weapon. "I'm gonna kill you!"

One more shot, aimed at his hand, missed and hit the floor.

"Stop!" she screamed. *Please stop. One bullet left.*

With a sudden lunge, he grabbed his gun and fired. The bullet grazed her left arm, just above the elbow. As a reflex, her finger squeezed the trigger. A look of astonishment froze on his face. The bullet entered between his eyes.

She collapsed against the faded wallpaper, numb and dazed.

Faint sounds, like an injured animal, made their way through the fog in her head. They grew louder until she realized it was Madison, still lying on the cot, her tiny face encased in duct tape. Panic gripped Vanessa. Bobby would be back any minute. She tried to sit up. The sudden movement shot a pain through her arm. She looked down. There was surprisingly little blood.

Madison was gagging. Vanessa made her way to the child and gingerly peeled off the tape, leaving her tender skin red and raw.

"You're okay now, little one," Vanessa whispered, taking her up in her arm, moving as quickly as she could to the back door. The locked deadbolt needed a key.

The setting sun left the house in shadow. *How long had she been there?* As she hurried toward the front door Bobby appeared, his outline visible through the sheer curtains stretched over the window in the door. The sound of the lock cylinders tumbled. She pulled Madison through the open cellar door and closed it behind them.

Madison cried out, "It's dark!"

Vanessa put her hand over the child's mouth. "Quiet," she whispered.

Bobby entered the house, greeted by his pal's blood-splattered body sprawled in the dark corridor. His dropped packages scattered.

He ran to the empty cot. "Shit!"

The night had stolen any trace of light. Vanessa steered Madison down the steep steps into the black abyss. Hitting the damp earth, she realized she'd left her shoes on the top step. It was too late to go back for them. Gripping Madison's hand, she stumbled across the uneven earth floor and fell into the far wall. Madison whimpered. But Vanessa couldn't stop. She felt along the wall until she found the ladder and hoisted the child up. The heavy wooden doors had been easier to open from the outside. She gave a shove. Once again, pain shot up her arm. The door gave way. Fresh air hit her face. She pulled Madison out, grabbed her tiny wrist, and ran.

Bobby hurried through the door to the cellar and pulled the string to a bare bulb suspended from the ceiling above the steps. Its swaying glow illuminated the cellar. As he stepped forward, he tripped over a pair of black suede shoes that rested on the top step, sending him tumbling down half a dozen steps before he grabbed the rail and righted himself. The cellar doors stood open. He ran down the remaining steps and up the ladder and peered out. The starless night covered the fleeing twosome.

Nearing the car, Vanessa pulled the keys from her pocket and opened the door. She helped Madison into the back seat and started the ignition. With headlights off, she sped past the house.

Whoever killed Bull and saved the kid would be back. Bobby scrambled for the front door, past the still blaring TV. He stopped dead and stared at the screen. An Amber Alert had been put out for Madison.

"One of the vehicles involved in the Thorne kidnapping," the reporter said, "has been spotted by a police helicopter. They're closing in on the area now."

"Fuck!"

He ran for the garage.

48

San Francisco, California

Half a dozen patrol cars turned the corner off Divisadero as Vanessa lurched toward the corner. She lay on her horn and blinked her lights, then pulled her car to a stop. The patrol cars fanned out and slammed on their brakes, blocking the street. Their emergency lights flashed; glaring searchlights fixed on Vanessa's car. Police jumped from their cruisers then ducked behind the open doors using them as shields.

"Get out of your vehicle with your hands up!" the sergeant yelled into a bullhorn.

Vanessa emerged. Hair disheveled, mascara-smeared eyes, and bare foot, she squinted in the glare of the lights.

"On the ground!" Someone shouted.

"You don't understand!" Vanessa said.

"You have one second to comply!" She heard the sound of guns at the ready.

Vanessa knelt, her hands raised in the air. "Please, don't shoot! I have my granddaughter in the car!"

"Lady, your second is up!"

Vanessa lay face down in the street, enduring the humiliation, as two officers ran to her. One bent next to her, yanked her hands behind her and slapped on the handcuffs. She screamed out in pain. The officers each grabbed an arm and hauled her to her feet. The sergeant leaned her against the patrol car and frisked her body for weapons. Two more officers approached Vanessa's car, guns drawn. Madison was hiding on the back floor. The officers made sure no one else was in the car before helping the frightened child out. Once she was seated in a patrol car, an officer tried to comfort the child.

"Please, listen!" Vanessa said. "He's still there!"

"Who? Where?"

"The kidnapper. The green house, down the street. He's going to get away!" Vanessa said.

The sergeant ordered the rest of the officers to surround the house.

"Thorne's maid gave us a description of your car. Why were you parked near the victim's house this morning and sped off after the kidnapping?" demanded the sergeant.

"I know how it looks. My ID's in my purse. I'm an attorney. My name is Vanessa Sterling, I'm Nicholas Thorne's ex-wife and Madison's grandmother." She struggled with the handcuffs, trying to stop her shoulder from throbbing. "I just learned today where my granddaughter lived. I only wanted to see her. I would never hurt her. I just risked my life to save her!"

An officer handed her purse to the sergeant who found her driver's license and ABA card in her wallet. The sergeant had a patrolman radio headquarters to verify her story. Once her identity was confirmed, he unlocked the handcuffs.

"Okay, tell me what happened," said the sergeant.

Scarpelli spotted the cop cars at the end of the street. Frantically, he climbed into the van, threw it in reverse, and floored it out of the garage, only to screech to a stop. He slammed his palm against the steering wheel. "Damn!" Squad cars blocked the driveway and officers squatted low, taking aim.

"Get out of the vehicle!" an officer called.

"Put your hands in the air!" yelled another.

Bobby Scarpelli leaped from the van, gun in hand. He never got off a shot.

The street exploded. Police and media helicopters, from overhead, swept searchlights, while television crews descended on the neighborhood. Paramedics loaded two body bags into a waiting ambulance, to be transported to the morgue. Reporters swarmed the patrol cars, searching for the story, curious about who was in custody. Dozens of cameras flashed, blinding Vanessa. She pulled Madison close to her, putting her coat around the child. A detective hurried over to block the reporters' view. In doing so he noted blood covering Vanessa's shoulder. Unsure who was hurt or the extend of the injury, he fired off an order, "Get these two to the hospital."

49

San Francisco, California

Under sedation, Vanessa could barely lift her head as they wheeled her into the emergency room on a gurney alongside Madison. As they came through the door, Nicholas, rushed toward Madison.

"Papa! Papa!" Madison cried out.

He bent low. She threw her arms around his neck and buried her face in his neck.

Looking at Vanessa, he said, "Where the hell did you come from?"

Before Vanessa could reply, Madison was wheeled down the hall, Nicholas following close behind.

Later that night, Vanessa awoke in a hospital bed. Kenny sat in the chair next to her bed.

"Pretty good excuse for standing me up," he said, when he noticed her eyes open. He brushed her damp hair off her face.

"How did you find me?"

"Are you kidding? You're famous. The story's all over the news."

"I shot a man," she said, tears burning her eyes.

He took her hand. "I know. You risked your life to save your grandchild. I think that makes you a heroine."

"How is she? I need to get out of here!" she said, ringing the nurses' station.

The nurse entered the room.

"I want to see my granddaughter!" Vanessa demanded.

"She went home with her father," the nurse said.

"Her father? You mean her grandfather," Vanessa replied.

The nurse looked confused. "Well, I'm pretty sure he was her father."

"Where are my clothes?" Vanessa looked around the room.

"Please, Ms. Sterling, the doctor hasn't discharged you," the nurse said.

"I'm not hurt…that bad," she said, wincing as she sat up, her shoulder rapped in bandages. "Give me my clothes."

Still wobbly from medication, Vanessa slipped out of the hospital gown and into her muddy, bloodied clothes.

"Vanessa, are you sure about this?" Kenny asked. Seeing her determination added, "The press is all over the place. Follow me, there's a back exit."

Driving Vanessa to the hotel, Kenny said, "I was listening to the radio while I waited for you at the hotel. What the heck happened?"

"I just wanted to see Madison. But it turned into a nightmare. I was outside Nicholas's house. Before I knew what happened, these guys pulled up. They grabbed Madison and took off. The rest was pure reflex. I couldn't let anything happen to her," she said. "I can't believe I shot the guy. I used to target practice at my grandfather's farm. One day when my father took me hunting, I shot a duck. I was heartsick for weeks after that. I hadn't held a gun since… until today."

He brought her hand to his lips. "I'm glad you're okay."

Vanessa could hardly wait to get into the shower.

She didn't pause on the way to the en suite. "Make yourself at home," she called over her shoulder.

About half an hour later she returned to the living room, the terry robe wrapped around her, wet hair cascading to her shoulders, a faux smile brightening her otherwise tense features. Kenny was focused on the network news updating viewers about the kidnapping.

"I almost feel human again," she said.

She helped herself to a glass of wine.

"Hey, go easy on that," Kenny said. "It doesn't mix well with whatever they gave you at the hospital."

"I'm fine. One glass won't hurt," she said, turning her attention to the TV.

Channel after channel reported on Madison's dramatic rescue. Photos of them, along with file photos of Bull and Scarpelli from previous arrests, flashed onto the screen. Kenny surfed the stations, until Vanessa caught a glimpse of Max Thompson.

"Go back!" she said.

"What?"

"The last channel. Wait! Go back!"

He punched the remote. They caught the reporter mid-sentence "... the daring daylight murder of Max Thompson. The shooting took place this morning, at the county jail. Thompson was being escorted to court for the third day of his trial for the murder of Rhio Diego. Both Diego and Thompson were reportedly former henchmen for the notorious Falcon."

The scene cut to the burly William Rowan, Assistant DA, looking uneasy in his role as spokesperson. "With Thompson dead, the Diego case is closed. We'll be following up on the murder of Thompson, but at this time we do not have any leads."

"I've got to go home!" Vanessa said, hurrying off to the bedroom.

"Why? Because some guy got killed?"

Vanessa didn't respond.

"What does he have to do with you?" he persisted, following her into the bedroom.

"I don't want you involved."

"Involved? I'm already involved. I took a risk telling you what you wanted to know. Now you need to tell me what's going on?"

Vanessa pulled her suitcase from the closet and proceeded to throw her clothes into it. She picked up the soiled outfit she'd worn back to the hotel and tossed it into the waste basket.

"Michael's involved," she said, heading back to the bar. This time for a scotch.

50

San Francisco, California

The next morning Kenny came through the bedroom door, balancing a coffee cup, cream and sugar on a tray.

"How's your head?" he asked.

"Ohhh!" she groaned. With great effort, she tried to lift her head off the pillow.

"I warned you, sedatives and alcohol don't mix. You passed out on the sofa. I carried you in here," he said. "I'd lay off that stuff, if I were you."

After setting the coffee on the night stand, he sat on the edge of the bed, leaned toward her and gave her a kiss. She stiffened and did not return the kiss. The other night she'd needed to be held. Now, her nerves were raw.

"Please try to understand," Vanessa said. "I'm sorry. I shouldn't have gotten you involved in this."

"Sure. Of course," he said eyes downcast.

Had he figured out she'd used him to get through a tough time? Judging by his eyes, she knew the answer.

Kenny was in the shower. Vanessa lounged on the sofa scanning *USA Today*, downing the remainder of the coffee, when the phone rang. It was Steven.

"I've been trying your cell for days. I didn't know where you were until I saw the news. The hotel wouldn't put me through until I threatened a law suit," he said. "Are you all right?"

Only five days since she'd arrived in San Francisco, but it felt like she'd been away for a very long time.

"I…I'm fine," she said

"You don't sound fine."

"I'll be okay, as soon as I get home. I'm leaving this morning," she said, trying to steady her voice.

"I'll meet you at the airport. Let me know what time your plane gets in."

The shower shut off. "I'll call you later," she said.

"I miss you," Steven said.

"I miss you, too." And she meant it. She hung up just as Kenny entered the room.

"I understand how you feel," he said. "I don't want to take anything for granted. But since you've had such a difficult few days, I've decided to pamper you today. What would you like to do?" Kenny asked toweling off his hair, another towel secured around his waist.

"I have to give my statement to the police. That will probably take most of the day," she said, unable to meet his eyes. "After that I'll be leaving as soon as I can get a flight."

51

San Francisco, California

The wind shifted, sending the morning fog back out to sea. Vanessa loosened the gray cashmere scarf from around her neck and plodded up the cracked cement steps into the bustling lobby of the Van Ness police station. She approached the harried desk sergeant; holding the card given to her by the detective the night before. The sergeant glanced at the card, took her name and case number, and directed her to a seat on the bench along the far wall. The only vacant spot was next to a tough-looking prostitute whose black spandex miniskirt barely covered the essentials.

"Got a smoke?" the woman asked.

Vanessa gave a weary smile and shook her head.

She'd been in police stations too many times to count, but now she was the one to be questioned. She preferred the role of attorney. Being on the opposite side of the process left her uneasy, somehow she felt as if she'd done something wrong. For what must have been a long while, she was lost in her thoughts.

The middle-aged, balding detective from the previous night, wearing the same ill-fitting suit, shouted her name over the din, jolting her back to reality. She followed him up the narrow steps into a cramped interview room.

"Ms. Sterling, I don't think I introduced myself last night. I'm

Detective Carl Polinski. I have to testify this morning, so we don't have much time. Let's get to it."

He pushed the button on a well-used tape recorder. "Case J-four-eight-nine-two-zero, Madison Katherine Thorne kidnapping, February twenty-five, two thousand four. Please state your full name and home address, followed by your description of the events that took place February twenty-four, two thousand four."

The strange conversation with Dean Stanton still haunted her. If Falcon could get to the District Attorney of San Francisco, he could get to anyone. Who could she confide in? How much did she dare say?

She related the saga detail by detail, omitting the fact she knew Scarpelli and Bull. Initially, she did so to protect Michael, but now, more to protect herself. If she told the detective about Michael's involvement with these men, he could construe a motive for her shooting Bull. He'd connect the dots, and maybe come to the wrong conclusion, never understanding she had simply been in the right place at the wrong time. All detectives were curious by nature and profession.

She'd finished her statement, but Detective Polinski wasn't through with her just yet. He left the recorder on as he leafed through his notes. Vanessa froze. The phone rang. He raised his hand to signal her to wait, turned off the recorder, and answered, all in one continuous motion.

He listened intently, before saying, "I can't do anything about that now."

Replacing the phone, he grumbled, "They want me in three places at once." He looked at his watch and pushed the record button.

"According to Thorne, he's the father of Madison Thorne. Which by any account, does not make you her grandmother. In fact, you're not related at all. So what were you doing at his residence yesterday morning?"

"Madison's birth record states that my son, Michael Thorne, is the father. I just wanted to see her."

"You admitted you shot one of the perps," he said, referring to his notes again. "A Roland Aguilera, aka "Bull." I couldn't find a registration for the gun."

She had a concealed weapon without a license. She couldn't lie about that. "I visited my brother in Oakland the day before. Someone broke into his house. I was frightened, so I borrowed his gun. I had no intention of using it."

All Polinski had to do was get a copy of that police report and he'd be full of questions. She was sinking deeper and deeper.

"Your brother's gun, huh?" he said and scribbled something down. "The investigation showed you fired three shots."

"He shot me in the arm and was ready to fire again. It was obvious he meant to kill me." she said.

The phone interrupted again. When Polinski hung up, he said, "They need me in court. I've gotta go. Thanks for coming in. I've got your number. I'll be in touch."

"I'm returning to Oregon," Vanessa said. She hated loose ends.

"I'll be in touch," Detective Polinski repeated.

52

Portland, Oregon
2004

Her flight touched down on the PDX tarmac, that afternoon. Once it was secured at the gate, she hurried off the plane. Steven waited, holding a bouquet of yellow roses. He beamed when he saw her run to him.

Holding her in his arms, he whispered, "Sorry, I've been so stupid."

They were finally settled into Steven's SUV, traveling southwest on Interstate 205, before she began to relate the chain of events in San Francisco. The load was too heavy to carry alone. The long ride home, through Portland, into the countryside, past dilapidated barns and ghostly sawmills, was a good time to tell him the whole story.

He'd listened without interruption, but when she stopped for a breather, he couldn't contain himself.

"You could have been killed!" he said.

"I know!" she said. "I just made a bigger mess of things."

"Michael's responsible for that mess!" Steven said. "And he had years to create it. How could you clean it up in a few days? Even if he didn't kill the guy."

"What!? You think... *my* son could kill someone?"

"I don't know," he snapped back. "But I do know he didn't contact you for years. And during those years he got involved with some dangerous people. You learned firsthand just how dangerous they could be." He released a deep sigh. "Face it, Vanessa, you don't know him anymore."

His words stung. *But, he was right. She didn't know who Michael had become.*

They drove in silence through the coastal mountains. Mounds of frozen snow banked the roadside. She was mad, but she wasn't ready to admit that. Steven drove along the coast to Depoe Bay. Just a mile south of the town was the home she longed for.

Gravel crunched beneath the tires as Steven navigated the narrow driveway. Vanessa stepped from the car and drew in a breath of the pungent pine trees mixed with salt air. Along the path, daffodils broke through the wet earth; a sign of pending spring. Gulls squawked overhead, welcoming her home.

Steven pulled her bags from the SUV while Vanessa unlocked the front door. He set the bags down in the entryway and took her in his arms.

"I don't want to argue. My main goal in life from now on is to keep you safe."

Vanessa wanted to change the mood. She stepped away from him, not wanting to deal with anything else tonight. She opened the bag that held the sandwiches they'd pick up on their way through town.

"Let's eat," she said.

"I'll start a fire," he said.

She kicked off her shoes and drew her feet up under her, settling onto the sofa. As they ate, the blazing fire warmed the cottage.

The last morsel finished, she cleared up the wrappers and threw them into the fire.

"I'd better check my messages," she said. Steven was already half-asleep on the sofa. "I didn't even think to check while I was away."

She hit the play button and Michael's voice echoed through the kitchen. "Mom! Call me as soon as you get back."

She held her breath while dialing his number. She didn't think she could take much more.

"You've been all over the news. I didn't know how to get in touch with you. I talked to Dad. Madison's shaken up, but she's all right. I can't believe you shot Bull! And Bobby and Thompson are dead, too!" His words tumbling over each other.

"The whole thing was a nightmare," she said.

"I've got to talk to you."

"Can it wait until tomorrow," she said. "I'm so tired I can hardly think. When I told Steven what happened he..."

"What!?" he said. "We need to talk. Alone."

She hung up, less impressed with his needs than she had been the week before.

After putting the teapot on, she returned to the living room. Steven stirred.

"Why don't you rest and I'll come back later and take you out for dinner," he said.

"I'm drained. I'm going to soak in the tub and go straight to bed."

"Okay," Steven said. "I guess I'd better go."

"I missed you," she said, snuggling up to him. "I hope you understand. This has been a traumatic week."

He'd already driven off, before she remembered she never told him about the strange behavior of the San Francisco DA.

53

Newport, Oregon

Michael slammed down the phone and smacked his fist into the Formica countertop. He'd been relieved that Thompson, Bull, and Scarpelli were dead, leaving only Mackey to deal with. But his mother blabbing to her boyfriend complicated things. He'd handle that later.

Living on the streets had taught him a few things. You couldn't make it in this world without fighting your way through. He was ready to return to San Francisco and take care of unfinished business.

After throwing away the unfinished sandwich, he drew on his jeans and buttoned his uniform shirt. *I won't be wearing this much longer.*

Working the night shift was the worst. Old biddies wanted their oil checked, and out-of-state tourists wanted to pump their own gas. The thought of seeing Jenny later that evening, kept him going. Once he finished work he jogged toward the Nye Beach Café, as he had been doing most every night since they met. He was comfortable with her; as if he had Kate back.

That night, he entered the tiny café to find her on her usual perch, the tall stool behind the counter, reading a book on herb gardens. He felt a rush from her smile.

She hopped down and began to fix his double espresso. The machine steamed and hissed. He watched her graceful body, fluid and assured. When she turned to hand him the cup, he admired her pierced navel peeking through the gap between her orange T-shirt and low-slung jeans.

He strolled over to a table and sat down.

"Not too busy tonight," he said.

"Uh huh."

"Why don't you come over here and keep me company."

She refilled her cup and joined him at his table.

"How's work?" she asked.

"Work sucks. I'm used to more excitement," he said, tilting his chair back on two legs. "I don't know how much longer I'll hang around this town."

"Where will you go?" Jenny asked, running her finger around the rim of her cup and licked off the froth.

"Back to San Francisco. Have you ever been there?"

"No. I haven't been too many places," she said, tucking a runaway curl behind her multiple-pierced ear. "I've been to Portland. When I was a kid, I used to go to my grandmother's in Sacramento every summer. I don't remember much, except they had walnut groves. When I was married I lived in Eugene."

"You'd love San Francisco," he said. "It's really cool. I made a lot of money there."

"What did you do?" she asked.

"I worked for my dad," he said. "Maybe we could go for a weekend sometime." He watched for her reaction.

"Really? I would love to! I'm sure I could get some time off."

"Okay. We'll go real soon…" He stopped mid-sentence. Wade Mackey had just wandered through the door.

Jenny stood up and slipped behind the counter.

"What can I get for you?" she asked.

Spotting Michael, Mackey ignored the question. He wasn't about to let this opportunity pass.

"Hey, Mike. Mackey's back in town," he said, holding his arms out like he was about to belt out a tune. "I've got some unfinished business with you, buddy boy."

Michael shrugged, "You're down a few comrades. Do you think you can handle me?"

"You asshole!" Mackey hissed.

His eyes darted to Jenny. She listened intently.

"I'll see you later!" he said and stormed out.

"What a creep," Jenny said, rejoining Michael at the table. "Does he live around here?"

"Yeah, right up the street."

"Lucky us."

"I'd better go," Michael said. He gave her a peck on the forehead and took out a crumpled five-dollar bill, leaving it on the table.

"You still tip too much," she said, reaching for the bill. "Remember, you promised to take me to San Francisco."

"Oh, yeah," Michael said, his thoughts already on other things. "You can count on me."

He hurried from Rosie's Café, his words to Jenny resounding in his ears. He'd made that promise before...

54

San Francisco
2000

Michael had grown tired of sneaking around behind his father's back. It had been several months since he and Kate returned from the lake house, and he longed to have her all to himself. Why did she keep putting him off? He'd begged her many times to leave with him. Finally, one night, they'd argued, and he'd walked out.

He drove through the city for hours, trying to calm the anger and hurt. Her reluctance to leave his father bewildered him. After all, if she really loved him, she'd want to be with him as much as he wanted to be with her.

Needing time to cool off, he checked into a downtown hotel. He wasn't about to go back to his father's house and continue the charade.

Alone in the hotel room he paced the floor, fighting off a growing urge to use. He'd been clean for over two years: this was the first real test of his sobriety. And he was failing. The TV didn't help. *I could get a drink. Alcohol's never been a problem.*

He stepped out onto the street into the bitter cold night, huddling next to the building to light a cigarette. He took a deep drag and slowly exhaled. A flickering red neon sign across the street caught his attention. 'Boulevard Bar.' Ignoring his gut, and with the wind at his back, he moved toward his destination. Toward his downfall. The lure as intense as a seductive woman.

In defiance of the smoking ban, a thick blue haze engulfed him as he entered the lounge. Tired black leather booths were jammed full with patrons. Rock music wailed from a crackling PA system. He strolled over to the bar and straddled a stool.

Michael had downed a few boilermakers when a slender, pocked-marked man in faded jeans and well-worn boots sauntered over and took the stool next to him.

The man ordered bourbon, straight, and gulped it down. He ordered another and looked around. Noticing Michael, he offered his hand.

"Name's Dan," he said, grasping Michael's hand.

With the camaraderie of two lonely souls, they struck up a conversation, shouting over the music, and hoisting a few too many. Tiring of the meaningless chatter, Dan leaned close.

"Say, are ya interested in something a little more exciting?"

Thoughts of Kate vanished, along with his sobriety.

"Whatcha got?" Michael asked.

"Mexican black," Dan said.

"Sweet."

Michael followed Dan into the howling night, both of them stumbled and weaved the few blocks to the boarding house where Dan lived. Michael followed his new found friend up a flight of stairs and down a dimly lit, debris filled hallway. There was barely enough room for the small dresser and unmade bed, that occupied the sparsely furnished room. With trembling hands, Michael made his purchase, then sat cross-legged on the mattress, anticipating the set-up. Dan handed him a clean needle and a cooker the size of a liter bottle cap, with a bit of wire rapped around it for a handle. Michael cut off a small piece of the black tar with his pen knife and put it in the cooker, pocketing the remainder. Dan tossed him a butane lighter which Michael flicked on, held under the cooker, and watched the smack liquefy. Smelling the familiar odor, his excitement grew.

"I'm gonna get messed up," Michael said, grinning. He drew the liquid into the syringe and sank it into his vein, laid back on the yellowed pillow, and waited.

"There's my old friend." The heroin kicked in. "Just like the first time."

He woke the next morning back in his own hotel room, his head heavy and groggy. *What the hell did I do?* He searched his pockets. The heroin was gone, and so was his wallet with the thousand dollars he'd been carrying. He considered himself lucky to be alive.

It had been so easy to backslide. Dan, like all the other low-life creeps Michael had met, would stab you in the back for a fix. With unparalleled clarity, he knew at that moment he could never go back to using. In that one night he'd proved how fragile life was. Kate meant too much to him to throw it all away. In his using days, he'd convinced himself he wasn't hurting anyone but himself. Now, he knew better. It affected everyone he loved.

He knew Kate would never take him back messed up. He slipped out of the hotel, unable to pay his bill, and drove a familiar route. Hung-over and deflated, he raised a trembling hand and rang the bell.

When Kenny answered the door, he wasn't surprised to see Michael standing there. Nor would he have been surprised if any other kid who'd gone through the program returned. Relapse was nothing new.

Uttering the hardest words an addict can say, Michael said, "I need help."

55

San Francisco
2000

A few days later, thanks to Kenny's connections and Michael's bulging savings account from the ample salary his father paid him, he admitted himself to Rising Sun Treatment Center, in Tempe, Arizona. Every day was crammed full of classes and therapy. It was tough, but he followed the twelve-step program, determined to make it work. He had everything to lose if he didn't.

He'd put off contacting Kate, fearing rejection. Since he talked about her endlessly in group sessions, he'd finally worked up the courage to call. All he could think about was being with her and what a jerk he'd been for leaving.

Predictably, she was still with his father.

"I'm okay. But I screwed up," he said.

"Where are you?" she asked.

"In a treatment program. I relapsed."

"I need you here," she said.

"What? You need me? Then why are you still with my father?"

"It's not easy to leave your father. He could make things very difficult for both of us," she said. "If I crossed that bridge and you weren't ready for a serious relationship, then where would I be?"

"I'll never leave you again. Please, tell me you want me back," he said.

"I need to tell you something first," she said quietly. "I'm pregnant."

"Pregnant?" he asked in disbelief.

"Yes."

"Kate, is it mine?"

"Yes."

He didn't have the nerve to ask how she knew.

"I've never stopped loving you," Michael said.

"You love me?" she snapped. "Then grow up! What am I supposed to do while you're in drug rehab and I'm getting bigger by the day? I need someone I can depend on."

"You can. Please, Kate. I can't leave now. I've got to do this right," he said. "Listen to me. Get out right now. Tell him to get lost. You don't owe him a thing. Find a place where we can be together. I love you so much it hurts. I'll be home soon and we'll get married."

"For real, Michael? Can you really be the man I need?" Kate whispered.

"You can count on me."

Kate wrote Nicholas a note to avoid an ugly scene. He'd never believe the child was not his. She had seen the rage in him that festered just below the surface. She remembered all too well the night she'd told Nicholas she was going to volunteer at the shelter. After that, he'd changed. She'd never been afraid of him until then. So tonight, while the servants were busy elsewhere in the house, she placed the note on his desk, picked up the small bag she'd packed, and left.

Kate stayed in a hotel until she found just the right house. Tapping into her inheritance, she bought a spacious Victorian overlooking the bay. For the first time in her life she had a home she'd chosen herself. She relished every purchase, making it her own, their own. She would soon have the family she'd always dreamt about. Sitting in the white-painted rocking chair in the baby's nursery, she surveyed the charming room she'd created for their child. An antique crib with seahorse and starfish quilt. Shelves that were filled with teddy bears and toys spanned one wall. She placed a hand on her bulging stomach, a reminder it was all true. She was content to wait for Michael, certain this time she'd find happiness.

After Nick divorced Vanessa and sent for her, Kate had thought her dreams had come true. She'd held Vanessa's hand just long enough to play the supportive friend, before flying off to join Nicholas. All the years she'd waited for him, only to find out what Vanessa had complained about was true.

All the men in her life had disappointed her, including her father...

Chicago, Illinois
1956

Raymond Stanley Remington had been obsessed with making money. He was the first to pull out of the poverty his ancestors had been mired in for generations. By the time Kate was born, he'd made and lost several fortunes. But he was on the verge of making his largest fortune yet. He convinced investors to fund high-rise apartments to be built along Lake Michigan in downtown Chicago. At first, people thought he was crazy. They gossiped about 'Remington's Folly.' Who would move to the squalid downtown and spend thousands of dollars to live in an apartment? But the idea caught on, and he couldn't build them fast enough.

Remington's obsession left him little time for his family. He was rarely home and when he was he isolated himself in his study, coming out only for a late supper with his wife, Lily. Kate longed for her father's attention. Sometimes she'd sneak into his study and sit by his desk listening to him talk on the phone or dictate into his tape recorder. When he'd discover her, he'd call for the nanny.

For a long time Kate was their only child.

With Remington occupied elsewhere, Lily doted on her daughter. Kate never wanted for anything. Lily spent her husband's fortune as fast as he made it, on everything from designer clothing and jewelry, to the finest furnishings and addresses. They'd moved to larger and larger homes until they purchased a ten-thousand square-foot mansion in affluent Winnetka, Illinois, in 1966. That same year, Remington bought his mother a house on the shores of Lake Michigan in Kenosha, Wisconsin, about seventy-five miles north of Chicago. Tycoons and socialites summered in the resort town and yachted on the choppy lake. That house became Kate's sanctuary throughout her life. As a child, she treasured her visits there with her beloved grandmother.

Her mother sought inclusion into the social life of upscale Winnetka, so she emulated the other families by sending Kate off to boarding school. Bridgeview Academy, only fifty miles from home, was the finest private girls' school in Illinois.

As Kate watched her mother drive away that first day, she felt abandoned. Those feelings were compounded when she tested at genius-level IQ, and the head mistress placed her two years ahead of her class. She'd never been on her own and having to compete with children two years older than herself was overwhelming. As an outsider, it was difficult for her to connect with the other girls. When Kate met Vanessa, they became fast friends. Vanessa opened doors for Kate, helping her fit in.

Kate and Vanessa became inseparable. It only followed that on school breaks they'd want to sleep over at each other's homes. At first, Vanessa's mother would have none of it. The Sterling family had a history, old money. Her great-grandfather had emigrated from England in the mid 1800's and begun the family fortune in industry. Those millions had been multiplied many times over when her grandfather invested in foreclosure properties following the 1929 market crash. He started the law firm Vanessa's father eventually inherited and where Vanessa cut her litigation teeth.

"Who is she?" Mrs. Sterling had inquired. "I've never heard of the Raymond Remington."

"Mother, she's at Bridgeview. That has to count for something. She's my best friend. Please!"

Vanessa had prevailed, and Kate became a frequent guest.

In addition to her exceptional mind, Kate's body had matured early. When she was only thirteen, it burst forth with a glory most women envied. This fact was not lost on Vanessa's oldest brother, Mark, then seventeen. He'd watch Kate when she and Vanessa swam in the pool or sunned on the deck in their daring two-piece bathing suits. He'd finally seduced Kate the summer she turned fourteen. They were together every time he could arrange it, until he left for college a year later. When he'd return during breaks, they would resume their tryst. Mark told Kate he loved her, and she imagined the day they'd be married.

During Mark's second year at college he returned home at Thanksgiving with Evelyn Hayes-Lockhart, heiress to the Milton Andrew Lockhart fortune. Her father was a Texas oil baron, and her mother came from the Emmett Hayes family who had made a fortune in Electronics. The Sterling family was ecstatic. Kate was devastated.

She'd never confided in Vanessa about Mark so she suffered in silence, making sure she was never in the same room with Mark again.

When Vanessa went to Illinois State, Kate attended the more prestigious University of Chicago. It came with a big price tag that suited her mother just fine. Kate handled the disappointment of losing her first love the only way she knew how, by filling her life with men.

With her beauty, deceptively sweet disposition, and curvaceous body, Kate had many admirers. She sailed through her courses with a four-point average, all the while keeping a very active social life. It was during this time she met Nicholas. He'd joined Vanessa on a trip to the lake house. Kate and Nicholas flirted and teased from the beginning, while naive Vanessa was pleased her friends got along. They had managed to get together that first night.

When Kate finished school her parents expected her to have a career and to marry well, since Kate had introduced them to several acceptable young men. Instead, she spent months at the lake house, traveled to Paris for the latest fashions, visited friends in Tuscany, and sunned topless on the beaches in Cannes.

At some point, Kate discovered she'd fallen in love with Nicholas's rough edges, bold behavior, and insatiable appetite for sex. None of the other men she knew could measure up. After that, her life revolved around him. When Nick began to travel on business, she'd join him, telling Vanessa she was off to another far-flung destination. There, Kate and Nick were free to be seen together, stay in the best hotels, and make love all night. She'd convinced herself that her life was just as she wanted it. Other times, when Nicholas would leave and not tell her where he was going, she suspected there were other women, but had no reason to be possessive. After all, she was the other woman, too.

Kate was only nineteen when Vanessa had Michael. She loved him as if he were her own. She took him to Paris for his thirteenth birthday. During summer vacations, she and Nicholas would sail the Lily I, often taking Michael along.

Vanessa loved Kate like a sister and was pleased that her husband and son loved her as well. Meanwhile, Kate had convinced herself that as long as Vanessa didn't know about her and Nicholas, no one got hurt.

56

San Francisco
2000

Shortly before Michael finished treatment, Kate saw a specialist. She'd been having intense headaches. She thought it was just the pregnancy, but her obstetrician wanted her to see a neurologist. The diagnosis was devastating. A brain tumor. Kate was worried about Michael, but most of all, she worried about the baby and refused to take the medication that would have reduced the tumor's size.

At last, Michael returned. He was overjoyed to see her, but the joy soon waned. Kate wasn't herself. Her energy was low. She was pale and drawn, distant.

"It's just the pregnancy," she said. "I'm a little old to be a first-time mother. I'll be fine. Don't worry."

He wanted to believe her. They married in a small private ceremony and waited for the birth of their child.

Madison arrived on Christmas Eve, healthy and beautiful. Michael and Kate were ecstatic. They couldn't think of a better present.

Over the next few years, Michael returned to working for his father after they called an uneasy truce.

Meanwhile, Kate doted on Madison, while keeping her condition from Michael. She began taking medication after Madison was born and believed she was improving. However, one morning, following a trip to the park with the baby, Kate collapsed. The hospital called Michael and he rushed to her side. The doctor assumed he knew how ill Kate was. When Michael learned the extent of her illness, that she only had a few years to live, his whole world crashed around him. He cradled her in his arms, rocking her back and forth. How could he go on living without her? The next months were torture. Kate grew weaker by the day. Michael hired a full-time nurse and a nanny to care for Madison.

In late May, 2003, Michael returned home very late, in a panic. He woke Kate.

"We need to leave," he said. "Tonight."

"What are you talking about?" she said, still groggy from a sedative. "I'm too sick to go anywhere. What happened? You can tell me. We'll work it out."

He looked into her tired, strained face, and knew he couldn't put her through that.

"I'm sorry," he said. "You're right. We'll talk in the morning. Go back to sleep."

"You promised. Remember?" she said. "You said I could count on you."

He kissed her gently and whispered to his sleeping wife, "Please understand."

He slipped into Madison's room. Tears clouded his vision as he bent low, kissed her rosy cheek, and closed the door behind him. He took only what fit into a back-pack, phoned his father, who seemed all too happy to watch over Kate and the baby, and stepped into the night. There was no other way. He couldn't believe what he'd witnessed that day. Just when he thought he had his life under control, once again people he trusted screwed him under. Locking the door behind him, he left for the airport and bought a ticket on the next flight out.

57

Newport Oregon
2004

The moon darted behind scattered clouds, casting eerie shadows under the street lamps. A cutting ocean wind had driven most casual walkers indoors. Lost in his thoughts, Michael didn't notice any of it.

He liked Jenny, she was the kind of girl a guy could depend on. Maybe she was just what he needed. Imagines of Kate flashed through his mind bringing pangs of guilt. What a coward he'd been for leaving her when she needed him most. He kicked a stone along the street as he made his way home.

And then there was Mackey. If it weren't for Mackey, Michael could make a life here. He could get Madison, hook up with Jenny. Have a real family again. If it weren't for Mackey, he could get his life back on track.

If it weren't for Mackey.

Michael came out of the funk and discovered he'd been wandering aimlessly. A block from home, the high beams of a slow-moving vehicle momentarily blinded him. *Mackey!* He cut across the neighbor's yard, entering his house through the back. Securing that door, he moved through the darkness, checking windows and locks, before sneaking a look out. The street was deserted. *Damn Mackey! I'm getting paranoid!*

Still unnerved, he left the lights out, and headed for the kitchen. By the light of the fridge, he retrieved a Coke and held the cold can to his throbbing temple before he popped it opened, taking a long swig.

What was that? Something darted across the yard! Michael ducked and made his way to the back of the house where he took a quick look out the small window into the night. At that moment, Mackey burst in, splintering the hollow-core door. He grabbed Michael and shoved him into the front room, onto the sagging sofa.

"Your family's a real pain in the ass," Mackey said. He retrieved a three-fifty-seven Magnum from his coat pocket.

Mackey pulled down the tattered shade on the front window and turned on the lamp. He planted himself in the chair by the door, then pulled a cigarette from a pack he'd drawn from his shirt pocket, all the while keeping his weapon aimed at Michael.

"You're such a piss ant. You sent your mommy to do your dirty work."

He clenched the cigarette between his teeth. "The bitch had me arrested, but I've got connections, too, buddy boy."

Michael's jaw tightened. "You're making a big mistake."

Mackey took several deep drags, before depositing the butt in an empty soda can resting on the lamp table.

"You thought you were in the clear when you left San Francisco. But you were wrong. Count the seconds you have left," Mackey said. "Tick, tock. When I'm done with you, I'll take care of your mother. Maybe I'll fuck her first."

Michael seethed.

"Michael! Are you okay?" Mabel Gaskin's voice called from outside the front door. "I heard a loud noise. What's going on?"

Mackey hissed, "Answer the fuckin' door! Get rid of her!"

Michael crossed the small room in several long strides. He extended his arm toward the door, only to turn toward his nemesis, landing a powerful blow to his jaw. Mackey dropped the gun, as he fell forward, taking the rickety end table down with him.

"What the hell?" Mabel screamed, pounding on the door. "Open up!"

Mackey staggered to his feet, reeling from the first blow. Michael grabbed the gun and slammed the butt into the side of Mackey's head. He collapsed on the floor. Michael aimed the gun.

"Jesus Christ!" Mabel screamed, hearing a gun discharge. Running from the porch, she yelled, "Help! Help! Call nine-one-one!"

58

Depoe Bay, Oregon

The phone jarred Vanessa out of a deep sleep. Her heart raced as she felt in the dark for the receiver. She cleared her throat and answered.

"Mom?" Michael said.

"It's the middle of the night! You scared me."

"Listen. I'm in jail."

"What!?" she said, bolting upright, suddenly very much awake.

"I shot Mackey."

"What!"

"You know how crazy he is. He broke into my house, I grabbed his gun...it went off."

"When is this going to stop? Tell me, Michael. When will it stop?" Vanessa's voice shrill, brittle. "What am I supposed to do? I can't be your attorney!"

"Mom, do something. I can't stay in this hell hole."

"What a mess. Maybe some jail time might straighten you out!" Her voice caught; she released a sigh. "You'll be fine for the rest of the night. I'll see you in the morning."

59

Newport, Oregon

Morning came all too soon. Vanessa had been up the rest of the night, trying to strategize what her next step should be. Could things get any worse? She called Matthew Strauss, a criminal attorney she'd known for several years, reaching him at home before daybreak. He was used to such calls.

Now, she waited for Strauss in the gray dawn just outside the jail, glad she'd grabbed her warm coat and knit hat. His deliberate steps picked up pace as he neared. He grabbed her hand and vigorously pumped it. Vanessa stood four inches taller, and from her vantage point, she could see the wisps of his comb-over that didn't quite do their job. His rumpled raincoat and narrow tie created more of a caricature of some TV detective, than the competent attorney she knew him to be.

"Sorry to meet under these circumstances," Strauss said, finally releasing her hand.

A guard escorted them to the attorneys' meeting room. Moments later Michael shuffled through the door, his hands and feet shackled. A guard held onto his arm.

"Sit in that chair and don't move until I return," the guard told Michael. "Good morning, Counselors," he said, nodding toward Vanessa and Strauss, familiar faces at the jailhouse. The guard had no idea Michael was her son.

Michael hadn't slept. Yesterday's rumpled work shirt was caked with dried blood.

"Didn't you get a shower?" Vanessa asked.

"Vanessa, it's a holding cell," Matthew reminded her.

"I don't think I would want to take a shower here," Michael said.

"Michael, I'm Matthew Strauss. Your mother has retained me to represent you," the attorney said, sliding his card across the table. "I need to know exactly what happened. Your mother can leave if you prefer. This can be between you and me."

"I have nothing to hide."

"Did you know the guy?" Strauss asked.

"Yeah. He's a dealer. I knew him from when I was using. In San Francisco," Michael said. He winced. The handcuffs were cutting into his wrists.

"Were there any witnesses to the shooting?" Strauss asked.

"The landlady was on the front porch. But I don't think she saw anything."

"Okay, let's start at the beginning," Strauss said.

Michael told the attorney about moving to Newport and finding Mackey living next door.

"He and his pals beat me up pretty bad about a month ago."

"All right, now we're getting somewhere," Strauss said, leaning closer. "When did this happen? I'll check the police report."

"We didn't report it," Vanessa interrupted.

"What!"

"I was afraid for Michael's safety. And apparently I was right," Vanessa said. "Mackey came to my house and threatened me, too. But before anything happened, a friend came to the door and he ran. I wasn't hurt."

"And you didn't report that either?" Strauss said, his eyes wide in disbelief. He ran his hand through his sparse hair.

The gathering fell quiet. Vanessa looked at Michael, but he averted his eyes. Strauss sat back in his chair and drummed his pen on the note pad.

"Let's see if I have this straight. Mackey and his buddies gave Michael a beating," he said. "Also, Mackey threatened Vanessa."

"Yes," Vanessa said.

"And you didn't report either incident," Strauss said.

"That's right. I went to San Francisco to find out about a murder they accused Michael of committing," Vanessa said. "But things went wrong from the start. You probably saw the news about the kidnapping."

"That was related to this guy? Do you two have any idea how bad this looks?" Strauss adjusted his reading glasses and scribbled a few notes. "Michael, are you telling me the truth? Was it self- defense?"

"Yes. Mackey was angry that Mom messed up the kidnapping and his buddies were killed. He was going to kill me, then Mom," Michael said, still struggling with his shackles. "He got distracted when Mabel came to the door. I went for the gun. We struggled. The gun went off."

"Okay. We have a hearing in an hour. I want you cleaned up and in a suit."

"I'll be back with some clothes in half an hour," Vanessa said.

Strauss waited for Vanessa to leave. "You're going to tell me everything you did leading up to the shooting. I want to believe you, Michael. So you better be straight with me."

When Steven pulled into the parking lot, he noticed Vanessa in her bright red coat near the jail entrance. She was so distracted she didn't see his silver Subaru. He made no effort to get her attention.

Once he was settled in his office, he closed the door and, once again, mulled over last night's event.

The call came just as he returned from walking his dog, Lexus. The lieutenant said there had been a shooting. A possible murder. Since murders were rare in Newport, the lieutenant wanted the DA in on it from the get-go. Steven was shocked to learn Michael Thorne had been arrested for the crime.

Since dating Vanessa, Steven had been concerned about the ramification of having a relationship with his opponent in court. That was minor compared to what he would have to face now. One of the best attorneys he'd ever had the privilege to know, she seemed incapable of rational thought when it came to her son. But Steven's gut told him that this guy was trouble. He was glad he hadn't met Michael before. That would have made facing him in court impossible.

He took the stairs two at a time, mentally preparing for the arraignment.

Clean-shaven, dressed in a blue, button-down shirt and khakis, Michael stood with Matthew Strauss, looking very different then the man from last night.

Vanessa sat in the gallery behind the defense table, the one she usually occupied. She straightened her skirt, and fiddled with a button on her jacket. When would she wake from this nightmare? She'd always reassured herself that the shady characters she defended had come from families with long criminal histories, people who'd never had a break from poverty and deprivation. But Michael had every advantage. When he ran away, she'd tormented herself night after sleepless night, rehashing every moment of his life, wondering where she'd gone wrong. The calm she'd finally carved out for herself in Oregon had ended when Michael returned. Since Kate's death, nothing had made sense.

Steven entered the courtroom. He couldn't look at Vanessa.

Strauss and Michael were awaiting the judge. Steven stood next to Michael. Michael and Steven, side by side. She closed her eyes, then looked again. Same height, same hair, same Grecian nose. They looked as if they could have been related.

The judge struck his gavel to begin the arraignment. He looked over his reading glasses at Vanessa.

"What brings you into court today, Counselor?"

"Good morning, Your Honor. Michael, the defendant, is my son,"

Vanessa said, her face flushing. She could think of a hundred places she'd rather be introducing her son!

"Your son? Well...hum...please proceed, Mr. Adams."

"The State charges Michael Thorne with voluntary manslaughter. The state requests he be held over for trial."

Judge O'Riley peered down at Michael. "How do you plead, son?"

Strauss nodded toward Michael. "Not guilty."

"Your Honor, Michael isn't a flight risk," Strauss said. "He has no previous record. He's a stable member of our community. He's employed and lives in the area. We're requesting bail."

"I have no objection," Steven said.

Vanessa posted the $50,000 bail and Michael was released. While standing together on the courthouse steps, she attempted to hug him, but his body stiffened. She held him anyway, wanting to make the nightmare go away, to have a chance to start over. He took her arms from around him and hurried away.

60

Newport, Oregon

Steven knew it was Vanessa before he picked up the phone. He hadn't been able to shake her from his thoughts since seeing the otherwise self-assured woman helpless and humiliated in court that morning.

Yesterday...was that just yesterday? So much had happened in the last twenty-four hours. Steven had made a mistake telling her what he thought of Michael. When she wanted to be alone, he knew he'd crossed the line. Not exactly the homecoming he'd planned.

He pushed his chair back, as if the physical distance from Michael's file lying on his desk would somehow separate him from the problem.

"Hello?" he said.

"Steven?" said Vanessa, sounding distant. "I know we shouldn't be talking about this."

"That's right. We shouldn't be talking at all," he said, wanting her.

"But, I haven't had a chance to tell you about Dean Stanton."

"Vanessa, please. Don't tell me anything more."

"But, Steven..."

"Don't make this any more difficult than it is."

"You should excuse yourself from this trial!" she snapped, anger colliding with hurt. "You're not able to be impartial."

"You've been blinded by your son's lies," he said. "I can't talk to you about this. I'll call you when the trial is over."

"Don't bother!" she said, ending the call.

With that disconnect, Vanessa cut herself off from her lover, friend, and confidant. The only person she could trust. She rose to gaze out the office window, arms folded against her chest. Beyond the jailhouse roof the sharp horizon line divided the shimmering sea from the crisp, clear sky. She wished life was that clearly defined, so that she'd know where the truth ended and lies began.

She turned and rested against the sill, surveying her office. Even though she'd occupied this drab cube of space for almost ten years, it felt temporary. Her usual flair was missing. No paintings graced the walls, nor were there family photos proudly displayed on the desk. Another time and place, she would have transformed it into her private oasis.

A shiver shook her body. Just moments ago, when Michael had pulled away, her heart sank. She scanned her blackberry for a number she'd entered while in San Francisco. She found it and dialed, needing to talk to the only other person who had ever cared for Michael as much as she had.

Harvard Law School
Cambridge, Massachusetts
1974

Almost nine months pregnant, Vanessa had her law school finals behind her and diploma in hand. Resting on the sofa in the tiny married student's apartment, she looked down at her immense belly and swollen ankles. Stress and pregnancy had put forty pounds on her otherwise slender frame. She reached for a sugar cookie from the opened package on the coffee table and wondered when Nicholas would return from his latest business trip. His schedule always seemed to be a mystery. Even the pregnancy hadn't changed that.

She'd already packed up the apartment with her friends' help and was ready to move back to Chicago. She'd planned to take some time off to be with the baby and to prepare for the bar exam before joining her father's law firm. Her mother had found her a luxury apartment in a high-rise overlooking Lake Michigan, ironically in a building Kate's father had built many years before. Her parents were paying the first year's rent, so she would have a proper place to raise their grandchild, as they put it.

She'd hoped to be settled before the baby came. But as she reached for another cookie, a pain shot through her back. The baby was coming early. No one was around to help her. Her friends had already left school heading back home, on to their new lives. She called a cab and wrote a note for Nicholas. When she arrived at the emergency room alone, her contractions were indistinguishable one from the other. Several hours later, she was holding her nine-pound baby boy.

The nurse took Michael from her arms so she could get some sleep. When she awoke, Nicholas was standing over her.

"He's perfect," Nicholas said, having viewed Michael in the nursery. He kissed her hand, then bent over and gently kissed her lips. "I'm sorry I've been so distant. We're a family now. I promise I'll be a good father."

Michael, bright and energetic, grew to be a handful. Nicholas was still an absentee husband and father, but when he was home, he doted on the boy. When he was gone, nannies quit regularly, unable to control the active child. At one point he was expelled from Bridgeview Academy for smoking pot on campus. Following in her mother's footsteps, Vanessa made a handsome contribution to the elite prep school and Michael was reinstated.

Then there was the other Michael. The handsome teen that could be engaging at Vanessa's frequent cocktail parties. He charmed the older women, making them giggle like school girls, a talent he'd inherited from his father. At that time, Vanessa had been proud of him, surprised by his adult demeanor. She'd even overlooked his transgression when she'd caught him pouring vodka into a water glass, in an attempt to camouflage the drink. They'd laughed about it. What was the harm? He was almost eighteen.

A few months later, Michael left. No note, no goodbyes. He just vanished.

With cell phone in hand, she dialed the number. It was time to involve Nicholas in Michael's spiraling mess.

61

San Francisco
2004

"Thorne residence," answered Josie. The maid put the call on hold and forwarded it to Nicholas in his upstairs office.

Hearing who was on the line piqued Nicholas' curiosity. Other than the hospital, he hadn't spoken to her in well over ten years.

"Vanessa?"

"Michael's been arrested!" she blurted out.

Silence.

"Nicholas?"

"Yeah, I'm here. Where is he?" he said.

"He's out on bail. It's horrible! He shot a man. Wade Mackey. Do you know him?"

"Know him? No. Why should I?"

"Mackey was somehow involved with Michael, I guess when he was using. He was seeking revenge for something that happened in San Francisco a few years back. Since Michael was living in your house and working for you...I just thought you might..."

"Michael's made his own life. I didn't keep track of his every move," he said, heading to the bar. He poured a scotch, although it was only ten in the morning. "How did it happen?"

"It's all so crazy. It's easier if I just start at the beginning."

"Please do," he said, settling into his easy chair by the fire. Scotch in hand, he listened.

62

Newport, Oregon
2004

Gus hustled from car to car, cleaning windows, topping off tanks, and making change, hating that damn kid he'd hired. Two hours late, Michael, still dressed in his court clothes, finally showed up. His release was contingent on his having a job so he'd better kiss some ass or he'd be back in jail. Gus wanted nothing more to do with this troublemaker. Michael followed Gus, from car to car, trying to explain, begging for another chance. But it was only making things worse.

"You're in a whole lotta trouble," Gus fumed, running a wet squeegee over a dirty windshield. "I don't need your kind messing up my business, so get the hell outta here."

"This job sucked anyway!" Michael shot back.

Gus shook his head as Michael stomped off.

Mabel Gaskin was on her hands and knees scrubbing the carpet in the living room, her immense rear end stretching the limits of her plus size-overalls. A carpenter in the back pounded nails, repairing the doorframe before installing the new door.

"Pack your bags! You're outta here!" Mabel screeched, as soon as Michael opened the front door. With great effort, she lifted herself onto the sofa. "I don't want to see your sorry ass around here again! No one's ever been killed in one of my houses. Look at this mess! I'll be at it for days."

"I'm sure you'll find more furniture at the dump," Michael said, heading to the bedroom. He grabbed his backpack from the closet floor, stuffed in his few possessions, and left. No job, no home, no money. But he wasn't going back to jail. With nowhere else to go, he headed down the hill to see Jenny.

She stopped filling the glass display case with pastries when she saw the look on Michael's face.

"What's wrong?" she said.

"You won't believe what happened," Michael said.

"You look awful."

"Do you remember the guy that came in here last night?"

"The smart ass? I sure do."

"He was waiting for me when I got home," he said, slumping into a chair.

"Holy shit!"

"He shoved in the back door." He watched her shock turn to fear. "Threatened me with a gun. I got it away from him."

"What happened then?" she asked, wide eyed.

They arrested me for manslaughter. I'm out on bail."

"You shot him?" she said.

"It was self-defense. The charges are bogus."

Noticing his backpack, she asked, "Are you going somewhere?"

"I wish. My place got trashed from the fight, and the old bitch threw me out. To make things worse, I got fired. I'd head back to San Francisco, but I'm stuck here for now."

While Jenny whipped up a double latte for a customer, she mulled over Michael's dilemma. By the time she'd rejoined him at the table, her mind was made up.

"You can stay at my place until you can figure out what to do. I don't have much room, but we can work something out," she said, reaching into her pocket for the key.

Michael hurried up the stairs to Jenny's studio apartment one flight above the Nye Beach Pastry Shop, a block from Rosie's Café. Thankful he'd have a place to crash, he turned the key and the door swung open to reveal a compact room with a kitchen at one end and a bathroom, the only room with any privacy, at the other end. Floral curtains and braided rugs brightened the otherwise dismal space.

Dropping his bag on the floor, he loosened his tie, and pulled it over his head. Removing his shirt and pants, he hung them neatly on the only hanger he could find. He unpacked his Levi's and tugged them on, before checking out the fridge. He found a Coke, then noticing the newly sprouted herbs in green plastic containers lining the windowsill; he popped the top of the can. Unwashed dishes were piled in the sink. He turned on the TV that sat atop a dresser, an obvious flea market find. He tumbled onto the bed, pulling a handmade quilt over his feet. Exhausted, he soon fell asleep.

A few hours later, Jenny locked up the café and hurried home. It was a gamble, inviting Michael to stay, someone she'd met only a month ago and now out on bail. She'd made that mistake before, more than once. But there was something about Michael. He was different. His stories fascinated her. He'd traveled to Europe when he was just a kid. He'd lived in San Francisco. Places she'd only dreamt about. Michael was nothing like her ex-husband. She didn't sense any hidden fury. And the way he looked at her, as if he could see deep into her soul. She couldn't help flirting back.

She took the stairs two at a time and flung the door open, catching it before it hit the wall. Michael was sound asleep. His muscular body stretched across her bed. She snuggled against him. Michael stirred. Half-awake, he nuzzled her hair. His arms encircled her. Then he fell back to sleep. She laid motionless, content to just be held.

63

Newport, Oregon

Steven stooped over the credenza, searching Westlaw for pertinent cases for an upcoming trial, but had a hard time concentrating. He tried to fight back the debate that had raged in his head for days now, ever since Michael's arraignment. He was about to divulge information Vanessa had told him in confidence. She saw Michael as the hapless pawn, when in fact he was playing her like a fiddle.

Steven turned from the computer and scanned the bulging Rolodex that held every name and number he'd had since law school. He found the one he was looking for and dialed.

"Steve, you old son-of-a-gun," said Carl Polinski. "How the hell are ya?"

Steven had known the detective from his days with the San Francisco DA's office.

"I'm fine, Carl," Steven said, glad to hear his friend's voice. "How's Agnes?"

"We got divorced coupla years ago," Carl said. "Not many women can handle an old fart like me. What's up?"

"I arrested a kid about a week ago by the name of Michael Thorne, for manslaughter. He's claiming self-defense."

"Oh, that's a *new* one," Carl replied with a chuckle. "Thorne, huh? Any relationship to Nicholas Thorne?"

"That's his father. His mother lives here in Depoe Bay."

"Well, I'll be damned! That'll smudge the reputation of the city's biggest philanthropist," Carl said, rummaging through the stack of reports on his desk. Finding the one he was looking for, he scanned its contents and continued, "Talk about a small world. I interviewed Ms. Sterling last week. Said she was the Thorne kid's grandmother. I was buying her self-defense explanation. Any reason I shouldn't believe her?"

"Vanessa isn't involved in anything her son hasn't dragged her into. You can believe her. She was in San Francisco because of him."

"Vanessa? Sounds like you know her well," Carl teased. "As I recall, she's a looker."

"And smart. Except when it comes to her son," Steven said.

"What did the kid do?" Carl asked.

"Seems he was involved with some drug dealers in San Francisco. Have you heard of Falcon or Wade Mackey?"

"Jesus! You've been in the woods too long. Those are some heavy hitters," said Carl. "You don't run into those guys on a street corner buying drugs."

"I knew it!" Steven said. "Michael was arrested for shooting Mackey. But I think that's just the tip of the iceberg."

"Sounds like he did us a service. Mackey was a real scumbag," said Carl.

"Mackey and his pals claimed Michael killed a guy named Rhio Diego."

"Interesting. Michael's accused of the Diego murder. He takes out Mackey. Scarpelli and Bull were shot kidnapping Thorne's kid, and his mother was involved in that," Carl said. "You think Falcon's somehow connected to the Thorne kid? Makes sense. Mackey worked for Falcon before he cut loose and left with Diego. I've suspected Falcon in the Diego murder, but the DA was satisfied that all the proof pointed to Thompson. There's no question in my mind Thompson was eliminated as a cover-up. Falcon's ruthless. Nothing stops this guy. We haven't been able to pin so much as a parking ticket on him.

There's no picture on file; no one's given us a description. I'm sure someone's being paid off and it ain't the cop on the beat. There's so damn much money in drugs, they can buy their way out of hell."

Carl changed the phone to the other ear and held it with his shoulder while he made some notes.

"Make a deal with the kid. If Thorne can ID Falcon and is willing to testify, maybe we can finally nail the SOB! But don't do anything until I get back to you."

"Thanks, Carl. I knew I could count on you."

No sooner had Steven hung up than the receptionist rang to say Matthew Strauss had arrived.

Strauss entered intent on business. Following a brisk handshake, he took a seat and rested his briefcase on his lap, snapping it open, and removing a folder.

"It seems Mackey and his cohorts beat up Michael and threatened Vanessa. I don't have any witnesses, but…"

"I'm a witness," Steven said. It would only be a matter of time before Strauss uncovered that fact. "I arrived at Vanessa's just as Mackey was about to attack her. He shoved me and ran."

"What's going on here? You of all people."

"I know, I know. But she wanted to wait. She promised to file a report."

"Well, well. I think we have a conflict of interest here, Counselor," Strauss said, with a sly grin.

Taking the bait, Steven slowly rose and leaned over his desk, bracing himself on his knuckles. "Don't make insinuating remarks you can't back up. Any personal relationship I may have doesn't affect my judgment." Steven said. "Michael's in up to his eyeballs. Mackey's death is one incident in a long line that leads back to his questionable life in San Francisco."

"You're flying by the seat of your pants, Adams," Strauss said. "That has nothing to do with the current charges. Hearsay and conjectures don't cut it. Under the circumstances, I want you to drop the charges against my client. The way I see it, you don't have a case."

"We'll let the Grand Jury decide," Steven said, taking his seat.

Strauss returned the unopened folder to his briefcase, snapped it shut, and stood.

"I don't think we'll get that far. I'll have a motion to dismiss on Judge O'Riley's desk by morning. Lack of evidence and conflict of interest should be sufficient for the judge to throw the case out."

Strauss stormed out of Steven's office, climbed into his pickup, and pulled a cell phone from his pocket. He dialed and waited for Michael to answer.

"We'll have a dismissal in the morning," he said. "Seems the DA has a thing for your mother. He also had some wild theory about you being connected to another murder in Francisco. That's totally out of his jurisdiction. I'll call you tomorrow to let you know how things turn out."

Michael slammed down the phone. He pulled on jeans and a sweater. So much for a lazy morning. Jenny was at work and wouldn't be home until late. He grabbed her VW keys and headed out the door. Coming to Newport had been a big mistake. What did he expect, some kind of happy reunion with his mother? He shouldn't have told her anything. Now she'd confided in her boyfriend, who intended to use it against him. The most important lesson he'd learned in San Francisco was to make sure people only messed with you once.

64

Newport, Oregon

Vanessa left the courthouse, still troubled by the call she'd made to Nicholas. He'd hardly reacted to the news about his son.

She drove the back streets, avoiding Highway 101. The often congested thoroughfare that connected one coastal town to another could be slow going. Turning north through Nye Beach, she drove past Michael's street. A flash of the court scene the day before made her neck ache.

The road followed the coastline's contour to Agate Beach, an expanse of sand where treasure hunters, braving the wind, searched for the beach's namesake stone. Rounding a curve, she pressed on the gas as the road rose uphill, past the new development that scarred the once-pristine vista, and merged onto the highway.

Nicholas had his quirks. She'd known that before she married him, remembering his rough treatment of a classmate over an innocent remark. She'd been shocked, but sure it was an isolated incident, until a knee injury ended his pro football career. After that, he'd turned against her, like she was somehow at fault.

The Jeep climbed the steep slope to Cape Foulweather where a thick layer of fog obscured the summit, spruce and cedar trees hung low, laden with dew. There the road began its descent.

She released an audible sigh when she pulled into her drive. The fading sunlight filtered through the newly-budding branches, casting a latticed pattern over the driveway. The view of the cove from the path leading to the front deck had never stopped amazing her. Today, the descending sun set the sky ablaze. Her life was spinning out of control, but the earth continued to circle the sun. Days beginning and ending, unimpressed with the mundane muddles of its inhabitants.

Standing in the hallway, she dropped her briefcase and hung up her coat, before heading to the kitchen in search of something to eat, settling for a glass of Chardonnay. After a couple of swallows, she refilled her glass, and headed to the bathroom.

She caught her image in the mirror and leaned in for a closer look. Her drawn face echoed the stress she'd been under for weeks. In the bedroom, she shed her business suit for sky-blue pajamas, and finished off the wine before dropping into bed. She pulled the comforter up to her chin and fell into a fitful sleep.

In a foreboding dream, she stood in front of Nicholas' house, still in her pajamas. Fog swirled at her feet. Her arms were folded across her chest to fend off the sharp wind. Through a window, she saw Madison playing on a scarlet rug in Nicholas' living room. The tranquil scene ended. Nicholas, Kate, and Michael stood at the window, glaring out at her, pulling the heavy drapery closed.

What was that? She sat up in bed, heart beating wildly. A draft caused her to shiver. She pulled the comforter from the floor where it had landed. Groggy and disoriented, she slid from the bed and went to the bathroom. She took two aspirins with a long drink of water. Returning to bed, she sat up against the pillows and tried to shake the eerie sense of despair that had haunted her since she returned from San Francisco.

She'd almost lost her brother and his wife. Thankfully, they were going to be all right. She nearly got herself killed, twice. She'd killed a man. And the lies and deceit of the three people she'd loved dearly. She wanted to push those memories to the furthest recesses of her mind, to revisit them at some other time. Or never. But her old ways of doing that no longer worked.

Four a.m. and she couldn't sleep. She crawled from bed, pulled on her robe, and walked barefoot along the pile rug in the hallway, on her way to the kitchen. Not eating dinner had left her famished.

She turned the corner to the living room and froze.

A male figure sat on the sofa.

"Hello, Mother."

"Michael! You scared me. What on earth are you doing here? How did you get in?"

"You gave me a key. Remember?"

"Don't do that again!" she said.

"Is it so strange I wanted to visit my mother?"

"At this hour?"

"Does it matter? Everyone's so interested in time. For some, time determines what they do and where they go. Instead of just doing whatever they want when they want to."

"What are you talking about?" Deciding not to play his game, she said, "I meant to call and see how you're doing."

She turned on the living room lamps.

"How am I doing?" he asked, leaning forward, clenching his hands. "Well, Mother, I'll tell you how I'm doing. I got fired from my job, kicked out of my house, arrested for manslaughter. How in the hell do you think I am?"

"Don't take that tone."

"Take that tone? My life's shit and you're worried about my tone!" he said. He stood and began to pace.

"Why are you here?"

"Do I need a reason to visit?" he said.

"Yes. When you intrude in the middle of the night. When you're obviously angry and not making any sense."

"Oh, I'll make sense. How dare you tell your boyfriend what I told you in confidence. Did it ever occur to you he'd use that information against me in court!"

"He wouldn't do that!"

"Oh yeah? He's looking into connecting me to Falcon and the Diego murder."

Vanessa felt the walls close in. Her vision narrowed.

"I don't believe you," she said.

"If it wasn't for you..."

"Did it ever occur to you if you had nothing to hide there wouldn't be anything for him to use?" Vanessa said, "You blame me! You're the one that's been lying to me for years."

"Yes, I blame..."

"Michael, shut up!" she said. "What about the danger you've put me in? All because you're protecting some murderous drug dealer!" The dam had broken. "And the lies and deception. You, your father, and Kate, living your secretive lives. What else, Michael? What else have you lied to me about?"

He turned towards the door.

"I'm not done!" she said. "What has your father got to do with this?"

"Leave him out of this! Your fucking job meant more to you than I did. I'd do anything for him," he said, coming back into the room. "Anything!" Spittle forming in the corner of his mouth.

"Michael, listen to me. He's lied to you, too. He can't be trusted," she said, putting a chair between her and her son. "He didn't want you to meet his family, so he told you they were dead. But the only one that died was his mother. Did he ever tell you that? His father killed her in a drunken rage. He never got over her death. He's lied to you and he's lied to me. Don't you see? It twisted him somehow. I don't think he cares about anyone but himself. He latched onto me for my money and prestige," she said, shaking with anger. "He divorced me when he found a way to make enough money without me."

He found a way to make more money! How could I be so blind? Michael met Falcon through Nicholas. That's how Nicholas could afford to live in such affluence. That would explain Madison's driver being armed. They didn't kidnap Madison to get to Michael. They did it to get to Nicholas! *Discussing murder was an everyday occurrence!*

"Your father's involved, isn't he?"

"You don't know anything!" he shouted, heading back to the door.

"Well, I sure don't know you anymore!" Vanessa said, reaching for the chair back to steady herself. "But I do know you're protecting your father!"

"Believe me, he doesn't need my protection!" he said, slamming the door behind him.

The next morning, Steven met with Strauss in Judge O'Riley's chambers. O'Riley had reviewed Strauss' motion to dismiss.

"If it was any other attorney but Steven Adams," the judge said, "I'd say you may have a case for dismissal. But if Steven tells me there's no conflict, then I'll go with that. As for lack of evidence, we'll let the grand jury decide."

65

San Francisco

This was the break he'd been waiting for. Detective Polinski had wanted to bust Falcon for years. If Steven was right about the Thorne kid, he'd finally have an eyewitness.

Polinski wasn't interested in fame or glory. He just wanted this guy off the streets. He dialed the DA's office. He'd known Dean Stanton since he was a rookie and was sure Stanton wanted Falcon as much he did.

"Dean, Carl Polinski."

"Carl, good to hear from you. What's up?"

"Do you remember Steven Adams?"

"Sure. I remember Steve."

"He's arrested a kid up in Oregon. It looks like the kid killed Wade Mackey."

"Good riddance," Stanton said.

"That's exactly what I told him," Carl chuckled. "But listen, I think the kid has ties to Falcon. It's worth looking into. I know you want this guy as much as I do. It would make your reelection a shoe-in."

"What's the kid's name?" Stanton asked.

"Michael Thorne."

"Thorne! Whada ya know? Sounds like you're on to something. See what else you can find out from the kid. Keep me in the loop."

66

San Francisco, California

Carl Polinski loosened his tie. He was in for a long night. Searching through cold case files, some years old, murder, extortion, drugs, all had escalated since Falcon arrived in town. Carl spent the night and most of the next day poring over every detail, cashing in a few favors from old contacts. He spun his theory to some trusted colleagues, and pulled together a plausible connection between Falcon and numerous unsolved crimes.

The next morning, he called Steven. "I talked to Stanton. He wants me to get information from the Thorne kid. If he can name names, verify what Falcon had his hands in, we've got the bastard. We have to make it worth something to the kid. How does the case look?"

"It's going to the grand jury," Steven said.

"Great. Make a deal. It sounds like he has first hand knowledge. Tell him we'll work with the FBI to give him immunity, a new identity. He's peanuts compared to nailing Falcon."

"You're bringing the FBI in on this? Let me think about that," Steven said.

"There's nothing to think about! There's too much evidence to be a coincidence..."

When Carl finished with the details, he said, "I'll Fed-Ex copies to you. Look 'em over and let me know what you think." Carl heard a call click in. "I've gotta go. I'll get back to you soon."

Carl answered his other line.

"Dean Stanton here. I just got a lead on Louis Ambrose, the ex-con you've been trying to track down."

On the way to join officers in their squad car, Carl deposited a package in the Fed-Ex drop in front of the precinct. Once he arrived at the address on Fell Street, he sent the officers around back, before ringing the bell. While he waited to be buzzed in, a dark sedan slowed just long enough to put two slugs in Carl Polinski's back.

67

Newport, Oregon

Jenny lay in bed; a smile spreading across her face as she thought about the night before. She and Michael had been together for only a week, but she was falling hard and knew she'd do just about anything for him. Michael opened the bathroom door, releasing a cloud of steam. His naked body glistened in the morning light. He saw her sleepy eyes and sweet grin and ambled over to sit on the edge of the bed.

"I'm a little shaky," he said. "I hope the grand jury doesn't buy Steven's bullshit."

"It's going to be okay," Jenny said.

She sat up and put her arms around him. He leaned towards her, nuzzling her hair.

"If we didn't have to be at the courthouse this morning, I'd screw your brains out right now," he said, running his tongue around her ear. He strolled over to the small closet where his clothes hung and began to dress. He pulled on the dress pants he'd last worn at his arraignment and tucked in the crisp light blue shirt Jenny had washed and ironed the day before.

She crawled from bed and stretched her shapely body before heading to the bathroom. She lingered in the shower, taking in the aroma of the lavender soap. Everything had a heightened sensuality since she'd given herself completely to Michael. She'd never felt so uninhibited.

"Jenny, hurry up. We're going to be late!"

She grabbed his towel off the rack and took in the scent that lingered in the cotton pile as she toweled off. She pulled on a sweater and tie-dyed skirt and let her hair dry naturally into a curly mop.

A gentle breeze ruffled Vanessa's scarf as she stood next to Strauss by the front entrance of the courthouse. Michael parked the yellow VW bug at the curb, then hurried up the front walk, hand in hand with Jenny. He shook hands with Strauss and nodded to his mother. They hadn't spoken since his late-night visit.

"I think you'll be a free man once we get this over with," Strauss said. "The DA has very little evidence to prove his case."

They entered through the main entrance and descended the flight of stairs to the DA's office. This was the prosecution's show. They would not be taking part, but they were all anticipating Michael's release and wanted to be on hand for the decision.

Steven came out of his office, hesitating when he saw Vanessa with her son and attorney, sitting on the benches that lined the hallway. He proceeded on to the grand jury room without a hello.

The four women and three men who made up the grand jury were seated when Steven stood before them.

His first witness was a ballistics expert, Harold Simpson. It was Simpson's umpteenth grand jury hearing. His brown tweed jacket that usually hung on a hook behind his office door, waiting for the next court appearance, needed pressing. He'd much rather be in his lab coat, but it was all part of the job.

"The bullets came from the three-fifty-seven Magnum that was found at the scene," Simpson read from his report. "Both Mackey's and Thorne's fingerprints were found on the gun. From the bullet's trajectory, it is apparent that the shots were fired from approximately three feet away."

"What would that indicate?" Steven said.

"The distance precludes an accidental shooting occurring during a struggle."

Simpson stepped down and Detective Ken Brown took the stand, nodding at Steven. They'd worked together on a number of cases. Brown had been with the Newport Police Department for fifteen years, working his way up through the ranks. Steven could count on him to notice the details others often missed.

The detective scanned his notebook before he began. "The alleged victim broke into Thorne's residence, splintering the back door. Mr. Thorne said he knew the victim and said they'd fought before. I asked him how he knew Mackey. He didn't answer," Brown said, flipping through his notes. "It appeared Mr. Thorne had taken time to wash up before the police arrived. This behavior appeared calculated. Overturned furniture substantiated there had been a struggle. Based on his behavior and the fact he fired two shots, I'd say he intended to kill Mr. Mackey."

Brown was excused, but he stopped long enough to hold the door for Mabel Gaskin. She'd foregone her usual flowered muumuu, opting for a black cotton dress that buttoned down the front, more suitable for a Sicilian funeral. Heavy support hose and black sandals finished the outfit. Her gray hair was neatly done up into a bun atop her head. Her reluctance to testify tempered her usual gregarious demeanor. She took the stand.

"I didn't see anything," she said, answering Steven's question. "I live next door. I heard a loud noise and went to see what caused the ruckus. I could see the lamp on, but Michael wouldn't answer the door. Next thing I know there's a fight, furniture was falling over, then gunshots. I ran and called nine-one-one."

"What was the time lapse between the end of the fight and the gun being fired," Steven asked.

"Well, I don't rightly know. I'd have to say not more than a minute or two. It was quiet, then suddenly, boom! It scared the wits out of me! I never liked that Mackey character. And Michael seemed like such a nice young man. It's hard to believe he'd do such a thing."

"Thank you, Mrs. Gaskin. That will be all," Steven said.

The morning passed quickly. It was almost noon when Steven stood to make his summation.

"The evidence presented proves the elements of voluntary manslaughter necessary to hold Michael Thorne over for trial for the shooting death of Wade Mackey. He made the decision to pull the trigger after the altercation had ended. Mrs. Gaskin testified that several minutes had passed before she heard the shots. A person has the legal right to protect himself. But the law requires we hold him to the standard of what an ordinary, reasonable person would do under the same or similar circumstances. It's apparent Mr. Thorne had control of the gun and he opted to kill Mr. Mackey."

Without any further questions, the jury adjourned to deliberations. Steven came out of the proceedings and the anxious group sat at attention, waiting for some sign. There was nothing Steven could, or would, say to anyone at that moment. He hesitated at his office door, poised with his hand on the doorknob and scanned their faces. Beautiful Vanessa, her face etched by the strain of this ordeal. Jenny, obviously enamored with Michael enough to get herself involved. Just another day for Strauss at $250 an hour. And Michael. Seeming nonchalant, but squeezing Jenny's hand, probably scared stiff. That was the first time Steven had taken a hard look at Michael.

"Mr. Adams, there's a Fed-Ex package for you," Steven's receptionist called out.

He took the package and retreated to his office. Just as he was about to open it, he noticed his message light blinking. *That couldn't be the jury already.* He hit the play button and discovered a message from Dean Stanton.

"Steve, something urgent has come up, and I think it directly relates to a case you're working on. It's important enough for you to grab the next plane and come down to San Francisco. Call me as soon as you get my message."

What did he have he couldn't email or fax?

Then Stanton added: "I'm sorry to be the one to tell you, but Carl Polinski has been killed in the line of duty. We've lost a fine officer and a friend."

Carl dead! The guy had twenty-five years on the force. He knew how to watch his back. Steven suddenly remembered Vanessa trying to tell him something about Stanton.

He ripped open the package and spread its contents on his desk. Carl must have combed every file. There were dozens of crimes indicating Falcon. He'd highlighted key cases and reports. This was huge and way out of Steven's jurisdiction. Carl had wanted to bring in the FBI, and now Steven knew it was time.

68

Newport, Oregon

Within the hour the grand jury had reached its decision. With Steven present, the jury read its findings. They had determined the elements of the crime were sufficiently met for Michael to be held over for trial. This gave Steven the leverage he needed.

He stepped from the jury room and motioned for Michael to come into his office. Michael's attorney, Vanessa, and Jenny followed. He stood silently while each filed in and found a seat around the conference table, before seating himself.

"The grand jury just returned a bill of indictment holding your case over for trial," Steven told Michael. "But I'm prepared to offer you a plea bargain."

"This is bogus!" Michael snapped.

"Quiet! Let me do the talking. What's your offer?" Strauss asked.

"I've received information linking Michael to the murder of a man in San Francisco by the name of Rhio Diego. I have information that indicates Joey Falcon was involved, as well. I had no alternative but to contact the FBI."

"The FBI!" Vanessa exclaimed. "Steven, what on earth are you doing?"

Ignoring Vanessa, he continued. "We're prepared to dismiss the charges in exchange for information leading to the arrest and conviction of Falcon."

"I need a few minutes with my client," Strauss said.

Steven stood. "I'll be back in ten minutes."

As soon as the door closed, Michael turned to his mother.

"This is your fault! If you hadn't blabbed to your boyfriend."

"Michael, don't," Jenny said. "Your mother was just…"

"Shut up, Jenny!" Michael snapped.

Jenny slumped back in her chair.

"Michael, you're the one that needs to be quiet!" said his attorney. "I'm old school. You need to treat women with respect. You told me you didn't have any connection with that murder. The only stipulation I made when I took your case was that you tell me the truth. I can't help you if you lie."

Michael's face was stone.

No longer willing to tolerate his theatrics and his growing list of lies, Vanessa snapped, "Afraid what else they'll find out? If you're found guilty, you could be sentenced to fifteen to twenty years. Take the offer. Do it for Madison, if not for your own sake."

"I agree with your mother," Strauss said. "You don't want to take your chances with a jury."

"There's something else you need to know that may help you make the decision," Vanessa said. "Grandmother Sterling left you a sizeable inheritance. It's been held in trust."

"What? You let me work at a disgusting job and live in that dump?"

"You're trying my patience. Show your mother some respect," Strauss said.

"If you recall," Vanessa said, trying to remain calm. "I didn't know where you were! And since you've been back, there's been nothing but trouble. Believe me, money can cause more problems than it solves. Anyway, there's enough to start a new life. Enough to make sure Madison goes to the best schools and lives in a good neighborhood. Remember telling me you wanted to make something of your life? Here's your chance."

Steven stuck his head through the doorway. Ignoring the tension that filled the room, he asked, "Have you made your decision?"

Strauss looked at Michael. "It's your call."

Steven took a seat.

"You'll let me go if I narc on Falcon?" Michael said. "No probation, no record?"

"Yes. But the deal is you lead us to Falcon, give us enough information to arrest him, and testify at his trial."

"Testify?" Michael said.

"You'll have security. We can put you into the witness protection program," Steven said.

Michael sat silently for a few minutes before he agreed.

"Okay. We'll meet on Monday with an agent from the bureau," Steven said. "Be prepared to tell him everything. Remember don't leave town, you're still under the jurisdiction of this court."

Steven pulled the prepared Order to Dismiss from his desk drawer. "Keep your end of the bargain, and you'll be a free man. If you screw this up, I'll pull your bail and you'll be back in jail awaiting trial."

Without another word, Michael stood and turned to leave. Jenny followed.

"I think you've made a fair deal. I'll have him here Monday. Don't worry." Strauss said. He shook Steven's hand and left.

Vanessa remained while the others filed out. She stood facing Steven.

"What the hell do you think you're doing?" she said. "I would never have confided in you if I'd known what you were going to do!" She stood, ready to leave.

Before she could open the door, Steven took one long stride and took her arm. The move caught her off guard. Her fortress crumbled. Engulfed in his arms, she took a deep breath. He helped her back into a chair. He pulled up another and sat facing her.

He took her hands and said, "I'm sorry I had to be so rough on you, but I had to handle the situation the best way I knew how. Will you forgive me? As for breaking confidentiality, I struggled with that, but we needed to get

240

that murdering scumbag Falcon. If Michael cooperates, we'll shut down the whole operation. Michael's lucky to be alive. Most people leave that business in a body bag, and if Mackey had been successful, that's exactly what would have happened."

Vanessa remained silent and Steven continued. "The timing's all wrong, but I have to ask you something. It can't wait. The last time we talked, you tried to tell me about Dean Stanton. I need to know what happened."

Vanessa contemplated where her loyalty stood. Certainly Michael had given her little reason to stand by him. She closed her eyes and took in a breath. At that moment, she realized what Steven had done! The reason he didn't excuse himself from the trial!

To give Vanessa a moment to think, he retrieved a bottle of water from the small refrigerator in the corner and handed it to her. She accepted the offering and took a long swallow.

"You did all this to help Michael, didn't you?" she said. "You knew you could get him off. You just needed to prove my theory that Falcon was the murderer."

"Yes," Steven said. "But we're not there yet. I need to know about Stanton."

"Okay. I told you I talked to the Assistant DA on Thompson's case. What I didn't tell you was he wanted to call Stanton. I knew you were friends, and I didn't want you to find out what I was up to. You'd try to stop me," she said, taking another sip of water. "But when that man broke into my brother's house, I thought Stanton could help. I was sure it was either Falcon or Mackey that sent that guy to scare me off, so I called him. Evidently the assistant DA had already told him I had an eyewitness to the murder. Someone who knew Thompson didn't kill Diego. He seemed interested. In fact, too interested. My gut told me something was wrong. So I lied. Instead of telling him I was at the hotel, I said I was at the airport. At that point, he became frantic. He didn't want me to leave town. He said he'd send a car. I hung up. He called me right back, so I threw the cell phone over the hotel balcony. I don't know if I overreacted, but he really scared me."

"I don't think you did. Listen to the message he left earlier today." Steven hit the play button and the San Francisco DA's voice filled the small room. When Stanton's message ended, Steven said, "I knew Stanton was up to something! I'll bet he had Carl Polinski shot."

"Carl Polinski? The detective on Madison's kidnapping? Why have *him* shot?"

"Carl and I go way back. He was a trusted friend, so I asked him to help. But I didn't know about Stanton. Carl talked to Stanton just before he was killed. If I'd listened to you..."

Steven's voice cracked. He looked down at his hands now resting on the table, composed himself and went on.

"Carl somehow saw through the cover-up, but he still didn't know Stanton was involved. He traced back evidence from the Diego murder, interstate smuggling, and numerous other crimes. You were right, the trail led to Falcon. Before Carl was shot, he sent me what he'd found. I'll be turning it over to the FBI."

Steven spread the papers out in front of Vanessa. She picked up one, then another, quickly scanning the contents. Her face grew pale.

"Michael paid me a surprise visit around four this morning. When I walked into the living room, he was there in the dark. He wanted to scare me," Vanessa said. "I wasn't sure what to make of it. But I blew up and told him I knew he and his father were connected to Falcon. I hit a nerve. He flew into a rage and left."

"If that's true, the FBI will indict him. I think Michael's in way over his head," Steven said.

"He may not be going to prison, but he'll always be looking over his shoulder," she said. "I can't believe the FBI is involved."

"It'll be over soon," he said, giving her hand a squeeze. "With Michael's testimony, the FBI will arrest Falcon and anyone else involved. He'll spend the rest of his life in prison. Michael will have a chance to start over."

Vanessa finished off the water. "God only knows what he'll do with it, but at least he's got a chance."

Steven's demeanor softened. "I'm going to get a reputation for bad timing. But here goes. There's something else I wanted to say. I've decided to resign. I'm going back into private practice. We can't go through this every time a trial comes up."

"You'd do that for me?"

"In case you haven't figured it out yet, I love you," he said, looking into her eyes.

"I...I don't know what to say," she said.

"You don't have to say anything."

When Vanessa stood to leave Steven tripped over the leg of his chair, stumbling back into her.

"I feel like I'm in junior high and just asked you to go steady. Vanessa, all this has been hard on us both. At least let me take you out for dinner tonight?"

"I've got to have time to absorb all this. I think I'd rather stay in. I'll settle for pizza at my place," she said, mustering a smile.

69

Depoe Bay, Oregon

It was the first time in months Vanessa had taken time to slow down and enjoy her beautiful surroundings. A blaze of color filtered through the shore pines as she set the table for dinner. She wrapped a cable-knit cardigan around her shoulders and stepped out onto the deck into the cool evening to take in the scene. Waiting a few extra moments after the sun disappeared, she was treated to yellow-tinged clouds turning to deep red, the silver-blue ocean absorbing the crimson tones. Steven found her there, her profile back-lit by the fading light.

"Hello," he called softly, trying not to startle her.

"Oh!" She jumped anyway. "Hi. You missed the sunset."

"I caught a glimpse of it as I drove past Whale Cove. It looked beautiful, but not as beautiful as you."

"Aren't we romantic this evening?"

"That's my plan," he said, leaning in to kiss her, balancing a pizza box in one hand and a wine bottle in the other.

She took the bottle and they made their way into the house. The table was set with her best china and crystal. Early blooming daffodils from the garden stood in an etched glass vase.

"This is quite a setting for pizza."

"Remember what you said earlier? Well, I wanted to make a fresh start, too."

He set the pizza box on the table and took her in his arms, softly kissing her lips. "Um, I've missed you."

In the candlelight, Vanessa looked lovelier than ever, her face more relaxed and youthful.

They sipped wine, ate salad, and munched the gooey cheese pizza, putting aside, as best they could, the recent chaos in their lives. They teased and laughed, two good friends on the verge of something deeper.

After finishing dinner, Vanessa gathered up the dishes and piled them in the sink. Calling from the kitchen, "You know what we need? Ice cream." She rummaged in the freezer for her stash of Rocky Road and returned to the dining room with soup bowls filled with scoops of the frozen treat.

"Sometimes, this makes everything seem better."

After a few bites, Steven ventured, "I had a revelation about Michael today."

"I'm sure you did. He's made a terrible…"

"No, Vanessa. Hear me out. Did you notice how much he and I look alike?"

"Yes, I noticed. I always wondered who he looked like…but… what…wait…this is crazy. What are you saying?"

"You and I met when we went to Harvard," he said. "Just one time."

The similarity between Michael and Steven *was* uncanny. The curious dream she'd had some weeks ago about the one exception to her no cheat rule, with a young man she'd met while still in law school.

"My last year there," he said, while the ice cream melted in the bowl. "I was with some buddies. We joined you and your friends at a bar."

Vanessa choked on her Rocky Road.

"I thought that was a dream!" she said. "We played pool. I drank too much."

"Yes, you did. Do you remember what happened after that?" he said.

"The dream was pretty vivid. You drove me home."

"We made love that night," Steven said. "The one and only time I ever cheated on my wife."

"When I first started working at the courthouse, I had a feeling we'd met before."

"Vanessa, you're not getting this, are you?"

"That we made love some thirty years ago and here we are...pretty amazing."

"That's right. Thirty years ago. Think about it. When did you have Michael?"

"January fifth, nineteen seventy-four. Why?"

"I graduated May, nineteen seventy-three. We met in April. Nine months before Michael was born."

"You can't be serious!"

"When I saw him this morning...the first time I've really taken a good look at him...it was like looking in a mirror."

"He never looked like Nick or anyone else in the family. But I thought nothing of it...I hadn't been with anyone else...or so I thought. Could it be?" Abandoning the Rocky Road she just scooped into her spoon, she continued. "In court the other day, you were standing next to him. Steven, he looks like you! Is this possible?"

"Seems incredible," he said. "But yes. I think it's possible."

Vanessa poured the last of the cabernet and downed it. "I can't believe this!"

"We could do a DNA test. They have Michael's on record now. I want to know for sure."

Vanessa smiled. Then almost to herself, "This is so strange. Life with its twists and turns."

She couldn't believe that Michael could be Steven's son. It was way too much to take in.

"Ah, the philosopher! I've wanted to make love to you from the moment I walked through the door this evening. Well, actually, since the last time we made love."

Just the distraction she needed.

The following morning, Steven was no longer by her side. She rolled toward the warmth of the springtime sun filtering through the window, listening to the gentle chirps of house finches welcoming the new day.

She managed to rouse herself from bed. After slipping into her red silk robe, she ventured into the kitchen. There he stood, scrambling eggs, with tousled hair, dressed only in boxer shorts.

He turned to greet her. "I wanted to surprise you with breakfast in bed," he said, feigning disappointment. In a flourish he dipped her back, kissing her fully on the mouth.

"Nice idea," she said, laughing. "But I think it's warm enough to eat on the deck."

"I'm glad it's Saturday." He pulled her robe off her shoulder and kissed her neck, making her giggle. "Oh swell, I try to be romantic and all I do is tickle you."

They settled into breakfast on the deck, sitting across from each other at the redwood table, nibbling eggs and toast. Somehow everything tasted better in the fresh air. They ate quietly, enjoying just being together. Only the breakers crashing against the rocks below, the occasional squawking seagulls, and the breeze whispering through the shore pines broke the silence.

The dense forest that surrounded the secluded cottage sheltered the deck most days from the wind. But the house sat in a clearing and, on this spring-like day, the sun's warmth brought a welcomed break from the long, wet winter.

"I've thought about doing the DNA test, to see for sure if I'm Michael's father," Steven said. "I've decided to go ahead and get that done."

"Could you wait?" Vanessa asked. Noticing Steven's disappointment, she continued, "It's just too much right now. I don't think I can handle anything else. It's been thirty years. Surely, a few more weeks can't really matter."

"Of course. I understand," he said. "I really sprang this whole thing on you at a bad time. I seemed to be pretty good at doing that lately. You throw me off my game."

Vanessa reached for the carafe, refilling both cups. "I love it here," she said, changing the subject. "I moved here for the peace and quiet. I grew up in a huge house that was surrounded by gardens, with a pool, tennis courts, and a stable. But it was never quiet. There were always gardeners and stable help. Maids and secretaries. And a constant flow of visitors. The only time I felt at peace was at Kate's lake house." She fell silent.

"What happened?" Steven asked, leaning forward. "You look so sad."

"I was thinking about Kate. When I was a kid, I spent at least two weeks each summer with her at her grandmother's house. It was paradise. Later, when she inherited the property, I spent as much time as possible there. I thought she was my friend...like a sister, who listened to my complaints about Nick. But all the while she was having an affair with him! What was I thinking?"

"Maybe she was the one who felt sad. She was torn between loving you and Nick. Anyway, that's what they did. You didn't do anything wrong," he said.

"I still have a hard time picturing Kate and Michael together. How sad the only child she had will grow up without her." She cupped her hand above her eyes, blocking the sun, looking up at the noisy jay in the spruce tree above them. "Madison will probably live with Michael. I may never see them again."

"Maybe, once we know it's safe, we could arrange a visit."

Vanessa said, trying to muster a smile. "It's time for Michael to grow up. Madison deserves a good father. Wait till you see her, Steven. She's so beautiful."

"Wait a minute. If Michael's really my son that makes me a grandfather!"

"You've grown more handsome with the years," she said, as she stood to clear the table. The sun dipped behind the clouds, sending them indoors.

"I'm going to take a shower," she said, leaving him on the living room sofa reading the sport's page in the Oregonian.

She lathered her hair and closed her eyes to rinse. The shower door silently opened and strong warm arms embraced her. Steven kissed her hard. Her body tingled. They made love in the steaming shower. The outside world seemed very far away.

Later that morning, Vanessa snuggled into Steven's arm, her legs curled under her, while they watched the news.

"There's something I want to tell you," she said, putting the TV on mute. "I wasn't going to say anything until I felt it was the right time. It's a funny thing to worry about. But, it's about money."

"Money? Oh, don't worry. I've put some aside. If you ever need anything…"

Vanessa laughed. "That's very sweet. But, that's not the problem. How do I say this? Um…well…I'm worth quite a bit of money."

"You are?" he said, a coy smile crossing his lips. "What's the problem?"

"Some men react strangely when their girlfriends are wealthy."

"You're wealthy? How much are we talking about?"

"Well, between investments, inheritance, income from the corporate practice in Chicago, about twenty-five million," she said. "Give or take."

"What! I can't imagine that kind of money. Wow!" he said, leaning back in his chair, smiling. "Humm. Let's see. I'm in love with a beautiful, smart, wealthy woman. What more could I ask for? I'm a lucky man."

"Money has a way of changing people. I think sometimes it's a curse. It certainly didn't bring my parents happiness. It didn't make me happy when I was married to Nick. Now, I hardly spend it. In fact, maybe I'll give most of it to charity."

"Let's not be too hasty here," he said, with a chuckle. Taking her hands and looking deep into her eyes, he said, "I love you, Vanessa. Nothing's going to change that."

70

San Francisco

Michael drove through the night, pushing the old VW bug to its limit. To pass the time as Jenny slept, he made a mental list of what he'd get when he had his hands on his inheritance, starting with a Ferrari. He was taking a chance leaving Oregon, but this had to be done in person. If he handled things right, he'd be back in Newport by Monday, with the DA none the wiser.

The cool, misty air swirled around the headlights as he drove over the Bay Bridge. At two in the morning, the noisy bug rumbled to a stop in front of his father's house. Lamplight filtered through the window from the upstairs library. His father still hard at work, as usual. The man never slept.

Michael took a few steps up the front walk when suddenly floodlights illuminated the front of the house. A figure stepped from the shadows, gun in hand.

"Javier!" Michael called out. "It's me. Sorry for the late night visit."

Javier walked toward Michael, holstering his gun.

"Michael, Amigo! Where the hell have ya been? I don't find nobody to beat at poker since ya left." Javier laughed, grabbing Michael around the neck, playfully, like a big brother.

Michael grew serious. "How's he doing?"

"Not good," Javier said, releasing Michael. "The doctor he say he shouldn't drink no more. But he don't listen."

"Look," Michael said, glancing at Jenny waiting in the car, "she doesn't know anything. Got it?"

"Yeah, sure," Javier said. "Ya shoulda seen him when he heard Kate died. I'm surprised he lasted this long."

Michael turned and motioned for Jenny to join them. Together they climbed the stairs and after introducing Jenny to his father, he settled her into his old room before rejoining his father in the library. Nicholas looked old and drawn, not the energetic man of just a few years ago. Once, he'd take the stairs two at a time. Tonight it took effort to move across the room.

"Still having trouble sleeping?" Michael asked.

"I get a lot done. In my line of work, there are no business hours," said Nicholas.

"How's Madison?" Michael asked.

"Just go about your life. She's fine with me," Nicholas said.

"I want to see her. I miss her. I want Jenny to meet her."

"Leave her be. It's only been a few months since Kate died. Have you no respect? Don't confuse her right now. Is that why you're here? You can't call your old man and let him know you're coming? You just show up with some woman in the middle of the night? What are you thinking? That she'll be Madison's new mother? Madison's mine! She's all I have left of Kate."

Michael was too tired to get into that argument tonight. He'd deal with that later.

"Dad, I have to talk to you."

Nicholas went on as if he hadn't heard Michael. "Your mother called. She told me about Mackey." He placed a hand on Michael's shoulder. "Good job."

"Dad, listen. Things have gone all wrong."

"What? Are you going to trial on this Mackey thing?" Nicholas asked, walking to the bar. He methodically poured scotch over ice. "I'll take care of it. Don't worry."

"No. Listen. They've cut me a deal," Michael said, watching the amber liquid fill the glass.

"That's my boy. How did you manage that?"

"I agreed to tell them everything I know about Falcon. If I do, they'll drop the charges."

"What!?" Nick said. "How did that happen?"

"Mom saw me after the beating. She saw Mackey and his buddies a couple of times before that and was already suspicious. I had to tell her something, so I told her about being at Diego's murder and that they thought I killed him. That's all I said. I thought she'd just help me leave the country," Michael said. "When she was here last month, she was trying to find some way to prove my innocence. That's when I called you. I thought Javier would scare her off."

Michael began to pace the floor. He had to make his father understand.

"She still didn't back down. Somehow she found Kenny Harper. Do you remember that guy? Kate worked with him at the shelter. Kate must've confided in him and he told Mom everything he knew."

"Don't worry about this Kenny character," Nick said, more than happy to take care of him.

"It's too late for that." Michael continued pacing, his hands emphasizing every point. "Let me finish. The next thing I know, she tells her boyfriend, Steven Adams, who just happens to be the DA up there, everything she'd found out. She somehow figured out who killed Diego. Adams used to work with Stanton and Carl somebody."

"Polinski," Nicholas said, taking a draw of scotch.

Michael stopped. "How do you know?" Michael asked.

"How do I know?" Nicholas asked. "When will you learn?"

Michael knew how powerful his father was, but was still amazed at how far reaching.

Nicholas strolled to the bar and refilled his glass, then took a seat in the easy chair by the fire. "Polinski started nosing around. Don't worry, I took care of him before it got too far."

"You were too late," Michael said. "Adams got the information. He already called in the FBI. The FBI, Dad! That's why they've offered me a deal. I'm small potatoes. If I tell them everything I know about Falcon, they'll put me in the witness protection program. They know you're involved. It's only a matter of time before they make the connection."

"You really screwed things up!" Nicholas lost his well-trained composure. He became that southside wise guy. "I've been busting my hump for years to make a name for myself. They respected me. I created an empire so vast, even Fontana, may he rest in peace, didn't know how big," Nick took a step closer to his son. "No one could touch me!" he muttered. His face turned red as the words spewed forth. "What did you tell them?"

"Nothing. I swear," Michael said, hardly recognizing the crazed man before him. "That's why I'm here. I've got it all figured out."

Nick grabbed Michael, pinning him against the sofa. Michael pried his father's feeble hands off and stood to face him. Nicholas slumped. The tough guy gone. He'd exhausted what little energy he had left. His failing health left him powerless to fight his son. And he knew it.

"We don't have time to argue. Sit down and listen!" Michael said.

"You little piss-ant. You're telling me what to do?" Nicholas said, looming over Michael, once again. "Do you remember when I took you to Diego's execution? I did that for two reasons. To make sure you'd never get into this business. And to get you the hell away from Kate. And it worked. You ran like a rat-bastard."

"Yeah, I did," Michael said. "I was a coward."

Nick drained his glass and got up to pour another.

"Dad, take it easy with that stuff," Michael said. "The doctor said…"

"To hell with the doctor!"

"There's only one way out of this," Michael continued. If his father wanted to drink himself to death, that was his problem. Taking a gulp of the Coke he'd taken from the bar fridge, he continued. "Go to Mexico."

Nicholas started to object, but Michael raised his hand and his father fell silent.

"Let me finish! You can sit back and enjoy life on a beach in Cancun surrounded by beautiful women," Michael said.

"What makes you think I'd run?"

"You've made more money than you'll ever be able to spend. It's time you took it easy. They have good doctors down there. You can kick back and enjoy yourself. I'll handle the FBI," Michael said. "Look, I took care of Mackey, didn't I? You told me never trust anyone. I've learned that lesson the hard way."

"I'll send Javier to take care of your mother and her boyfriend."

"Dad, you can't do that. It's over," Michael said. He finished off the Coke. "Now, here's what we'll do."

Michael's late night meeting with his father had left no time for sleep. That morning, he was eager to see Madison. And he wasn't leaving without setting things right with his father about her, too.

He joined Nick in the solarium that morning. Josie stopped mid-pour when Michael entered the room. She smiled, pleased to see him.

"Welcome home. Do you still like your eggs scrambled?" she asked.

"Just toast this morning, Josie," Michael said. She finished pouring Nick's orange juice and left the room.

Michael sat opposite his father. "We need to talk about Madison."

"So it's come to this?" Nick said, pushing his chair back.

"Javier told me what the doctor said. You're living on borrowed time. You can't take her with you. She's better off with me. Jenny and I will spend the day with her. Before we leave, I'll tell her who I am."

Nicholas slumped in his chair, feeling very old.

Madison awoke with the robust energy of a four-year-old, slowing down just long enough for the nanny to bathe and dress her. She wiggled impatiently until her braids were done up with sky blue ribbons and her buttons were fastened, before she flew down the stairs.

"Papa, Papa!" she called out. "Good morning, Papa."

She stopped in the doorway, when she saw a stranger at the table.

"Don't be shy. It's okay. Come and meet Michael," Nick said. "He and Jenny are going to take you to the zoo today. What do you think of that?"

"The zoo?" she said, still standing against the doorway.

"Yes, it's okay. Michael's known you your whole life," Nick said. "As soon as you eat breakfast, you can go."

Madison was bright and talkative, naming the animals in the zoo and telling Michael and Jenny all about school and her friends. They had hot dogs and cotton candy from a vendor, and later, played at the park.

Exhausted from her big day, she fell asleep in the car on the way home. Back at Nick's, Michael carried Madison into the house, up to the library, where Nicholas waited. He'd been drinking, his face flushed. Michael laid Madison on the sofa and soon she woke.

"Papa," she cried, hopping off the sofa and running over to Nicholas. "You should have seen the baby rhi-nos-ris! It was pink and round."

"I'm sorry I missed that." Nicholas picked up the child and set her on his lap. "Papa has to tell you something. You need to be a big girl." Nicholas squeezed Madison close to him. "I have to go away."

"Papa, no!" Madison said.

"Oh, sweetheart, I don't want to leave you, but I have to."

"Who's going to take care of me? Josie?"

"No, no. Now listen carefully. This is very important. Michael is your real daddy."

"You're my daddy!"

"I'm Papa. That means grandfather. Your daddy's back and it's my turn to go away for a while," Nicholas said. "You can visit me."

Madison clung to Nicholas. The room fell silent. He carried her over to Michael and placed her in his lap.

"Didn't we have a good time today?" Michael said. "We can have fun every day. I love you, baby. I promise I'll never leave you again."

Madison squirmed out of Michael's lap to stand by Nicholas.

Eyeing him apprehensively, she asked, "Are you really my daddy?"

"Yes, Madison, I'm really your daddy."

"Is Jenny my mommy?"

"No, sweetheart," he said. Kate's death suddenly overwhelmed him.

"Did you know my Mommy?"

It was more than Michael could bear. Tears ran down his cheeks. He choked back a sob. "Yes. She was as beautiful as you are. But your mommy's with the angels," he said.

Nicholas poured another scotch and left the room. In twelve short hours, he'd lost everything.

71

San Francisco, California

On Monday morning, as was his routine, Dean Stanton arrived at his office an hour earlier than anyone else, with a large black coffee and the day's Chronicle. He'd spotted the headline when he bought the paper at the newsstand downstairs, but managed to contain himself until he was inside his office. Now he laid the paper out on his desk, staring in disbelief.

'Prominent Businessman and Philanthropist, Nicholas Thorne, Dies in Yachting Accident.'

Stanton took a gulp of coffee, taking a moment to let the news sink in.

'An explosion aboard the fifty-five-foot yacht *Kate's Voyage* engulfed the vessel in flames. The yacht belonged to Nicholas Thorne. His body was burned beyond recognition. His assistant verified he was spending the day on the yacht, preparing for an extended trip to Mexico. Two crew-members perished along with Thorne.'

The article went on about Thorne, the upstanding citizen, and listed all the charity boards he sat on.

Stanton stared out the window at the sun-dappled bay. Falcon dead!

His cell phone rang.

"Have you seen today's paper?" said Mayor Richards.

"I can't believe it!" Stanton said.

"I couldn't have come up with a better way for him to go. May his soul burn in hell."

72

Depoe Bay, Oregon

Vanessa sipped herbal tea, while she caught up with the latest news on CNN. Steven made soft sputtering noises asleep on the sofa still tired from the previous day's drive to Cannon Beach. They'd awakened early Sunday to a glorious spring day and decided on a long drive. Before starting out, they put the convertible top down to enjoy the unusually warm coastal breezes. Along the way, they visited art galleries and boutiques, walked on the beach, and ate crab at a local café before making the long drive home. She'd been happy to put some distance between her and Depoe Bay, leaving Michael and his problems far behind. At least for the day.

Vanessa stopped on her way to the kitchen for more tea when she heard the CNN newscaster say, "Today's top story. Financier Nicholas Thorne is dead at the age of fifty-nine."

"What?!" Vanessa exclaimed.

The tea-cup fell to the floor, shattering to pieces.

Steven sat upright, not yet fully awake. "What's going on?"

"Nicholas is dead!"

"What!"

"Shh!"

The broadcast continued, "Thorne was best known for his savvy business dealings that helped him amass a fortune."

The camera turned to Mayor Richards. "He will be missed," Richards said. His round face filled the screen. "He was truly a fine citizen. His contributions to the city are immeasurable."

"I can't believe this!" Vanessa said. "I need to get to Madison!"

"Let's not move too fast here. Michael can check on her. You said Nicholas had a staff; they'll take care of her for now. He's got enough to deal with, as do you. Let's get this Falcon thing over with this morning. Michael will be free to go to Madison and take care of funeral arrangements as soon as we wrap this up. The sooner the better for all of us."

73

Oregon, California

FBI Special Agent Daniel Forsythe had driven in from Salem that morning and was waiting with Steven when Michael and his attorney arrived. Forsythe's navy blue pinstripe suit and yellow power tie, together with his hard-set steel gray eyes, confirmed he meant business.

Steven waited for them to be seated around the conference table, before he gave Michael his condolences. "I'm sure this was a blow."

"I can't believe he's gone," Michael said, his face haggard from the all night drive. "In light of my father's death, there's really no reason for us to continue."

"What's your father's death got to do with this?" Steven asked.

"He was Joey Falcon."

"What!" Steven said.

Strauss's mouth fell open. Agent Forsythe removed his glasses and pinched the bridge of his nose.

"You're saying that Falcon and Thorne were one and the same?" Forsythe asked.

"Yes." Michael leaned back in his chair.

"For fifteen years he carried on a double life...?"

Michael cut in. "More like twenty."

"Do you have any proof?" asked Forsythe.

Michael reached inside his coat and removed a wax-sealed, cream-colored envelope and handed it to the agent.

"My father drew this up some time ago, fearing he'd be assassinated someday. There were very few people he trusted. This letter should clear up the whole matter."

Forsythe put his reading glasses back on and read:

To Whom It May Concern: My name is Nicholas Thorne. I assumed the alias Joey Falcon, to work without interference as I organized the sale and distribution of drugs along the West Coast. Because of this line of business, there are people who would like to see me dead. They may go to great lengths to accomplish this.

In the event of my untimely death, the individuals most likely responsible are San Francisco Mayor Donald Richards and San Francisco District Attorney Dean Stanton. They have worked for me through the years and have suppressed evidence in numerous crimes, including the murder of Rhio Diego.

This letter will be locked in my safe deposit box until my death.

My son, Michael Thorne, is the only person with access to it.

Sincerely, Nicholas Thorne

Notarized by Gilbert Van der Dam. Ninth day of June, two-thousand and two.

"How do we know this letter is authentic?" Forsythe said.

"Check murder records in San Francisco for the date it was notarized. You'll find Van der Dam's death remains unsolved. Why would my father write such an incriminating letter defiling his presumed good name if it wasn't true?"

"Isn't it a little too coincidental that your father dies the day before you're to blow his cover?"

"He had a way of knowing what was going on. If he'd gotten word things were going wrong he may have decided to commit suicide rather than face prosecution. He's been very ill."

"Even with your father's death, there are others involved. You worked for him. Tell us who they are."

"Michael, I think at this point we need to stop," said Strauss. "This was not in the agreement. Michael was to identify Falcon. He's done so, upholding his part of the plea agreement. I'd like to reschedule this meeting after I've had a chance to confer with my client."

"No, I have nothing to hide," Michael said. "Let's get this over with. I need to get to my daughter." He turned to Forsythe and said, "I worked for my father for a short time a few years ago. I did some bookkeeping. Nothing more. Everything was coded, so I had no idea what was going on. But he did tell me about the letter."

"You told your mother you witnessed Diego's murder. That's why Mackey and his men were after you," Steven said.

"Those guys had me mixed up with someone else," Michael said. "My father wanted to keep me out of that part of the business."

"But your mother was almost killed." Steven persisted.

Michael interrupted. "My mother has a vivid imagination."

"What? Are you saying your mother lied?" Steven said, unable to control his escalating anger.

"Adams! That's enough!" Forsythe said. "Act professional or I'll have to ask you to leave."

"I think you're a little too close to the situation to see things clearly," Michael said, with a smirk.

Steven's face reddened. He stood and leaned toward Michael. Before he could speak, Forsythe got up and put a hand on Steven's shoulder, pushing him back down into the chair.

"Michael, you've said enough. I can't help you if you continue," Strauss said, trying to calm the tension-filled room.

"Shut up, Strauss. I'm done with you," Michael said. He leaned back in his chair, crossing his legs.

"Adams, what's he talking about?" Forsythe demanded.

"Oh, don't you know?" Michael answered. "He and my mother are very close."

"Is this true, Adams?" Forsythe asked.

"Yes, but…"

"That's it! I'm taking Michael into custody until we can straighten this whole thing out."

"You made me a deal! Strauss, do something!" Michael said.

"Sorry, Michael, you fired me," Strauss said, gathering up his notes and placing them in his briefcase. "You need to find another lawyer." He snapped his briefcase shut and left the office.

Agent Forsythe rose. He pulled his jacket back, revealing his holstered revolver, then pulled out his handcuffs.

"You don't get it, do you?" Michael sputtered, losing his smug demeanor. "Even if I had information, it would be worthless now. The whole system changed when my father died. Someone else will step in and hire new people. We had a deal!" Michael slammed his fist on the table. "The charges against me were supposed to be dropped if I cooperated. Well, I'm here. I told you what I know."

"I'm taking you into custody until we can decide what to do with you," Forsythe said. He cuffed Michael, then called for backup. Moments later, two uniformed officers arrived to escort Michael to the county jail next door.

A backup plan had been devised for just such a contingency. Michael used his one phone call to contact a District Federal Judge his father had helped get appointed. Within hours, the charges were dropped and Michael walked from jail a free man.

74

Newport, Oregon

When Steven learned of Michael's release, he felt a sense of relief. The kid had been right. He'd held up his end of the bargain. They'd had no business re-arresting him. The days dragged on and after a hectic week, Steven looked forward to spending a quiet weekend with Vanessa. He sorted through his files, placed several in his briefcase, and snapped its metal clasps shut. He took his coat from the hook. Remembering the warm temperature, he folded it over his arm, then picked up his keys, turned off the overhead lights, and opened the door.

The phone rang.

He looked at his watch. Assuming Vanessa was checking on how late he planned to work, he stepped back into his office and answered the phone.

"Nicholas is alive!" A woman's voice spoke softly, not wanting to be overheard.

It sounded familiar, but he couldn't quite place it.

"Vanessa's in danger! I think he's going to kill her," she whispered. Then more to herself then Steven, "What have I gotten myself into?" The phone went dead.

He recognized the voice. It was Jenny!

He drove at break-neck speed, pressing speed-dial as he sailed over Cape Foulweather.

Vanessa lounged on a deck chair, reading a mystery novel, watching the blue sky fade to gray. Night closed in quickly. She set her book aside to enjoy the early moon illuminating the water.

The air cooled, but she wasn't ready to go inside. She picked up the sweater that lay on the chair and wrapped it around her shoulders. The phone rang. She didn't want to answer it, but did so reluctantly, hoping Steven was calling to say he was on his way.

"Vanessa!"

"Steven? What's going on? You sound…"

"Listen! Something…"

His cell phone was cutting out. Trying to make sense of Steven's frenzied voice; she was unaware of the footsteps approaching.

"Lock your door!" Steven yelled.

"Why? What's going on?"

The footsteps drew closer.

"Who's there?" she called out.

"Vanessa…" Steven's voice trailed off as she dropped the phone.

Steven listened helplessly as he sped along the coast road, praying he wouldn't be too late.

"Surprise!"

"I thought you were dead!" A sudden gust of wind took her breath away. "What are you doing here?" Steven's panic suddenly made sense.

Nicholas stood on the footpath that led to the driveway. He'd effectively blocked the only escape route.

She stepped down from the deck, as if to join him. But when she reached the footpath, she started to slowly back away, crushing pine needles under foot.

"Before I left the country I wanted to say goodbye," he said. "It would be rude of me to leave without seeing you."

"What are you talking about?" she asked, stifling a scream.

"I never had a chance to tell you what you've meant to me," he said. He began to slowly walk toward her.

She was counting the steps. She knew the way.

"What I meant to you?"

"Yes. How you screwed up my life!"

Steven left tread marks on the main road as he swerved onto Oceana.

Nicholas stepped closer.

"You're the murderer!" Vanessa said. "You've messed up your own life!"

The moon emerged from its shroud of clouds, illuminating his contorted face. He didn't notice the black abyss that lay just inches from where they stood. Vanessa's heart raced. She'd always hated this cliff with its shear drop to the ocean below. The combination of high tide and full moon had created massive waves that slammed into the cliffs, shaking the earth under their feet.

Just as her heel caught the edge of the cliff, she grabbed a prickly branch of the shore pine and swung her body sideways. At the same moment, Nicholas lunged for her. His weight propelled his body forward. The crack of a bullet cut through the trees, the sound muffled by the breaking waves. His body careened over the bluff. The wind snatched her sweater, fluttering it to the sea below, like a wounded sea gull. The pine needles stung her arms and face, but she clung for her life.

Steven kept his foot heavy on the gas as he maneuvered the dark narrow road. He passed a black limousine parked off the side of the road. Not sure what he'd find, he stopped at the edge of the driveway and stealthily made his way up the drive, heading for the footpath. In the moonlight he could barely make out someone on the edge of the cliff. As he ran in that direction, he could just make out Vanessa. He reached her just as she'd pulled herself up onto solid ground.

Vanessa sat huddled on the sofa in her living room wrapped in a blanket Steven had retrieved from the closet. "It's still unreal. Nicholas looked demented. He blamed me for everything."

"He's out of your life for good now," Steven said, taking Vanessa into his arms. "It's not your fault. You were protecting yourself."

75

Newport, Oregon

Shielding her eyes from the glaring summer sun, that cut a path across the expansive ocean, Vanessa spotted an agate. Letting go of Steven's hand she retrieved it from its sandy bed. Steven walked on ahead. A sudden, sharp wind caused Vanessa's body to shiver. Michael flashed through her mind. It had been months since she'd last heard from him. Shaking herself free from the past, she hurried to catch Steven.

"You come in handy on cold walks," she said, snuggling close. "Let's stop for a latte."

They continued up the ramp to the parking lot, where just beyond, Nye Beach boutiques and shops were closing for the night. They gazed into the darkened windows until they reached the coffee house. Still open, they entered and abruptly stopped. There, sitting behind the counter, was Jenny. She looked up from her paperback novel, then jumped off the stool and ran around the counter to hug Vanessa.

"What on earth! Where'd you come from?" Vanessa asked, holding Jenny back a bit to get a look at her. "Where's Michael?"

Jenny glanced across the café at a group of young women just finishing their drinks. "Why don't I get you something, then we can talk."

By the time Jenny had finished making their lattes, the other customers were gone. She joined Steven and Vanessa at their table, setting steaming cups before them. She slid her slender body into a chair, clasped her hands and lowered her head as if in prayer. It took a moment before she began.

"Michael's in San Francisco, where I left him about a week ago. It's not good. I mean he's really down. You can imagine how he feels," Jenny said, checking over her shoulder to make sure they were still alone. "I tried to be patient, but he'd get mad at me for the stupidest things. He didn't want me to discipline Madison. So I go, 'What the hell am I doing here?' I probably coulda had everything I wanted. That's never happened before. But it's not worth it, you know?"

"Yes, I do know," Vanessa said, stealing a glance at Steven. "I'm sorry for all he put you through. You made the right decision. I don't know if I could ever look him in the eye again, after all he's done."

Jenny got up and locked the door, turning the closed sign on. After returning to her seat, she continued, "There's something else you need to know. Michael saved your life."

"You saved my life, Jenny. What Michael did was set his father on me."

"Michael knew his father was coming here. He was at your house that night. The night Nicholas died. He hid in the trees and when Nicholas closed in on you, Michael shot him."

"No, that's not how it happened. Nicholas fell off the cliff."

"All I know is Michael was there and he did fire his gun and then his father fell."

Vanessa looked in disbelief at Steven.

"I can't believe it!" Vanessa said. "He tried to save my life?"

"What a horrible choice he had to make," said Steven.

"After that he became even more difficult," Jenny looked down at her hands. "At first, I thought we were going to San Francisco for Madison because Nick was dead. So I was shocked to see Nick still alive. And he was one angry guy. He blamed you for ruining everything. I had no idea at the time what he was involved in. When I overheard a conversation between them I was stunned. It's like 'what have I gotten myself into?'" Jenny stirred her coffee and floated far away for a moment. "I loved him, you know?"

"I know you did." Vanessa patted Jenny's hand. "I'll always be indebted to you. Steven's call gave me a moment to think what to do."

Steven encompassed Vanessa's hand in his.

"When I found out Nick wanted you dead, I had to do something. It was horrible," Jenny said. "The two of them argued. I guess Michael figured he couldn't stop Nick, so he somehow got back here."

"Well, however it happened Nicholas is dead, so no more Joey Falcon. Michael has a second chance not many people get. He's his own man." Steven said.

He glanced at Vanessa. The DNA had come back positive. Steven was indeed Michael's biological father. One day they'd tell Michael. But that day would have to wait.

"I hope he's not getting involved in his father's business," Steven said.

"He's not. Things are a mess. Most of the men that worked for Nick scattered. Javier's the only one that stayed with Michael," Jenny said, taking a sip of the warm frothy drink. "Anyway, Michael inherited the house. He has no idea where his father's money is. He guessed in off-shore accounts. He has his grandmother's inheritance. He'll be okay. But he's a broken man...," her voice caught. "He loves you...just give him some time."

"The one good thing in his life is Madison. I hope he'll be a good father to her," Vanessa said.

"He's staying in San Francisco. Why not, I mean he's got the house and all. And anyway, Madison can stay at the same school. Poor kid's been through a lot," Jenny said. An odd sort of smile crossed her face. "They treated Madison like a princess."

"Did you hear the Coast Guard found the body?" Steven said.

"Oh," Jenny said. "What happens now?"

"However it happened, Nicholas is dead," said Steven. "There won't be any charges against Michael."

"After all, you can't kill a dead man."

www.ingramcontent.com/pod-product-compliance
Lightning Source LLC
Chambersburg PA
CBHW031156050726
47495CB00019B/1879